T

y

my Story

Love

V Simcox

The Magic Warble

The Magic Warble

Victoria Simcox

Two Harbors Press

Two Harbors Press
212 3rd Avenue North, Suite 570
Minneapolis, MN 55401
612.455.2293
www.TwoHarborsPress.com

ISBN - 978-1-935097-17-4
ISBN - 1-935097-17-2
LCCN - 2008909901

Book sales for North America and international:
Itasca Books, 3501 Highway 100 South, Suite 220
Minneapolis, MN 55416
Phone: 952.345.4488 (toll free 1.800.901.3480)
Fax: 952.920.0541; email to orders@itascabooks.com

Cover and Interior Artwork by Amanda Swanson
Cover Design by Alan Pranke
Typeset by Peggy LeTrent

Printed in the United States of America

Contents

The Last Day of School

Kristina awoke when the jangling of her alarm sounded right in her ear. She reached over to her night table and gave her clock a good whack and then stuffed her head under the pillow. "Oh, I don't want to get up," she mumbled.

It was the last day of school before the Christmas holiday break, and it was so hard to drag herself out of bed. Twelve-year-old Kristina wished she could have slept at least another hour.

Even with the pillow over her head, she could hear the familiar sound of the old floorboards creaking in the hall. Then she heard her door open, followed by the tap-tap of her mother's footsteps as she approached Kristina's bed.

Ingrid Kingsly sighed. "Kristina, I know you're awake. Please get out of bed before you miss the bus again—for the fifth time this month."

"Okay, Mother," Kristina said sleepily. "I'm getting up."

As soon as she heard her mother leave the room, Kristina took the pillow off her head and sat up. Her flaxen hair was tousled about her head as she got out of bed and walked over to the window. There was a small crack at the bottom through which the wind was whistling. She pulled her nightshirt sleeve over her hand and rubbed the condensation off the window. Her pale blue eyes peered through the circle of clear glass, at the snow that was lightly falling. *Wouldn't it be nice if the busses weren't running today?* Kristina thought. Then she realized it was highly unlikely that school would be canceled—the snow wasn't even sticking to the ground.

Kristina could not have cared less about missing the last day of school. She didn't have many friends there anyway; in fact, a couple of the kids were downright nasty to her.

It was a good thing she had great parents who made up for her lack of friends. Even though she was adopted at birth, everyone said she looked just like her father Wilhelm, who had the same color blond hair and blue eyes as her. He'd always say, "Don't worry about it, if you don't have many friends at school, you're a unique girl and if you find a few unique friends in life, be grateful for that."

Kristina Kingsly was somewhat of a loner, spending a lot of time reading books, drawing, or playing with her pet rat, Raymond. But even though she disliked school, there was one good thing about it: her teacher, Miss Hensley. She was a really nice lady, and a unique friend in Kristina's opinion.

The sound of Raymond drinking from his water bottle brought Kristina back to reality, and she looked at the clock on her wall. "Oh, no!" she gasped. The time was 8:05 a.m., and the bus would arrive at 8:30 a.m.. It took seven minutes to walk to the bus stop—maybe four and half if she ran.

She got dressed as fast as she could, pulling on mismatched socks because all the rest were in the wash. She ran a comb quickly through her hair, then picked up Raymond and stuffed him in a leather purse that she had just for him.

She ran down the old staircase to the kitchen, gulped down a quick bite to eat, grabbed her loose-leaf binder with all its papers hanging out, and threw on her coat, hat, and scarf.

"Bye, Mom!" she yelled.

"Good-bye, dear. Please try to organize yourself a little better," her mother said as she watched her daughter scurry out the door.

"I know, I know—I'll try harder next time," Kristina called over her shoulder.

Outside, the snow was falling gracefully, and it made everything seem so quiet. Kristina could see that the bus was turning onto her street, so she started to run toward it, but a brisk wind suddenly knocked her loose-leaf binder out of her arms and scattered her homework all about the snowy sidewalk. The bus driver, Mr. Macgregor, a stout old Scottish man with jolly red cheeks and a missing front tooth, caught sight of Kristina running in circles, frantically trying to retrieve her papers. When she finally grabbed the last one, her foot hit an icy spot on the sidewalk, and she slipped and fell.

"Ouch!" she winced. Even through her heavy winter coat, she

could feel that she had scraped her arm on a chunk of ice.

Mr. Macgregor swung the bus door open. The children on the bus were looking out the windows, and Kristina could see them pointing at her and laughing.

"Hurry, young lassie, before ye catch yer death," Mr. Macgregor said, looking very concerned. "It's more'n a wee bit nippy out."

With wet papers hanging out of her binder and her hat on lopsided, Kristina trudged up the steps of the bus. Then she squared her shoulders and held her head high as she walked to the empty back seats, not once glancing at the other children, who snickered and laughed as she passed them.

One girl, Hester Crumeful, stuck her tongue out and whispered, "Aw, the little weirdo has a boo-boo."

Kristina thought that Hester, a slightly rotund, spoiled rich kid, was weird herself. She always wore a ribbon tied at the top of her head and had a different colored one for each day of the week. Kristina sat down in the back of the bus and opened her purse to look at Raymond. "We'll be just fine, Raymond. At least Miss Hensley will be happy to see us," she whispered.

Miss Hensley let Kristina bring Raymond to class. She said it was educational for the children to observe him. He even had his own special cage with toys in it.

Kristina liked to be the first one to come to class so she could visit with Miss Hensley before the final bell rang. When she entered the classroom, she placed Raymond in his cage. After feeding her pet, she organized her assignment as best as she could and placed it on Miss Hensley's desk, just before the final bell rang. The other kids came running into the classroom, and Graham Kepler, Hester Crumeful's thirteen-year-old cousin, made a paper airplane and threw it at Kristina. It hit her on the forehead, and she scowled at him but didn't tell Miss Hensley. Graham tossed his carrot-colored hair and smirked, like a Cheshire cat, at Kristina. He had so many freckles on his face, it resembled the stars in the sky on clear night.

I don't quite know why he's so mean to me, Kristina thought. *Maybe he thinks that Miss Hensley likes me better than him.* Kristina really didn't care what the reason was; she just wanted the school day to be over.

Finally, the clock on the wall said 2:15 p.m.—only fifteen more minutes until the final bell. School would be out, and the Christmas holiday would begin.

Miss Hensley had finished grading everyone's papers and was passing them back to the class. Kristina could hardly believe her eyes—she got a B+ on her paper. This was the best mark she had ever gotten. When all the graded papers had been passed back, Miss Hensley went back to Kristina's desk.

"I was really impressed with your work. Great job!" she said.

"Thank you, Miss Hensley. I can't believe it—a B+!" Kristina replied.

"Could you please stay a few minutes after class?" Miss Hensley asked. "There's something I'd like to give you."

"I'd be glad to," Kristina replied enthusiastically.

After the final bell rang and all the students had been dismissed, Miss Hensley went to the storage closet at the back of the classroom. She unlocked the door and stepped inside. She pulled a string connected to a light bulb. The storage room lit up, and a large spider skittered up the light bulb. Kristina watched from her desk as her teacher pushed a step stool toward the dusty shelves along the wall. She reached up to the top shelf. "Ah, there you are," she said, pulling out a dusty burgundy hatbox. Miss Hensley brushed the dust from the top of the box and said quietly, "The time has come for you to be passed on."

Kristina wondered what Miss Hensley was doing. She watched patiently as her teacher blew some more dust off the old hatbox. She walked out of the storage room and over to her desk. "Come here, Kristina," she said. "I have a present for you."

"You do?" Kristina said excitedly, feeling very honored. "What is it, Miss Hensley?"

"I wish that I had time to tell you about it, but I don't want you to miss your bus," Miss Hensley said. She handed the hatbox to Kristina.

"Thank you very much, Miss Hensley."

"You're very welcome. Now hurry along."

Kristina glanced up at the clock. "Yes, I'd better hurry," she agreed. She turned and began to walk to the classroom door.

"Kristina," Miss Hensley called after her.

"Yes, Miss Hensley?" Kristina replied.

"Aren't you forgetting something?"

"Oh, yes, of course! I almost left without him!" Kristina said, rolling her eyes. Then she quickly put Raymond in his purse.

As Kristina headed out of the classroom, Miss Hensley nodded and said quietly, just barely loud enough for Kristina to hear, "May you have a wonderful Christmas holiday."

- 2 -

Davina Pavey

Once again, Kristina barely got to her bus in time, and when she did finally get on, she headed straight for the back seats. On her way there, Graham Kepler stuck his foot out into the aisle and tripped her, causing the hatbox to slip out of her arms and roll down the aisle toward the front of the bus. Hester Crumeful snatched it up, just before it rolled down the bus steps. She stared at Kristina with a devious, smirk on her face.

"Give that back to me right now, Hester Crumeful!" Kristina yelled angrily.

Hester didn't answer. Instead, she threw the hatbox to Graham, who caught it like a football. The rest of the children watched with great enthusiasm to see what the next play would be. When Mr. Macgregor looked through his rear-view mirror and saw what was going on, he quickly brought the bus to a halt at the side of the road. Then he got out of his seat and went down the aisle toward Graham. Graham sunk down in his seat, holding the hatbox in his lap, looking very cowardly.

Mr. Macgregor pointed his stubby finger at Graham's face. Squinting one eye, he said in a heavy Scottish brogue, "Now ye

8

listen t'me, young laddie. Anymore trouble outta ye, an' it'll be the last time ye ride the bus for the rest of the year!"

Though reluctant, Graham handed the hatbox back to Kristina. She quickly sat down in the last row of seats.

Mr. Macgregor went back to his seat, and when Graham was sure he wasn't looking, he turned to Kristina and whispered, "Just wait; I'll get you back. You'll see."

Kristina ignored him and looked out the window.

"Teacher's pet. Sissy baby! It's probably just something for self-improvement in there anyway, like a book on how not to look like a nerd," Hester scoffed as she chomped loudly on her chewing gum. She blew a huge bubble that popped and stuck to her entire face.

Kristina looked over at Hester and couldn't help laughing.

Graham and Hester knew that Kristina had been given a gift from Miss Hensley, because they had been eavesdropping at the classroom door the whole time Miss Hensley had been talking with Kristina. The two of them got off at the stop just before Kristina's, and Kristina watched from the window as Graham made a large snowball and threw it at Hester, hitting her in the back of the head. Soon after, Mr. Macgregor pulled the bus to a stop and opened the doors.

"Now you an' your critter have a merry Christmas, an' try to stay out ay mischief," he said as Kristina exited the bus.

"Thanks Mr. Macgregor. You have a merry Christmas also," Kristina replied.

~ ~ ~

Ingrid Kingsly came into the entryway just as Kristina got home. "Put your things away upstairs and hurry back down," she instructed Kristina. "Your dinner is on the table. I have to leave here in fifteen minutes to meet your father for his office Christmas party."

Kristina put Raymond in his cage and shoved the hatbox under her bed. She wanted to take her time with opening it, and enjoy the moment, so she planned to do it after she ate. Then it dawned on her that if her mother was going to her father's office Christmas party, she'd be getting a sitter. *Oh, I hope it's not Davina Pavey,* she thought.

Davina was two years older than Kristina—fourteen and a half, to be exact—and she lived three houses farther down the street. Whenever she came to watch Kristina, she'd spend her time either eating the cupboards empty or following Kristina around the house, hoping to see her do something for which she could snitch on her to Mrs. Kingsly.

Kristina could just imagine it: Davina, with her long, greasy black braids, Coke-bottle glasses, and beady little eyes, standing in her bedroom doorway. She'd be eating potato chips that would get stuck in her braces, and she'd watch every move that Kristina made.

Kristina entered the kitchen, where her mother was busy doing dishes, and sat down at the table to eat. At least dinner was a plus—macaroni and cheese out of the box; her favorite.

"Oh, I forgot to mention to you," her mother said as Kristina squeezed large amounts of catsup onto her macaroni. "That nice girl, Davina Pavey, is coming to be your sitter tonight."

"Oh, great," Kristina muttered.

"What was that?" her mother asked.

"Uh, I said that's great," Kristina replied, trying to act more chipper.

"I have to hurry and get ready," her mother said, heading out the kitchen, just as the doorbell rang. "Would you get that, Kristina?"

Kristina walked to the front door and peeked through the peephole. "Just as I expected—Davina," she said. She opened the door. "Hi, Davina," she said flatly.

Davina wiped her nose with the back of her hand and walked into the house. "Where's your mother?" she asked.

"She's upstairs, getting ready," Kristina answered. She stood there, uncomfortably, for a few minutes until her mother appeared at the top of the stairs.

"Hello, Davina," her mother said brightly.

"Hello, Mrs. Kingsly. Wow, you do look beautiful tonight," Davina replied.

Kristina rolled her eyes in disgust. Davina would always try to butter up her mother.

"Why, thank you, Davina," her mother answered. Then she slipped on her long coat and applied her lipstick in the entryway

10

mirror. "We'll be home by ten o'clock. Help yourself in the kitchen," she said to Davina. As Kristina started up the stairs, her mother looked up at her and said, "Now, you do as Davina tells you, and remember, Grandma's coming tomorrow, so we have to get up early and clean this place. Bedtime's at 9:30 sharp!"

Davina looked up at Kristina with a hideous grin on her face. She loved having the power to dictate orders.

As soon as Kristina's mother left, Davina headed for the kitchen to see what type of food she could devour. This meant that Kristina finally had a chance to open her present without being bothered—or so she thought. She got the hatbox out from under the bed, but just as she was about to open it up, she heard Davina's heavy steps coming up the stairs. *How predictable,* Kristina thought.

Davina opened the door and sauntered into Kristina's bedroom, eating a large corned beef sandwich drenched in mayonnaise.

"It's impolite not to knock," Kristina said, irritated.

Davina ignored her remark. She was much too interested in the hatbox that Kristina had pushed behind her back. Smacking away on her sandwich, she sauntered over to Kristina, and asked, "What's that you're hiding?"

"It's none of your business," Kristina snapped.

Davina placed her sandwich, still oozing mayonnaise, on the dresser. Then she reached behind Kristina and grabbed the hatbox.

"Give it back!" Kristina yelled.

"Does your mother know your hiding this?" Davina snapped,

11

a chunk of bread flying out of her mouth. "Your mother will thank me for catching you sneaking around like this!"

As Davina started prying at the clasp, Kristina felt anger bubbling up inside her, and she clenched her fists, wanting to punch Davina.

"What's wrong with this thing? Why won't it open?" Davina asked, her eyes growing very squinty and her face turning plum red. When she couldn't open it, she tossed it back to Kristina. "Well, if I can't open it, then neither can you. Have fun." With that, she picked up her sandwich, licked the dripping mayonnaise off its edge, and sauntered out of the room.

Kristina got up and slammed the door behind Davina. Then she picked up the hatbox and tried to open it, but it was no use; the clasps wouldn't budge. "Why did you have to give me this thing, Miss Hensley? It's caused me nothing but trouble, and to top it off, it's so darn old that it won't open anyway." Feeling very frustrated, she shoved it back under her bed.

An Irritating Sound

It was in the middle of the night, when most people were fast asleep that an irritating buzzing noise woke Kristina. She tossed and turned as the sound of it seemed to go deep inside her ears. Thinking it must be an insect that had crawled inside her ears, she dug her fingers inside them, but nothing was in there. So she cupped her hands over her ears to dull the sound. It became a little softer, but as soon as she took her hands off her ears, the noise grew louder once again. *Where in the world could that bothersome noise be coming from?* she thought. Weren't all the troubles from the day before enough? Now she had to deal with this.

The moonlight spilled through the window and lit up the room, but Kristina still couldn't see where the sound was coming from.

"All right, where are you?" she called out in frustration. She got out of bed and walked over to the window to see if the noise might be coming from outside. Nothing seemed unusual—all the other houses on her street were dark, and the snow was falling pretty hard, at least that was something good; she could go sledding the next day.

Suddenly, the sound grew even louder, and she realized that it was coming from inside her room. She spun around quickly to see if she might catch sight of whatever was making the sound, but when she did so, it was nowhere to be found.

There was a piece of paper on her dresser, so she grabbed it and quickly rolled it up. If it was some sort of annoying insect making the noise, she would use the paper to swat it. "Come on out, wherever you are," she coaxed, now standing in the middle of the room, tapping her foot. "Where are you?" she continued, slapping the rolled-up paper onto her other hand. She just couldn't figure out where the sound was coming from. She started walking back toward her bed and noticed that the closer she got to it, the louder the weird noise became.

Raymond had woken up and was standing in his cage, looking at the floor near her bed.

"What is it, Raymond? Where do you think the noise is coming from?" Kristina said.

Raymond just kept staring down at the floor with his eyes wide and his whiskers twitching.

"So, you're hiding under my bed, are you?" she said, reaching for her bedspread. She pulled it up and threw it to the other side of the bed. The buzzing noise grew louder. *Insects aren't that loud. This is becoming a little freaky*, she thought. She went down on her hands and knees to look under the bed. It was dark, and there was no sign of any strange insect. She got up and scratched her head, thinking, *This is too weird.* Then she remembered that she had shoved the hatbox under the bed. She looked under her bed again. The buzzing seemed to definitely be coming from the hatbox Miss Hensley had given her. *What in the world could be in there?* she thought.

Raymond stood on all fours, staring at the bottom of the bed, as though being drawn to the strange sound. She quickly touched the hatbox with her rolled-up paper. There was no zap of electricity or anything of that sort, so she decided to pull it out. She slid the box out from under the bed and picked it up. It didn't feel weird, so she shook it. Then she remembered that it wouldn't open, so, feeling frustrated again, she tossed it on the floor, where it slid across the room and bumped into her dresser. She crawled back into bed and stuck her head under her pillow, but that didn't help—the buzzing just grew even louder, and then it suddenly changed into what sounded like one continuous melodic, quavering note being

14

sung. "Would you shut up!" she finally yelled, grabbing hold of her pillow, ready to throw it at the hatbox. But just before she did so, the lid slowly opened. Kristina's eyes grew wide with surprise and she jumped out of bed. Inside the box was a little leather sack, the kind one would put a marble collection in. It had a gold tassel tied around the top of it—and the strange sound was coming from inside it. She quickly untied the tassel and peeked inside it, hoping to find something spectacular. But instead, what she found was not spectacular at all. Sitting in the bottom of the sack was a tarnished silver ball, about the size of a golf ball.

"This is what I got myself so worked up about," she said, looking up at Raymond. "It's just a crummy silver ball with an electronic buzzer inside it."

Feeling very disappointed, Kristina closed the sack and placed it back in the hatbox. The moonlight shone directly on the little hatbox, giving it a soft glow, and the tarnished ball inside kept right on singing its strange quavering note.

As Kristina sat staring at it, some thoughts popped into her mind: *Maybe I shouldn't be so ungrateful. After all, it's the thought that counts, not the gift itself. Miss Hensley really didn't have to give me anything at all, and besides, the ball could have some sentimental meaning to her. I was the only student who got to stay after school and be honored with a gift from her.*

"Oh, well, what the heck? I may as well play with it," she said to Raymond.

Once again she opened the hatbox, took out the leather sack, and untied its gold tassel. Then she dropped the ball onto the palm of her hand.

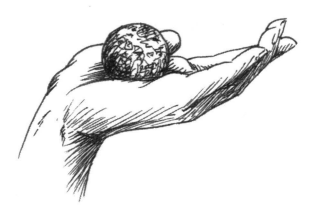

"You sure are tarnished, and I must say very unusual, with your mysterious sound. I bet that you used to be beautiful, shiny silver." While rolling the ball around on the palm of her hand, she noticed that it was perfectly smooth and seamless. "How peculiar. I wonder how that annoying sound got inside of you." As she held her hand directly in the moonlight, the ball suddenly began to get very warm. She swirled it around on her palm a few times, and then clasped her hand tightly shut around it. All of a sudden, it turned scorching hot. "Ouch!" she yelled, dropping it and shaking her hand to relieve the pain.

The ball bounced once and then a second time, right into her clothes closet. She quickly went over to the closet, hoping to find it on the floor, but when she couldn't see it anywhere, she realized that it must have gone down the laundry chute.

The laundry chute was connected to a steel tunnel, which ran down into a large canvas sack on the basement floor. She poked her head into the opening of the chute, but it was too dark to see anything, so she crawled down into the tunnel until she was up to about her waist. She listened again for the strange sound, but she couldn't hear anything, so she crawled in a little farther until she was hanging from her ankles. Suddenly, her right ankle slipped off the corner of the opening of the chute, and then her left ankle slipped as well, and she went sliding, headfirst, down the dark tunnel into the large sack on the basement floor. Luckily, there was a pile of laundry at the bottom of the sack to soften her landing. *Wow, that*

16

was fun! I should of thought of doing this a long time ago, she thought.

It was dark in the sack, and as she sat quietly, she could hear the noise once again. It was a faint sound, coming from the bottom of the pile of laundry. She dug her hand down into the dirty clothes, and as she did, she noticed that what she was feeling was different than clothes. It was dry and crisp, almost like paper. Her hand suddenly felt the little ball. It was no longer hot but just a little warm. She pulled it out from the bottom of the pile, and the melodic tone became louder once again. Then, suddenly, she heard someone whistling, and she felt the laundry sack lift off the ground—with her inside it. The little ball suddenly stopped singing and she felt herself being dumped out of the laundry sack. Clearly, what was happening to her was nothing short of magical.

- 4 -

Bernovem

A fraid to make a move, Kristina lay curled up in the place where she had been dumped out. The laundry sack was gone. The pile of laundry had been replaced by a pile of leaves, and instead of the basement floor, it seemed to be grass. She cautiously poked her head out the pile of leaves and saw a lovely manicured garden. In the middle of it sat a small cottage made of stones and with a thatched roof. The garden itself was circular and along its perimeter was a dense forest. The weather was slightly cold, and the sky was overcast. A cold breeze blew by her and made her shiver. She felt very strange, being in the garden, and wondered if she was simply dreaming. *If this is a dream, I sure hope it's more exciting than yesterday*, she thought.

She suddenly heard the sound of whistling again, and when she poked her head out of the pile of leaves, she saw a man—or at least she thought it might be a man—coming around the corner of the cottage. He looked old, and he seemed to be even shorter than herself. He had a stout stature, distinctly sharp facial features, icy blue eyes, pointy ears, a long white beard, and silver hair. Upon his left shoulder he carried a large sack, and in his right hand he held a rake. He walked toward the pile of leaves, and Kristina ducked

18

back down so he wouldn't see her. He dumped out the large sack onto the pile of leaves, which brought another pile of leaves upon her head. Kristina tried not to move or make a sound.

Then the little man struck a match and was about to throw it on the pile of leaves, right where she was hiding, but she jumped out just before he did so yelling, "Wait! Please don't throw that match!"

The little man almost fell backwards. "What in our lady's name is this?" he said, steadying himself.

"I didn't mean to end up in your leaf pile," Kristina said nervously, while backing away. "As a matter of fact, I have no idea how I got here."

The little man walked closer to her, leaning forward slightly and holding the rake in front of him, as if to protect himself. He stared at Kristina as though he'd never seen anyone like her before.

"You may find this hard to believe," Kristina said, "but I was only trying to retrieve a little silver ball."

The little man's eyes grew wide. "A little silver ball, you say."

"Yes, Sir I…"

The little man seemed impatient. "Well, go on. Go on, spit it out."

"My teacher, Miss Hensley, gave it to me on the last day of school. It was a Christmas gift," Kristina continued.

The little man twirled his beard around one finger as he thought for a moment. Then he looked up at her and, seeming relieved, said, "Why, yes, of course! How soon I lose my memory." He dropped his rake on the ground.

"I'm very sorry if I upset you," Kristina said.

"No, no. No worries! Come with me to my cottage, and we'll

have a nice cup of tea. I could use a little break anyway. My back's about killin' me," he said, stretching backwards.

He picked up his rake, and then put it down on top of a wheelbarrow that was nearby. Then he motioned for Kristina to follow him. Kristina wasn't sure if she should trust him, but he seemed friendly enough, so she walked after him. When they arrived at the cottage, he pushed open the small wooden door, and they went inside. He took a lantern down from a hook on the wall and led the way into the front room. There was a fire burning in a fireplace, and it made the room—probably the living room—feel cozy and warm. Kristina noticed that everything in the room was smaller than normal.

"Come, child, sit down," the little man said, pointing to a small couch. "Now, how about that cup of tea?"

"Oh, yes, please. I'm a little chilly and that would warm me up," Kristina said.

The little man picked up a basket filled with tiny red flowers. Then he took a big handful of them and dropped them into a black kettle that was sitting on top of the fire. As the flowers fell in, the water in the kettle spat out the top.

"Now, then, let's discuss matters while we wait on our tea," he said, sitting down in an armchair across from Kristina. "This little silver ball… do you have it with you?" he asked, while lighting a pipe.

"Yes, I have it in my pocket. Would you like to see it?" Kristina asked.

"Yes, but let me get the tea for us first." He got up and poured tea into two cups and handed one to her. The tea was fluorescent red, and Kristina had to squint because of its brightness.

"I've never seen tea like this before. Its color is such a brilliant red," Kristina said. She took a sip of it. "Yum, this is very good. I would say it tastes like…" She paused for a moment and then continued. "Well, actually, I can't describe it at all, but it is very delicious."

"It's fairy blossom, very hard to come by nowadays," the little man said as he sat back down. He took a big puff off his pipe, then stuck out his knuckle-swollen hand and said, "The name's Rumalock."

20

Kristina took hold of his hand and shook it. "I don't mean to ask a silly question or seem rude, but are you a human?"

Rumalock chuckled and said, "No, I am what you would call a dwarf."

"I've heard of dwarfs in fairy tales." She looked a little embarrassed. "I never thought they... or, I mean, you were real. I mean, no one I know of has ever met one," she said, getting a little tongue-tied and turning red. "I hope that I'm not saying the wrong things."

Rumalock chuckled again. "No need to feel bashful, my dear. I'm sure you don't run into many dwarfs where you come from, and for that matter, I guess, I could say that I don't get the chance to meet many of your type either."

Kristina took another sip of her tea and then said, "My name is Kristina."

"Pleased to meet you, Kristina," Rumalock said. "Now, should we take a look at this little ball?"

"Oh, yes, of course." She took it out of her pocket and dropped it onto the palm of his hand. He held his eyeglasses with his other hand and peered down at it. He rolled it around and then clasped his hand tightly shut around it.

"Yup! It is the one," he said. "This, my dear, is a very special day, to say the least."

"Oh, why's that?" Kristina asked, looking a little confused.

"This little ball is called the Magic Warble. It is what everyone in our land has been waiting for, for many years," Rumalock said excitedly. Then, looking very serious, he narrowed his eyes. "After it was given to you, did anyone else come into contact with it or even with anything that it was stored in?"

Kristina had to think for a moment and then answered, "Yes, three people, to be exact. Wait a minute, four, actually, if you include my pet rat, Raymond." She started to count on her fingers. "So it would be Graham Kepler, Hester Crumeful, Davina Pavey, Raymond, and, of course, me."

"My, my, that many, and a rat also. I haven't seen one of those little fellows in years. This could make matters very complicated," Rumalock said.

"How so?" Kristina asked.

Rumalock placed the Magic Warble back in Kristina's hand and said, "After the Magic Warble was given to you, whoever touched it or even anything it touched, like a container it may have been resting in, will be brought here."

"Where is here?" Kristina asked.

"The place you are in, child, is called Bernovem," Rumalock answered. He took another long drag of his pipe and blew out a large number of perfectly round smoke rings. Then he got out of his chair, walked to the fireplace, and took a dusty book off the mantel.

"What is that?" Kristina asked.

"This, my dear, is the Book of Prophecy, and it is the only one in the whole land of Bernovem." He opened it and ran his finger along the page. "Ah ha! Here it is, just as predicted: Kristina Kingsly," he said.

"Do you mean I'm in that book?" Kristina asked, getting up off the couch to take a look inside it.

Rumalock pointed his finger on the page. "Is your name Kristina Kingsly?" he asked, while glancing up at her through his round glasses.

"Yes," she answered, looking puzzled. "But how come I've never heard of Bernovem?"

"Bernovem is a land very far from your land, or any other, as a matter of fact. It's in a totally different galaxy than where you are from. You see, child, you have been brought here by the Magic Warble to deliver it to its resting place."

Kristina's face went pale.

"Is something the matter?" Rumalock asked her.

"I'm just worried that I won't know where to bring it," Kristina said.

"I thought you might feel that way. I must tell you that I can't promise you that your journey will be a smooth one, but if you trust that the Magic Warble will lead you to where it needs to go, you should be fine. And besides, you might even get some help along the way."

Kristina looked back into the book. "Why are so many of the pages blank?" she asked.

"Oh that's because the prophecies in this book will only appear on the pages a few minutes before they actually come to pass. Look here—it says, '*Kristina's scrape on her arm was healed.*'"

"How could that be? The scrape is right here on my arm. It couldn't possibly heal within a few minutes," she said, showing him the scrape she had gotten from falling on the icy sidewalk the morning before.

"Ah! But are you sure? Give me your arm." Rumalock said.

Kristina stretched her arm out, and Rumalock poured a few drops of his tea onto her scrape.

"*Ouch!* What are you doing? That's very hot!" she said, shaking her arm to relieve the pain.

"Take a look at your scrape now," Rumalock said excitedly.

"It's gone!"

"That's right! The tea is also magic."

"This is all so cool," Kristina said excitedly.

"Yes, yes, I suppose you could say that," Rumalock said as he placed the Book of Prophecy back on the mantel. "Now, child, you look hungry. How about a nice warm meal?"

"I'd like that very much," Kristina said.

Kristina ate a delicious meal of cheese, brown bread, boiled potatoes, and the best chocolate cake she had ever tasted. Afterward, while sitting by the crackling fire, she still could hardly believe where she was or how she had gotten there, but she was much too sleepy to figure it out. She took the Magic Warble out of her pocket to take another look at it, and when she stared down at it; her sleepy eyes suddenly grew two sizes bigger.

"The Magic Warble! Its color has changed. It used to be tarnished silver, but now it is light purple," she said.

"Yes, of course, Kristina, it is all part of its journey," Rumalock said. He sat across from her in his armchair, smoking his pipe.

"All part of the journey?" Kristina repeated, yawning. Her eyes grew so heavy that she couldn't keep them open any longer. Once she fell asleep, Rumalock got up, and placed a warm woolen blanket over her. Then he blew out his lantern and left the room.

- 5 -

Clover and Looper

It was early morning when Kristina awoke. She sat up, stretched her arms in the air, and yawned. Then she looked around at her surroundings and remembered once again that she was not at home, and that meeting Rumalock and having fairy-blossom tea with him had all been real.

She suddenly heard voices coming from the other side of the window, so she got up, walked over to it, and drew the curtain open. She could hardly believe what she saw next. Right in front of her on the window ledge were two little fairies about three inches in height. One of them was a girl, who appeared to be a teenager and was very pretty, with hazel eyes, chestnut-colored hair, and lots of freckles on her nose. She was standing with her hands on her hips, talking to a younger boy fairy, who had curly auburn hair and bright green eyes. He was sitting on the edge of the windowsill, swinging his legs.

Kristina stood quietly, hoping that they wouldn't notice her. They were the most fascinating creatures she had ever seen. The window was cracked open slightly so she could hear them conversing.

"Why do you always complain when you don't get your way?" the girl said.

"You know that I've been waiting for this event all year, but do I get to go? No! Instead, I get to come here and miss all the festivities," the boy whined.

"Stop being such a baby," the girl said.

Kristina suddenly sneezed, startling the girl fairy and causing her to lose her balance and fall backwards off the windowsill. Quickly, she flapped her wings so she didn't hit the ground.

Seeing the girl fairy fall, the boy fairy couldn't control himself from laughing, which in turn almost caused him to fall off as well. Kristina found it quite funny also, and she, too, began to laugh along with the boy.

"Do you always go sneaking up on fairies' conversations and try to cause accidents?" the girl fairy snapped at Kristina.

Kristina, taken by surprise, stopped laughing and swallowed awkwardly, not knowing what to answer.

"Well, maybe you were right, Looper. This does seem to be a waste of our time," the girl said to the boy, who was still sitting on the window ledge, chuckling.

"What did I tell you? Let's get out of here. I can still make some of the games if we leave now," the boy said.

Kristina's feelings were hurt by the fairies' attitude, but she didn't want them to leave, so she tried to think of a way to make them stay. She turned and looked around the room and saw that the chocolate cake from the night before was sitting on the coffee table under a glass dome. She turned back to the fairies and said, "Could I offer you some of Rumalock's chocolate cake?"

The girl fairy seemed to be about to snap at Kristina, but then she answered, "Well, I guess we could accept your offer, seeing what trouble you have put us through."

Kristina quickly went to the coffee table, removed the glass dome from the chocolate cake, and cut a large piece of it. Then she laid it on the plate. "Would you like to come in and eat it? It might be easier then setting the plate on the window ledge," she said.

The girl fairy looked at the boy fairy and then back at Kristina. "I suppose so," she said.

The fairies crawled through the crack in the window, the boy first and then the girl. As the girl was crawling through she got her wing stuck and, without thinking, Kristina reached out with her finger to help pull her wing through. But the fairy pushed her away abruptly and snapped, "Well, you sure aren't very smart now, are you?

Don't you know that if you touch a fairy's wing you can prevent the fairy from ever flying again?"

"Come on, Clover, give her a break. She is trying to be nice to us," the boy said.

"Okay," the girl agreed. "I guess I should have let you know about the wing bit. Let's just forget it."

Then they flew over to where the plate of chocolate cake was sitting on the coffee table and landed on top of it. They scooped it up with their tiny hands and then stuffed their mouths full of it.

"Rumalock does know how to make great chocolate cake," the boy fairy said with his mouth still full.

The fairies were enjoying the cake so much that they seemed to forget that Kristina was sitting on the couch. She cleared her throat in order to get their attention.

They looked up at her, and the boy, whose face was covered with chocolate said, "Oh, I'm sorry. I guess we should formally introduce ourselves." He stuck out his tiny hand, covered in chocolate, and said, "My name's Looper." Then pointing to the girl fairy, he said, "And that's my grumpy sister, Clover."

Kristina took his tiny little hand between her two fingers and gently shook it. Clover didn't offer her hand; instead, she smirked.

"My name's Kristina."

The fairies ate only about a quarter of the slice of cake, and when they were done, they flew back to the windowsill. There was a crack in the wood that had some dew in it, and they dipped their tiny hands in it to wash the chocolate off. Once cleaned, Looper stretched his arms in the air, yawned, and said, "I sure could take a nap right about now." Then he sat down and leaned against the windowpane.

He was just closing his eyes when Clover grabbed him by the arm and said, "There's no time for lazing around. We've got to get this human child to the Indra River before nightfall."

Looper jumped up suddenly, shook his head to get his wits back, and said, "Well come on, Kristina, let's get going."

"What do you mean; take me to the Indra River?" Kristina questioned.

"We must get you and the Magic Warble to the Indra River before nightfall, because Queen Sentiz will be sending out her wicked zelbocks to find you. They're probably in the forest right now, and believe me, they'd love to capture you for the queen. So the sooner we get you on your way, the better chance you have of not getting caught," Looper said.

"Hey, hold on a minute! This all sounds a too weird. I'm not sure I'm cut out for all this adventure stuff. Is it possible to just zap me back to my world?" Kristina asked.

The fairies looked at each other as if Kristina was crazy, and then, in unison, said, "*No!*"

"Actually, the only way for you to go home is by placing the Magic Warble in its resting place," Looper said.

"Kristina, go and get the Magic Warble. We can't waste any

more time," Clover said impatiently.

"It's right here in my pocket," Kristina said. Then she pulled it out and held it on the palm of her hand. "Wow, how cool! Its color is different again. This time it changed from light purple to dark purple!" Kristina said excitedly.

"It won't be so 'cool' if we don't get a move on," Clover replied.

"Okay, okay, I'll go!" Kristina said.

With that, she pushed up the window and crawled through it, following the fairies.

6

The Zelbock

Clover and Looper were suspended in midair as they waited for Kristina to crawl through the window. Their wings were fluttering so fast that if anyone were to glance quickly at them, they might be mistaken for hummingbirds.

When Kristina landed on the soft green grass, Clover took notice of what she was wearing. "Where did you get those ridiculous clothes?"

Kristina looked at herself. She had on one white sock and one pink, and old cloth sneakers that she used for slippers around the house. Her pants were too short, and her sweater was buttoned wrong. "I got up late the other morning, and I had to rush to catch my bus. Then I fell asleep in my clothes because Davina—"

"Oh, don't worry about it, Kristina," Looper said kindly. "Clover has a tendency to find something wrong with everyone."

"Whatever!" Clover said, tossing her head and crossing her arms.

"Let's head that way," Looper said, pointing to a trail that led to the forest. Then he made a few loops in the air and began leading the way toward a trail.

"Wait a minute! I haven't had a chance to thank Rumalock for his hospitality or even say good bye to him," Kristina said.

"It's okay. He had to leave very early this morning to gather fairy blossoms," Looper replied. "Besides, he didn't want to wake you, knowing you had such a long journey ahead of you."

"Rumalock had mentioned that the fairy blossoms are rare and hard to come by. I would have thought that they'd grow like weeds in such a lush forest as this," Kristina said while following the fairies.

"They used to, but ever since Queen Sentiz had her zelbocks destroy most of the magic herb, it's very hard to come by. She has had her zelbocks plant thorn bushes in their place; even so, there are still small amounts growing on the lower mountain regions, but the problem is, not to many of the dwarfs or gnomes can travel that far, especially the old ones," Looper said.

"But why would the queen want to destroy the magic fairy blossoms?" Kristina asked.

"She hates the dwarfs, gnomes and almost every other creature that lives in the land of Bernovem," Clover said.

"And she has total control over everything," Looper added.

"I don't get it. How would she control the dwarfs and gnomes by destroying the fairy blossom?" Kristina asked.

"Well, you see, Kristina, before Queen Sentiz took over the rule of Bernovem, the dwarfs and gnomes were able to harvest the fairy blossom, and they could pick as much of it as they pleased. It is what kept them youthful, because when they made tea of it and drank it regularly, they wouldn't age. They could stay youthful indefinitely, but without it, they age much more rapidly, and I'm sorry to say..." Looper suddenly looked very sad.

"Go on," Kristina said.

"Well, I hate to have to say it, but without it, they become very weak and they die."

"Oh, I'm sorry," Kristina said. She continued following the fairies for what seemed hours, and her legs grew very tired from walking. The sun was starting to set and fog was beginning to roll in, making it hard for them to see.

"How much longer until we get to this river?" she asked.

"Sh-h-h! You mustn't talk louder than a whisper. We have

already fallen behind schedule, due to your nonstop gabbing," Clover said.

"Queen Sentiz's zelbocks are surely out in the forest, searching for anyone suspicious who may have..." Looper flew very close to Kristina's ear and in a low whisper said, "The Magic Warble."

Kristina reached into her pocket for the Magic Warble, but Looper suddenly stopped abruptly in midair and glanced from side to side nervously. Then he flew to a nearby tree and landed on one of its branches. He looked all about the forest.

Kristina wondered what he was doing and was about to ask Clover, but then he turned around and whispered, "Quick! Take cover!"

As quick as a flash of light, Clover flew off to a nearby tree stump. Then Kristina looked around to see where she could hide.

"Over here!" Clover called out to her. She was sitting with her knees curled up, inside a knothole of a stump. Kristina ran, jumped over the stump, and hid behind it.

"Hey! Watch out!" Clover snapped.

Kristina was about to respond, but then she heard something coming toward them. She poked her head over the stump and saw a horrible creature, slightly taller than a dwarf but very ugly. Its face was covered in warts. It had a crooked, turned-up nose, and its back was hunched over. It stood very near Kristina and Clover, with a suspicious, evil look on its face, sniffing the air like a dog. Kristina dared not make a move in case it might see her.

She glanced up at the tree where Looper was standing, straight as
a pin, against its trunk, not moving a muscle. The horrible creature
couldn't see anything, so it started to leave. But then a branch
Kristina was sitting on suddenly snapped. She gasped, and the
creature turned around to face her. It stared directly into her eyes
and grinned from ear to ear. Drool dripped out of the corner of its
mouth, and it rubbed its large, knuckle-swollen hands together.

Kristina glanced back at Looper, who was now motioning for
her to run to the tree he was in. She looked over at Clover.

"Hurry! Run to the tree and climb it!" Clover said franticly.

The creature started toward Kristina, so she ran as fast as she
could toward the tree.

"Quick, Kristina, jump and pull yourself up," Looper said.

The branch was much higher than the top of her head, but she gave it her best shot. She jumped once but failed to reach it. The creature was right behind her.

"Don't give up, Kristina! You must reach it," Looper said fearfully.

She jumped again, and this time caught hold of the branch. Then she swung her legs upward, just as the creature lunged up underneath her, scratching her back with its long, grimy fingernails. She got her legs around the branch, and then pulled herself up to sit on it.

"Give me the Magic Warble," the creature hissed.

Kristina was barely balanced on the small branch, and she felt her heart pounding very fast in her chest. Then, to make matters worse, the Magic Warble slipped out of her pocket and fell to the ground. Like a flash of light, Looper swooped down out of the tree to try to lift it. He strained with all his might to pick it up and managed to get it a few inches off the ground, but it was too heavy, and so he dropped it. The creature dived toward the Magic Warble but while in midair, an arrow hit the creature in the middle of its back. It gave out a shrill screech and then landed, face down, inches from the Magic Warble. It dug its grimy nails into the ground and tried with all its strength to reach the Magic Warble, but when it was about an inch away from it, its body went limp.

A boy—Kristina thought he looked like he must be in his early to mid-teens—came running toward the horrible creature. His breathing was labored as he approached its lifeless body. He put his foot on its back and pulled the arrow out of it. Then he turned around and looked up at Kristina, who was still in the tree.

Is this handsome young man coming to rescue me? she wondered.

He wiped the blood off his arrow, and said, "What do you think you're doing, wandering these parts of the forest? Stupid girl."

Kristina's feeling of being a maiden in distress who would be rescued by a handsome young warrior suddenly melted away. She jumped down out of the tree and walked over to where the Magic Warble had fallen to the ground. The boy was putting his arrow back in his quiver and was not paying attention when she picked it up and put it back in her pocket. Looper flew over to the boy and landed on a rock in front of him. Then Clover pushed herself out of the knothole in the stump, wiped the dirt from herself, and flew to Looper.

Looper knelt down on one knee and bowed before the boy, and Clover gave a little curtsy.

"Thank you, Your Highness, for saving us from a most certain death," Clover said to the boy.

7

Prince Werrien

Kristina wondered what the bowing was all about, and as she stood watching, Clover flew over to her and whispered in her ear, "Don't you have any respect? Bow!"

The boy slung his quiver and bow across his shoulder. "Thanks, guys, but no need for the formalities," he said.

"But the respect is due to you, Prince Werrien," Clover said.

"Not as long as that villainous queen—oh, excuse me, Her Majesty, is in power," the boy responded.

Looper made the introductions. "Prince Werrien, this is Kristina. Kristina, this is Prince Werrien."

"Are you really a prince?" Kristina asked.

"I guess you could say that, but the way things are now, I just go by Werrien." There was silence for a moment, and then Werrien continued, "Well, it's been a pleasure, but I'd best be off. I've got plenty of things to do." He turned to leave.

"Wait!" Looper said, in a slightly anxious tone.

Werrien turned around.

"There's something you ought to know."

"Oh? What is it?" Werrien asked.

Looper flew up to his ear and whispered, "We are in the presence of the chosen one."

Werrien wrinkled his nose and smirked. "Let me guess—this little girl?" Werrien asked.

Kristina marched over to Werrien. "Little girl? If you haven't noticed, you're not really that much taller than me." She stared up at Werrien, who was about a head and a half taller than she was.

"Oh, I get it. You're the one who has come to save Bernovem from all its troubles." Werrien crossed his arms and stared right back at her.

Looper landed on the rock again and tried to stand taller than he really was. "As a matter of fact..." he began. He swallowed nervously and continued. "Yes, I mean, that is the reason she came here."

The smirk on Werrien's face grew more pronounced. Then he rolled his eyes, turned around, and proceeded to walk away. "You can usually find me in these woods, so let me know when she's done saving Bernovem. We'll have a big celebration," he said.

Kristina felt herself losing her temper. *"Hey, Prince Charming!"* she yelled.

Just as Werrien turned around in response, she tossed the Magic Warble to him. He caught it, and then looked curiously at it. "What's this?" he asked.

"Oh, I'm not quite sure, but I've been told it's called the *Magic Warble!*" Kristina said haughtily.

"What? This colored ball?" Werrien asked, tossing it up in the air. When it landed in his hand, it was so hot that he had to drop it.

"It hurts, doesn't it?" Kristina said, feeling a bit of satisfaction.

Werrien bent down and cautiously picked it up. It was no longer hot but just a little warm. He looked up at Kristina; she could see the shock in his blue eyes. "You really *are* the one," he said. Then he suddenly smiled. "Well, I was hoping this day would get better. Whoo-hoo!" he hollered with joy. He went over to Clover, who was still standing on the rock, and lifted her by her tiny hand and spun her around in the air. Then he placed her back down on the rock. Clover blushed as she straightened her skirt and tried to find her balance. "Wow! I can hardly believe that the Magic Warble is really here in Bernovem," Werrien said. He rolled it around on the palm of his hand, still in awe of it. Then he tossed it back to Kristina and right after that, he took notice of her mismatched socks. He grinned at her in a way that made Kristina feel embarrassed, and the odd thing was that she had never really felt that way before, not when other kids teased her or laughed about the way she dressed.

Looper could see how she was feeling, so he said, "We really need to get to the Indra River before we run into another one of the queen's zelbocks."

"Mind if I go with you?" Werrien asked.

"Would you?" Clover promptly replied, her eyes lighting up. "I mean, if it's not too much trouble, we could always use your protection." Her freckled cheeks blushed red.

"I thought that you had plenty to do already," Kristina said, still feeling annoyed with Werrien.

"Look, I'm sorry for treating you the way I did. It's just that I would never have thought that the Magic Warble would be returned by a..."

"A dumb little girl?" Kristina said, finishing his sentence.

"Well, not a dumb little girl, but a..."

"I get the point. Let's just drop it. I guess I wouldn't mind having you come along," she said.

"Well, then, it's settled. What are we waiting for?" Looper said.

They started to leave, but then Kristina stopped and said, "Wait! What about that dead creature? Are we just going to leave it out here in the open?"

"Don't worry about it. Zelbocks don't last very long after they die," Werrien said.

Kristina turned to look at the zelbock, but it was gone. "Where did it go?"

"It disintegrated; even Bernovem's soil can't stand zelbocks," Werrien replied. "Though I must say, that was pretty good thinking, to try to cover our tracks. I mean, for a girl, that is."

"What do you mean, for *a girl*?" Kristina snapped back. *For such a handsome boy, he sure doesn't have the personality to match it*, she thought.

~ ~ ~

The sun had totally disappeared, and the woods were covered in a blanket of darkness. Looper and Clover flew a little ahead of the two children, lighting the way with a soft glow, like fireflies. Looper seemed to hear something, and he suddenly stopped in midair. "Listen! Can you here it?" he asked.

They all stopped to listen.

"Yes, I can. What is it?" Kristina asked.

"It's the Indra River," Werrien said.

"Not much longer and we'll be there," Looper said.

Clover shivered a little. "I feel a storm coming," she said.

No sooner had she said this than a swift wind came at them and picked up Looper and her and took them for a twirl in the air. Lightning flashed across the sky, and then thunder pounded the atmosphere. Kristina looked up, and a drop of rain fell on her nose. A few seconds later, the rain began to fall with such heavy force that it felt like buckets were being dumped on their heads.

"I think you'll have to carry on from here without us!" Clover yelled. "We can't fly in this downpour."

"Come on, Clover! We can try to make it," Looper tried to coax her.

"You listen to me, little brother. The road stops here for you and me, so don't get any big ideas," Clover said sternly.

"I guess that means you two are on your own from here on," Looper said sadly, trying to steady himself in the rain.

The four said their good-byes. Then Clover and Looper took cover under a large leaf to wait out the storm.

Werrien continued to lead the way through the brush and pouring rain. "Lucky I met up with you guys, for if I hadn't, you'd have to find your own way to the river," he said as he tried to cut through a thick mass of tangled thorn bushes that were blocking their way.

"I am appreciative, but on the other hand, I came here to your land, which I'd never heard of before, to deliver this thing called a Magic Warble, which I didn't ask to do, and believe me, at this moment I'd rather be home in my comfy, dry house than trudging through this wet forest with an arrogant boy like you," Kristina said.

An arrow hit a tree just behind Werrien's head, and before she could even blink, he grabbed hold of Kristina and pulled her to the other side of the tree. As the two of them sat crouched on the ground in the darkness, they could hear what sounded like a horse trotting toward them.

"Wait here," Werrien said.

He crawled to another nearby tree, stood up, and cautiously peered around it. He could see a black-cloaked figure upon a jet-black horse. He motioned to Kristina with a twitch of his head to come over to where he was. She crawled as quickly as she could over to the other tree.

"Can you see that little clearing through those trees?" he asked.

"Yes," Kristina answered, having to squint to keep the pouring rain out of her eyes.

"When I say go, we must run—and I mean faster than you've ever run before," Werrien said.

Kristina felt butterflies in her stomach.

"Okay, one, two, three, *go*!" Werrien whispered. He took off running very fast, but Kristina could run fast too, and she kept right up with him. "There's no stopping from this point on!" he yelled.

The black-cloaked figure caught sight of them and began charging after them. It quickly gained on them. Werrien and Kristina kept running as fast as they could.

"I don't know if I can run any farther. I'm getting a sharp pain in my side!" Kristina yelled.

"It's not much farther. You have to keep going!" Werrien yelled back.

Suddenly, Kristina's foot hit a rock and she went flying, face first, to the ground. The black-cloaked figure was about a hundred yards behind them. Werrien helped her up. They started running again, but the black-cloaked figure shot an arrow at them and it skimmed Kristina's shoulder, causing a burning sensation. The sound of the horse's hooves pounding the ground got louder and louder, and she could hear its heavy breathing behind her.

"I hope you're not afraid of heights!" Werrien yelled.

"What do you mean?" Kristina yelled back.

"Take my hand!"

Kristina grabbed his hand—and suddenly there was no ground beneath them. They had jumped off a high cliff and were about to land in the Indra River.

8

Four More Arrive in Bernovem

When Kristina entered into the land of Bernovem, the time there had no correlation to the time in her own world. All the while that Kristina had been in Bernovem to this point; Davina, Hester, and Graham were still sleeping soundly in their beds on the same night that Kristina had been awakened by the annoying buzzing sound.

Davina, Hester, and Graham all woke up at the same time, approximately the same moment that Kristina entered into the land of Bernovem. Raymond, who was already awake, stood staring at the open laundry chute. The same thing had woken all them as it had Kristina—the continuous buzzing sound. The annoying sound went deep in their ears, like a noisy creature had crawled inside them. Davina, Hester, and Graham tossed, turned, and shoved their heads underneath their pillows, until finally they all woke at the same time. They even sat up at the same time, except for Raymond, who was trying to bury himself in his shavings. Then, while all of them looked around their rooms to try and figure out where the annoying sound was coming from, it happened.

Poof! They all disappeared into thin air, and as quick as a flash, they were magically transported to the land of Bernovem.

Davina found herself falling at a high speed from the sky, clutching her bed sheet, which the wind caught hold of and turned into a parachute. She slowly drifted down, and then, with quite a *bump*, landed on the soft green grass in the same spot where Kristina had been dumped out of the sack. Feeling a little stunned, she glanced about the beautifully manicured lawn and, just like Kristina had, thought that she must be dreaming. As she sat there, she suddenly heard noises coming from a nearby bush. It sounded like some wild beast had been caught in a trap. She got up and walked toward the bush, passing the rake that Rumalock had left on top of the wheelbarrow. She stopped for a moment and glanced from side to side to make sure no one was around, watching her. Then she ran over to the wheelbarrow, grabbed the rake from it, and held it over her head. She then cautiously tiptoed toward the bush. *If the wild beast tries to lunge at me, why I'll just whack it a good one over the head with the rake*, she thought.

A few feet away from the bush, she heard a voice come from inside it. "Whoever you are, you'd better come out now, or you'll be sorry you were ever born!" she said angrily.

The voice didn't respond, so she proceeded toward the bush. Then, when she was close enough, she cautiously stuck her foot into it and wiggled it around to see if she might feel something. When she didn't feel anything, she took one step inside the bush.

"Ouch! Get off my foot!" an annoyed voice said.

Davina jumped back, but still kept the rake over her head, ready to slam it down. More rustling came from within the bush, and then, suddenly, a girl in a nightgown came crawling out of it. It was none other than Hester Crumeful.

"If you even try to hit me with that rake, my mother will call the police, and you'll be hauled away and thrown into jail faster than you could hit yourself over the head. And believe me, you'll wish you would have, once you know who you're dealing with!" Hester said.

Davina dropped the rake. "Who are you?"

"Who are *you*?" Hester asked in her snooty tone.

"I think I might recognize you, though I'm surprised you don't recognize me. My name's Davina Pavey. I was president of the book club, as well as Library Assistant of the Year at Webster Elementary last year. You should have known that—you go there, too!"

"Oh, really?" Hester asked in a doubtful tone. "So how come I haven't seen you there this year?"

"Well, duh!" Davina said, rolling her eyes. "I now attend Wallendon High. Isn't it *obvious* that I'm much older than you?"

"As a matter of fact, I'm twelve and a half, and you don't look more then a year or two older then me, and I don't recall seeing or hearing of you at all, though I'm sure that you must know my family," Hester said.

Davina shrugged her shoulders. "No, I..."

"Does the name Crumeful ring a bell?" Hester went on.

Davina suddenly looked like she had swallowed a frog. "You mean the Crumefuls who live in the mansion in Eastwood Manor?" she asked.

"Yes, I certainly do mean the Crumefuls who live in the mansion in Eastwood Manor," Hester said, rolling her eyes. "I suggest that the next time you have inkling to kill somebody with a rake, you first better find out who you're dealing with."

Feeling very embarrassed, Davina dropped the rake and walked up to Hester. Then she bent down and started brushing the dirt and leaves off of her nightgown.

"I'm so sorry," she said. "What did you say your name was?"

"It's Hester Crumeful."

"Oh, yes! How could I forget, Hester? That is such a beautiful name. Were you named after anyone special in your family?" Davina asked smoothly.

"Yes, as a matter of fact, I was named after my great-aunt, the late Hester Crumeful II. I am the third," Hester answered.

"Well, isn't that special?" Davina went on, oozing with false compliments.

Suddenly, they heard noises coming from the nearby forest, so they both stopped talking to listen.

"What do you think that could be?" Hester asked.

"I don't know," Davina answered.

The two of them started walking toward the forest.

"Aren't you going to grab the rake?" Hester asked.

Davina smiled. "Oh, yeah, good thinking."

As they got closer, the sound—a moaning noise—got louder and clearer. They entered the forest and once again, Davina put the rake above her head. There was a fallen tree up ahead of them, and the sound was coming from just beyond it.

Scared, Hester hid behind Davina. "Get ready to bash it a good one," Hester said.

Davina tightly gripped the rake and jumped on top of the fallen tree, ready to let whatever was moaning have it, but suddenly a voice spoke.

"*Ah!* Please don't! I'll do anything you say!" the voice said, coming from a person that was covered in mud.

"Wait! Stop! I know that voice!" Hester said, surprised. "That's my dorky cousin Graham Kepler! Besides, only he would moan like a baby over something as little as sitting in the mud."

Graham jumped up. "Give me that rake!" he yelled, lunging at Davina. He grabbed hold of it and tried to pry it out of her hands. "I'll show you who's the baby!" he went on hysterically. Graham, being smaller than Davina, was no match in the struggle over the rake.

"Oh, yeah? You think you can mess with me, do you?" Davina clenched her teeth and turned purple in the face. She gave Graham a kick with her foot, and he fell back in the mud with a big splash! Once again, Graham sat up, covered from head to toe in fresh mud. Davina and Hester started laughing.

"Okay, I give up," he said. "But can anyone tell me where I am and how I got here?" As he was speaking, he felt something crawling out of his nightshirt and then onto his shoulder. It crawled on top of his head, and he jumped up, screaming.

"Stop jumping around like a scared chimp!" Hester said to him.

Graham stopped and rolled his eyes upward to try to see what was sitting on top of his head.

"It's that pesky little critter of Kristina Kingsly's," Davina said. She grabbed hold of Raymond.

"Hey, watch where you're squeezing me. I just finished my midnight snack, and I'm still quite full," Raymond said.

Davina was so startled to here Raymond speak that she dropped him.

"Clumsy girl," Raymond said, just before scampering off into the woods.

"This is too weird, being in this strange place, and to top it all off, talking rodents! I must be dreaming," Hester said nervously.

"Well, then why don't I splash some mud in your face? That should wake you up," Graham said, while trying to rub some of the mud off his freckled face.

"I must admit, it is kind of freaky," Davina said. Then she turned to Graham. "Hey, aren't you the kid who put that stinky Limburger cheese in the classroom heater last year?"

"Yeah, how did you know?" Graham asked.

"What do you mean, how did I know? Everyone heard about it. My brother Marvin told me that it stunk up the hallway for over a month."

"Yeah, wasn't it great?" Graham laughed.

"Hello? Aren't you guys forgetting something," Hester said impatiently. "We're standing here in some weird forest, in our p.j.'s, and to top it off, we heard a rat talk!"

"Yeah, and aren't you a fine sight to see," Graham teased. Hester did look kind of funny, with her hair all messed up. "I can't believe it. This is the first time ever that I've seen you without that stupid bow in your hair, Hester."

Hester made a face at Graham, and said, "I wouldn't be surprised if all of this is just another one of your ridiculous pranks."

"Thanks for the compliment, but I'm in enough trouble. I'm practically grounded for the entire Christmas holiday break. I certainly don't need anything else to add to my list. Besides do you think I would have gone to this much trouble to prank you guys, being that I'm the one covered in mud and all?"

"Good point, but then how did we all get here?" Davina asked.

"Do you think I look that smart?" Graham said."

"Definitely not," Davina said.

Hester looked around the moss-laden forest. "I'm feeling kind of scared," she said.

"Stop being such a baby," Graham said coldly.

Davina looked about and noticed a trail leading back to the finely manicured lawn. Then she noticed Rumalock's cottage. "Hey, look, there's a little house. Let's go see if there's anyone home," she said.

"Yeah, maybe there'll be some grub we can eat. I'm starving," Graham chimed in.

"I could go for that," Davina said.

The three of them tromped over to Rumalock's house, stomped down the little steps, and knocked on the old wooden door. Nobody came to answer; Rumalock was still out. Graham pounded a second time on the door. Then he put his ear up against it to see if he could hear anyone walking around inside. "Doesn't look like anyone's home," he said.

"Let's check to see if any windows are open," Davina said.

"What do you mean, like break in?" Hester asked.

"Well, we are hungry, aren't we?" Graham responded with a

big grin on his face.

"Starving," Davina answered.

The three of them walked around the cottage.

"This place is really weird. Everything is so small," Graham said. They came to a window. "It looks like I'll have to crawl in, seeing that there's no way either of you will fit through it," Graham said.

"Hey, you watch your tongue, Graham Kepler. You'd better remember it's my family who lets you spend summer vacations at our horse ranch, and I could change those arrangements real fast," Hester said.

"Yeah, yeah," Graham replied, brushing off her comment.

Suddenly lightning flashed across the sky, and a few seconds later, they heard a loud clap of thunder. The rainstorm had finally hit Rumalock's neck of the woods.

- 9 -

Queen Sentiz

Queen Sentiz was nervously pacing the floor when the large ornate door cracked open. Her head servant, a dwarf named Ugan, dressed like a court jester, sheepishly poked his head into the elaborate meeting room. "Your son has arrived, Your Majesty. Do you wish for me to send for him now?"

The queen walked briskly toward the door, grabbed the doorknob, and flung the door wide open. Ugan scurried backwards like a dog cowering with its tail between its legs.

"Send him here at once!" she yelled, clenching her fists and digging her long red nails into the palms of her hands.

"Right away, my lady," Ugan responded timidly. He headed down a long winding staircase, almost tripping over his own feet.

Queen Sentiz slammed the large door shut and started to pace the floor again. Not long after, the sound of a horse's hooves on the cobblestones below the window caught her attention, so she went to look outside. As she approached the window, a brisk wind blew her long black hair about her sharp-featured face. One of her zelbocks was leading her son's horse away to its stable and steam was coming off the exhausted animal's body.

The rainstorm had arrived and a bolt of lightning flashed across the sky, followed by a loud clap of thunder. It frightened the horse, causing it to rear up on its hind legs. The zelbock took its whip and snapped it on the tired animal's back. This brought a smile to the queen's face.

While she was still glaring out the window, a knock came at the door. "Enter!" she yelled in an irritated tone.

Her son Ramon, a big, awkward young man with a large bulbous nose, squinty eyes, and a permanently quizzical look on his face, walked into the room. His jet-black hair hung like a wet mop over his face, and it dripped all over his already rain-soaked clothing.

"Well, don't just stand there like an idiot. Give me the Magic Warble," the queen commanded.

"I...I didn't get it, Mama," the prince stammered, looking worried.

"*What?*" the queen yelled, her thin lips almost disappearing around her clenched, protruding teeth. "You're an imbecile, just like your father. I tell you, if you weren't from my blood, I would have already imprisoned you as well."

Queen Sentiz had banished her husband, Prince Raspue, to a horrible prison on the remote Treachery Island, located south of Bernovem.

"Our plan failed, Mama, when Zitrot tried to snatch the Magic Warble from the girl, he was shot with an arrow through his back."

The queen's blood seemed to boil inside her. "*Who shot him?*" she yelled, sticking her ski-slope nose in his face.

Prince Ramon put his arms up, as if to defend himself from being hit. "I'm sorry to say, but it was that troublesome boy, Werrien," he answered, while cowering away from his irate mother.

In a furious rage, the queen marched to the door and swung it open. Ugan was standing at attention right outside. "Get Rupert right now!" she yelled.

"Yes, right away, my sweet queen," Ugan answered. Then he bowed many times while moving backwards toward a long, winding staircase. As he descended, the bells on his clothing could be heard jingling. A short while later, he returned with Sir Rupert, who had been given his title by the queen, due to his ability to perform magic.

Sir Rupert, the queen's advisor, was an old man, very tall and lanky, with small dark eyes, and a thin long nose that pointed downward over a pair of tense, thin lips. His skin was almost transparent, due to his ill disposition.

Ugan knocked on the large, ornate door.

"*Enter!*" the queen yelled.

Ugan bowed to Sir Rupert and then summoned him into the queen's quarters. Hunched over and carrying a black leather suitcase, the old man entered the large meeting room.

"Ah, Sir Rupert, please come in and sit down," the queen said in an unusually soft tone.

Very slowly, Sir Rupert walked into the room, stopped, and bowed to the queen; then he proceeded to a large meeting table. But before he could sit down, he started to cough. The queen's eyes grew wide as she waited for him to stop, and she impatiently drummed her long red nails on her chin. When he didn't stop, she couldn't stand it any longer, so she yelled for Ugan to come back into the room. Ugan, being right outside the door, came quickly back into the room. He then took one of the chairs from the large meeting table and slid it over beside Sir Rupert. He crawled up on it, made his hand into a fist, and proceeded to hit Sir Rupert on his back to stop him from coughing. Finally, the old man indicated with a hand gesture for Ugan to stop. Ugan crawled down off the large ornate chair and pushed it behind Sir Rupert. As the chair hit the back of the old man's knees, he fell into it in a sitting position. Using all his strength, Ugan pushed the chair up to the meeting table.

"Will that be all, Your Highness?" Ugan asked.

"Yes, yes, be on your way," the queen answered and impatiently waved her hand for him to leave.

Ugan bowed humbly and once again left the room. The queen brought her attention back to her son, Ramon, who was staring out the castle window with a dazed look on his face. She cleared her throat to get his attention. When he finally looked over to her, she said, "Sit down, you idiot, and this time take better note of what's going on."

Prince Ramon blew his nose loudly with a silk handkerchief that had the queen's face embroidered on it, a present from his father,

Prince Raspue, when he'd still lived at the palace. Prince Ramon walked over to the meeting table and sat down. Once again the queen yelled for Ugan. Ugan entered at once, and seeing the queen standing, waiting for him, he pulled out her ornate, plush chair from the head of the table. He walked over to the tall queen, who towered over him, took her by the hand and led her to the chair to sit down. After she was seated, she held out her ring-clustered hand toward him. Ugan bowed and kissed it. The queen smiled slyly, patted him on the head, and with one of her long red fingernails, flicked one of the bells that hung from his court jester's hat.

"You're such a well-behaved little dwarf," she said calmly. Then as if she had a change in personality, she said angrily, "Now get out of here!"

Sir Rupert, who was sitting across from the queen, bent over and almost fell out of his chair while trying to pick up his suitcase. Queen Sentiz pretended not to notice and didn't even think to lend a hand to help. It took all of Sir Rupert's strength, but he somehow managed to lift the case and place it on the table. As he opened it, the queen looked like she might start drooling with anticipation. As for Prince Ramon, he sat slumped on his seat, seeming quite bored with the whole situation.

Sir Rupert reached into his suitcase and removed a purple silk cloth. Underneath it, cushioned in a bed of purple velvet, was a shimmering crystal, about the size of a small foam football. With his long bony fingers, he took it out of its bed and lifted it high above his head. He closed his eyes and mumbled something. Sitting beside him, Prince Ramon bit his fingernails and rolled his eyes impatiently. The queen was so entranced with the crystal that she didn't notice her son's behavior.

"Please remove the suitcase from the table," Sir Rupert said.

Queen Sentiz looked to Prince Ramon, who was not paying attention, and she slapped the table hard in front of him. The prince, startled, jumped and knocked against the underside of the table with his large knobby knees. Sir Rupert jumped as well and almost dropped the crystal on his own head. He gave Prince Ramon a look of disgust that encouraged him to quickly take the suitcase off the table.

Once again, Sir Rupert proceeded to lift the crystal above his head and chanted something again. When he was finished, he slowly brought the crystal down in front of him and carefully balanced it on the table. Then he waved his bony fingers around it and as he did so, it started to glow with a bright, multicolored light, which reflected off the walls. The crystal began to spin around in circles, flashing its colors on the walls. Suddenly, it stopped spinning and all the bright colors were sucked back inside it. Prince Ramon eagerly leaned forward to look inside the crystal. He could see the rushing Indra River with all its splashes, curves, and drop-offs.

"There they are!" he blurted out, hitting the crystal with his large bulbous nose, almost knocking it over.

"If you'd move your enormous head, we could see also," the queen snapped.

"Oh, sorry, Mama," Prince Ramon said sheepishly. He moved his head out of the way, and Queen Sentiz and Sir Rupert leaned forward to look into the crystal.

"Where are they? I can't see them," the queen said abruptly.

"Look closely to the right side of the river, my lady," Sir Rupert said.

"Ah ha! Yes, there's the little human scum," the queen grimaced.

While they were glaring into the crystal, the Indra River suddenly disappeared, and the crystal lit up once more. Its kaleidoscope of colors started to spin around the room again.

"What is the meaning of this?" the queen asked Sir Rupert.

"The crystal has found something else important to show us," Sir Rupert answered.

The colors funneled back into the crystal, and it stopped spinning. The three huddled around it. This time it was not the Indra River that was brought into view but the inside of Rumalock's house.

"More humans!" Prince Ramon said, surprised as well as disgusted.

They could see Davina, Hester, and Graham in Rumalock's cottage, standing around the chocolate cake, gobbling it down like it was their last meal.

"They're popping up like a bad skin rash, the retched little gluttons," Prince Ramon went on.

Just as he finished speaking, the crystal went dark and tipped over. The queen turned to Prince Ramon and said, "Saddle your horse at once, and this time take at least one hundred zelbocks with you. We can't afford to let them slip away again." She marched over to the door and swung it open. On the other side sat Ugan, leaning against the wall, sleeping. She stomped her foot loudly, and he jumped up to stand at attention. "You pathetic little dwarf! Get up! I've got a chore for you," she snapped.

"What is it, Your Majesty?" Ugan asked, still feeling groggy.

The queen grabbed him by his beard and lifted him up. "You will go to the house of that good-for-nothing brother of yours, Rumalock, and lead the humans back here into my trap," she said.

Although Ugan didn't like the idea, his only choices were either to obey the wicked queen and keep his servants life, or to disobey and be banished to Treachery Island forever. He chose to obey.

Leacha's House

After jumping into the Indra River, Kristina and Werrien were separated, and the raging water swiftly dragged Kristina down its course. Barely staying afloat, she managed to grab hold of a tree branch that was dangling over the river's edge, but the limb was almost completely broken off from the tree. As she bobbed up and down in the ice-cold water, gasping for air, her hands grew numb, and she could barely hold on to the branch. The chilly water made her body weak, and she grew weary. One of her hands slipped off the branch, and then the branch snapped and floated away from the tree. She was so exhausted and cold that she could only allow the river to pull her along its course. As she was pulled along, many thoughts began to pass through her mind: *Will I ever see my family again? Who will look after Raymond? Is this how my life is going to end?*

Suddenly, the worrisome thoughts stopped and she began to feel very peaceful—so peaceful, in fact, that she was just about to close her eyes and let the river have its way. But then she glanced up to see something fluttering above the surface of the water. She felt a surge of adrenaline flow through her body, and it gave her the strength to pull herself up. When she surfaced, the rain pounded on her head. She gasped for air and then opened her eyes to see Looper hovering in front of her. Then she saw a tree branch in front of her.

"Grab on!" Looper shouted.

She looked up to see that it was Werrien who was holding the tree branch out to her. She grabbed hold of it, and he pulled her to safety. Once on dry land, she tried to stand up but couldn't; she fell over from exhaustion. Werrien placed a blanket around her, and then carried her to his home in the forest. It wasn't until the next day that she finally roused herself, and as she was slowly waking up, she could hear a conversation.

"She seems okay to me. What do you think?"

"Well, if she's not, it's probably because she grabbed onto the broken tree branch. You'd think she'd have had enough sense to grab hold of a branch that was still connected to the tree."

Kristina opened her eyes to see Clover looking at her reflection in the window and fixing her hair.

"I thought it might be you guys," Kristina said weakly.

The sound of footsteps could be heard approaching the bedroom. When the door swung open, there stood a short, plump, strange-looking elderly woman. In one hand she carried a cup with something steaming in it, and in the other hand she had a dish towel. Seeing the fairies sitting on the bedpost, she took the dish towel and flicked it at them.

"Shoo! Shoo! You pesky little critters," she said, as though they were nothing more then common houseflies.

Looper and Clover flew toward the open window, but Clover, being the feisty fairy she was, quickly flew behind the old woman and yanked as hard as she could on a couple of her hairs.

"Ouch!" the old woman yelled, almost spilling the hot substance in the cup. She turned around quickly and glanced about the room. "I'll lay tree sap out where you least expect it. That'll fix you little pests!" she said angrily.

As she spoke, Clover was just outside the window, mimicking her.

The old woman turned her attention back to Kristina and, in a more soothing tone, said, "My dear child, you're finally awake."

She sat down on the bed. "My name is Leacha. I am Werrien's mother," she said proudly.

Kristina found it quite hard to believe that Werrien could have such a strange-looking mother—she looked nothing at all like him. The strange old woman's ears were pointy, like Rumalock's, but she didn't look like a dwarf. Her face and nose were much rounder and she had a few gray whiskers sticking out of her double chin. "You'll be as good as new after a cup of hot, nourishing soup," she said, her warm smile revealing an almost toothless mouth.

Kristina sat up, and Leacha handed her the steaming cup.

"All I remember is being pulled out of the river by Werrien," Kristina said, after taking a sip of the hot broth, which she thought tasted quite nasty.

"You fainted," Leacha said, "You were starting to worry us, sleeping as long as you did."

"My name is Kristina."

"Yes, I know," Leacha said.

"Are you a dwarf?" Kristina asked.

Leacha giggled a little, and her eyes seemed to disappear into the folds of her fat cheeks. "Oh, no, child. I'm a gnome."

Kristina handed the soup back to Leacha. She started to reach into her pocket, but to her surprise, she had no pockets. Then she looked down at herself and said in a panic, "These are not my clothes, and the Magic Warble—it's gone! I must have lost it in that raging river."

"Don't fret, child. I had to give you dry clothes," Leacha said. She pointed her chubby finger to a chair in the corner of the room. "Yours are now clean and dry, hanging over there, and as for the Magic Warble, well, it's safe with Werrien."

A knock came at the front door, and Leacha left the bedroom to go answer it. Kristina could see from the bed that it was Werrien. He entered the house and embraced Leacha.

"How is she, Leacha? Is she awake yet?" Werrien asked.

"Yes, she is, and she's doing just fine," Leacha said.

"That's good to hear; I've been really worried," Werrien said.

Kristina felt strange after hearing Werrien say those words.

"She should be as good as new after a cup of my turnip-root fairy-blossom soup," Leacha said.

"Thank you, Leacha, for all your help," Werrien said.

"You know I would do anything to help. You are like my own son."

"You're too kind," Werrien went on.

"I still have some soup left on the fire. Sit down, and I will serve you."

"I'd love to have some, but I'm afraid I won't be able to. There's news that Queen Sentiz has sent out more of her zelbocks to find Kristina and me, so we must be out of here within the hour."

Tears welled up in Leacha's eyes, and she used her apron to wipe them. "I've always known that this day would come, but now that it's here, it's hard to take," she said.

Kristina got out of bed and stood near the door to better hear the conversation. She was surprised by Werrien's concern for her well-being, and it made her feel good that someone near her own age cared about her. She certainly hadn't experienced that with the kids at home.

A mirror hung on the wall across the room, and when she viewed her own reflection, she took notice of the clothes that Leacha had dressed her in. They were made of soft suede and looked very similar to the clothes that Werrien wore. They were very comfortable, and she liked how they looked on her. She looked once again at her own clothes hanging on the chair and decided not to change back into them. A hairbrush was on a nearby table, so she took it and brushed her hair. When she was finished, she walked into the living room.

Werrien noticed her and his eyes lit up. "Wow, you look great!"

"I do?" Kristina asked.

"Yeah! You kind of look like you could be my little brother—I mean, except for your long hair."

"Thanks! My dream has always been to look like someone's little brother," Kristina said sarcastically.

Werrien walked over to her, and in a chummy way, gave her a light punch on her shoulder. "Now that you're all better, we'd best be on our way," he said.

Leacha hurried off to the kitchen to pack food for their journey.

"I'll be outside with Taysha while you're getting ready," Werrien said.

Kristina wondered who Taysha was and kind of hoped that it wasn't another nasty fairy like Clover. She went into the kitchen and saw that Leacha was busy filling a sack with food. Leacha took a large wooden canister off the counter and tried to untwist the lid. Kristina could see that she was having trouble getting it off.

"Could I help you with that?" she asked.

"Would you be so kind?" Leacha handed her the wooden canister. Kristina gave it a good twist, and off the lid came. "Such a strong girl," Leacha said.

"I think you must have loosened it for me," Kristina said. She handed it back to Leacha. Leacha looked inside the jar and a sad expression came across her face.

"Is there something wrong?" Kristina asked.

Leacha pointed to a small leather pouch hanging from a hook on the wall. "Would you hand me that little pouch, dear?" she asked. Kristina took the little pouch off the hook and handed it to Leacha, who poured the contents of the wooden canister into it. "I hope that nothing will happen, but just in case, you will need this if you or Werrien get injured on your journey," she said. She handed the pouch to Kristina. "I know it's not much, but it's all that I have left."

"What is it?" Kristina asked.

"It's dried fairy blossom. Please don't tell Werrien that I gave it to you."

"Won't you need this to keep up your own strength?" Kristina asked.

"Don't you worry about me. I'm an old lady and I have lived a poor yet very blessed life. If my days are shortened, then at least I will know that I did my best to help the true prince of Bernovem." She smiled and took Kristina's hands in her own. "Please take it."

"Will you be able to get more for yourself?" Kristina asked.

"I'll be just fine, child. Now no more questions. We need to get you two on your way."

Kristina accepted the little pouch and was about to put it in with the sack of food, but Leacha stopped her.

"No, child, you must keep it with you, just in case you two get separated from these other things," she said.

The door in the kitchen opened and Werrien walked in. "We must leave at once. There are many zelbocks looking for us. A dwarf passing by told me that he has seen them. They're less then two hours away," he said.

Kristina followed Werrien out of Leacha's house, and once outside, she was surprised to see that the house was in the bottom of a large tree. Not far off, under another tree, stood a horse. Werrien walked up to it and threw a saddle onto its back. Kristina had never seen such a beautiful horse. It was so elegant, with a snow-white coat and a shimmering silver mane. She wondered if she was going to ride on it. She went up to it and stroked it on the nose.

"It's not that bad. Besides, it beats walking all the way."

Kristina quickly pulled her hand away. *Was that the horse talking?*

"What's the matter? Haven't been around horses before?" Werrien asked her.

"I'm sure that I just heard it talk," Kristina said.

"What's the big deal? All animals talk," Werrien said.

"Not where I come from," Kristina said.

"Well they do in Bernovem. Come here; I'll give you a lift up on Taysha."

Kristina had never ridden a horse, and she was a bit nervous to do so, but there was no way she was going to let Werrien know—she'd had enough of his sarcasm as it was. She calmly walked over to Taysha's side, where Werrien was standing with his back toward her. When she came close enough, he turned around to face her, holding a knife in his hand. Kristina looked shocked.

"Don't be afraid. I just thought that this would go good with those old clothes of mine you're wearing. Besides, it might come in handy along our journey," he said.

Kristina wasn't sure if she should take the knife. Her mother and father would have never allowed her to carry one around. Werrien sensed her apprehension and was about to put it away.

"What are you doing?" she asked.

"By the look on your face, I figured you didn't want it," he said.

Kristina laughed nervously. "I'd love to carry that knife," she said.

Looking a little puzzled, Werrien handed it to her. "Now you look like a true warrior," he said.

Kristina blushed. Even though it wasn't a compliment she would have expected, she kind of liked it.

Werrien helped her onto his horse, and then he jumped up onto the front of the saddle. They said good bye to Leacha, and as they headed into the moss-laden forest, Leacha stood outside her tree house door, crying and waving farewell with her handkerchief.

- 11 -

A Pain in the Rear

After tripping over a rock, Ugan toppled down a slope and landed on a nasty thorn bush. He moaned with pain as he looked to see that his bottom was stuck with many thorns, some as large as toothpicks. Just above in a tree, a black raven cawed down to him. "Oh, quit your squawking, or I'll knock you out of that tree," Ugan said, his voice straining from the intense pain.

"Give me some of your food, and I'll pull those thorns out for you in a jiffy," the raven said.

Ugan ignored the raven and tried to reach around himself to pull out the thorns. The raven felt Ugan was ungrateful and so he flew away. Ugan realized that he wasn't able to reach the thorns with his short arms, so he yelled after the raven, "Okay! I'll take your offer, but just for a few crumbs of bread."

Brushing the top of Ugan's head, the raven landed on a rock next to him.

"Well, come on, I don't have all day," Ugan said, while leaning against the rock and sticking his bottom out.

The raven hopped to the ground behind him and took a thorn in his beak. As he pulled it out, Ugan's face went scarlet red, and his usually straight beard hairs curled up from the agonizing pain. The raven kept pulling away at the thorns, and Ugan stuck his fist in his mouth and bit down on it to take his focus off his pain. Finally, the raven pulled the last thorn out of Ugan's bottom. Then it hopped back onto the rock, and Ugan stood up with a very stiff back from bending over so long. The raven watched with large, hungry eyes as Ugan began untying his lunch sack from his waist. Just as he had finished untying it, the raven snatched the small sack from Ugan's hand and flew off with it.

"Why, you good-for-nothing..." Ugan yelled. With fumbling hands, he tried to untie his slingshot from his waist. But it was no use; by the time he finally held it to the sky, the raven was a mere speck off in the distance. Ugan sank down against the rock, and as his bottom touched the ground, he moaned in pain. *Now what am I supposed to do?* he thought.

He had neither food nor the measly amount of fairy blossom rationed to him by the queen. Feeling such despair, he drifted off to sleep and began to dream about his life in the past, when things had been much better. Prince Raspue was still at the palace and had treated him with kindness. The prince had allowed Ugan to have clean and comfy sleeping quarters, healthy meals, and plenty of fairy-blossom tea, which gave him ample energy to do his job, for which he formerly had been paid. He would have two days a week off, during which he could spend time outdoors, fishing, working in the garden, or just basking in the sun. His dream was so relaxing and peaceful, but then it suddenly changed. Four zelbocks were taking Prince Raspue as a prisoner. They handcuffed him and dragged him out of the palace. Queen Sentiz watched from the palace window, laughing at the sight of her husband being humiliated as he was dragged away. While she stood there, her face grew larger and larger, and her laugh grew louder and louder, until her mouth was about to swallow Ugan's head. Ugan woke up, shocked from his dream. Sweating and shaking, he sat there with his eyes wide and his breath heavy.

It was dark out and hard to see. An owl screeched loudly and made him jump to his feet. He realized that it would be too dangerous to travel any farther in the dark, so he made the decision to find a safe place to take cover for the night. He would try to sleep and would get an early start in the morning to Rumalock's house. He hoped that he could make it by mid-afternoon the next day. He crawled up the slope that he had fallen down earlier and when he reached the top, he felt winded, so he stopped to rest. He poked his head between a thatch of grass to view the trees in the forest ahead. He could see a small fire burning, and he noticed a dwarf coming toward the fire, carrying wood. The dwarf placed the wood down and then knelt by the fire to stoke it. Ugan sat quietly, hoping the other dwarf wouldn't notice him. He didn't want to take the chance of any more bad encounters, for he had had enough for one day. The other dwarf rolled out a sleeping mat beside the fire and then laid down on it. Ugan waited until he was sure that the dwarf was asleep before he tiptoed closer to the fire to get a better look. He could see a large knapsack across the fire from the sleeping dwarf. Ugan was usually not one for stealing, but he had not eaten since the day before, nor had he had any fairy blossom, which he desperately needed for his stamina.

The other dwarf began snoring away, so Ugan cautiously approached the knapsack, but as he did so, the sleeping dwarf tossed himself over to lie on his other side. Ugan hid behind the knapsack, hoping that the sleeping dwarf wouldn't wake up. He waited a few more minutes until the dwarf was snoring again. Then he untied the tassels of the sack. As it opened, a pot and a spoon fell out, clanking loudly on the ground. The sleeping dwarf sat up abruptly, and Ugan quickly hid behind the sack and tried not to make a sound. The other dwarf glanced nervously about the woods, but when he didn't see anything, he went back to sleep. Ugan cautiously dug his hand into the sack to see if he could feel any food. He pulled out an apple and some fairy blossom—finally, something to ease his nervous mind. He took only enough for a few days; after all, he didn't want to leave the sleeping dwarf without any for himself. He retied the tassels on the knapsack and quietly tiptoed off into the forest to find a place to rest for the night. He found a large tree with a smooth base where he could build a fire as well as sleep. Then he settled down for the night.

While sitting by his own cozy fire, drinking the fairy-blossom tea he had stolen, the raven, named Roage picked through the stolen lunch with some other ravens. As they rummaged through it, Roage came across a napkin with the queen's face on it. Queen Sentiz had made sure that her portraits were on almost everything in the palace. The largest ones were in gaudy, ornate frames that hung on all the walls of every room in the palace, and the smallest ones were on the sides of each and every quill pen. Captured fairies were made to work as slave laborers to paint many of the portraits.

Noticing the portrait of the queen on the napkin, Roage became very angry. No animal in Bernovem, even the most sneaky and conniving, supported the queen. Anyone from her household would have to be pretty brave—or pretty stupid—to travel alone in the deep woods. Ugan really was neither of those—except maybe a smidgen of the latter.

"We can't let this imposter loose in our forest," Roage said to his comrades, who were busy gobbling down some stale bread. "The little sneak," Roage went on. While the other ravens fought over the last few crumbs, Roage spread his wings and cawed loudly to get their attention. They dropped the bread crumbs out of their beaks and stood silent, looking at him with their beady black eyes. "We must leave at dawn to find him," Roage said.

As dawn rolled in, the ravens left their tree to find Ugan, but after searching for a long time and finding nothing, they were ready to give up. The five of them flew up to a tree and perched on a branch to rest. It was foggy, damp, and miserably cold out.

"It's no use; he's not out here," one of the ravens said.

"That's what I'm thinking, and I'm getting hungry," another raven chimed in.

But suddenly, they heard some rustling.

"Quiet! I hear something!" Roage said, tilting his head sideways to look down from the tree where they were perched. At the base of it, huddled under a small gray blanket with the queen's portrait embroidered on it, lay Ugan, sleeping soundly. The five ravens dropped to the ground and hopped toward the gray mound. They grabbed hold of the blanket with their beaks and, all at once, yanked it off of Ugan.

Ugan woke abruptly. "What, when, where am I?" he said, still half-asleep.

With their wings stretched out, the ravens circled around him, cawing loudly.

"What do you want from me?" Ugan asked, backing himself up against the tree.

"We know who you are," one of the ravens said.

"A dirty traitor," another one said.

"You work for that wicked Queen Sentiz," Roage said.

"You don't understand. I'm really only her slave," Ugan responded.

But the ravens had no mercy, and they began to close in on him. They pecked at him with their long, pointed beaks. Ugan managed to kick them away, but they had already torn his pants and nipped his legs until they were bloody. When he finally broke free of them, he began to run as fast as his little legs could carry him.

Through the foggy forest, the ravens tailed close behind him, swooping down and pecking at his head, making it very hard for him to see in which direction he was going. But he dared not stop. He had heard stories of ravens like these actually killing dwarfs. These stories were always thought to be no more then old dwarfs' tales, the kind that would be told late at night while sitting around bonfires, but even so, he wasn't taking any chances.

As the chase went on, the weather changed, and it started to rain heavily. Lightning struck a tree and it fell, almost hitting Ugan on the head. Luckily he managed to outrun it, but just barely. The ravens were also having a hard time chasing him in the heavy rain, and so they flew up to a tree branch to rest.

"He's lucky this time, the traitor! But I'd better not catch him again in our neck of the woods," Roage said as he and the other four sat, drenched, on the branch.

As Ugan kept running, the forest started to look familiar. The rain began to lighten up, and he noticed that the ravens were gone. He finally stopped and leaned against a tree to catch his breath. While panting heavily, he stared through the tall mossy trees, and to his surprise, he could see, directly in front of him, his brother Rumalock's cottage.

- 12 -

A Special Invitation

It was quite a surprise for Ugan that he had run all the way to Rumalock's cottage, for he was expecting the journey to take much longer. He leaned against a tree, trying to catch his breath, and with a shaky hand, he wiped the sweat off his brow and thought about the task that lay ahead of him. He really wasn't looking forward to it, especially with his nerves so wrenched from the frightful chase and his legs in pain from the cuts that the nasty ravens had made. Leading the three human children into Her Majesty's trap only gave him a sick feeling in his stomach to add to it all.

Her Majesty—what an unsuitable title for such a horrible being, he thought. But that was beside the point; his life was at stake, and what had to be done just had to be done. He hated to be deceitful, but at the same time, he wasn't going to risk maybe being banished to Treachery Island. He had been there many times with the queen, and it was not a pretty place. Prisoners were held in locks and chains, in cold damp cells, and he could still recall their screams of anguish. Most of them would go insane over time from being there so long. The mere thought of it sent a chill down his spine.

A hope of a new Bernovem was something Ugan didn't have. The reality of living in the dismal palace with the self-absorbed queen was as far as he could see. He was a dwarf of little faith, and he envied his brother Rumalock for opting to live a simple life. Though Rumalock had to live poorly and spend a lot of his days in search of the almost-extinct fairy blossom, it still seemed much better than Ugan's life at the palace. *Luxuries and riches are not always what they are chalked up to be*, he thought. If he'd only listened to Rumalock's advice years ago, about not taking the position at the palace, he would have been much better off. But then again, how was he supposed to know that Queen Sentiz had such a plan to oppress and dictate over Bernovem? Her beauty and charm were so convincing, and it just seemed too farfetched, all the talk among the so-called believers about a Magic Warble being returned someday to bring peace to Bernovem. Besides he wasn't the only one not taking it seriously; most dwarfs and gnomes didn't believe it. The believers were in the minority.

Ugan thought again to the task that lay ahead, and he hoped that Rumalock wouldn't be home, so that he could just pretend that the cottage was his own. He took a deep breath and started off toward it, hoping what he needed to do would just come to him as he went along. He walked very quietly, so as not to be seen or heard. As he drew near the cottage, he could see a light coming from the front window and smoke coming out of the chimney. He peeked in the window. There was no sight of Rumalock, but sitting on the couch were two girls, and in Rumalock's armchair sat a boy. The three of them were playing cards, and the boy was smoking Rumalock's pipe. They were arguing over the game.

"Graham, I saw you looking at my cards, you cheat!" one girl said.

"I was not, Hester!" Graham replied.

"That's why you've been winning every time," the other girl added.

"Right, Davina. He's nothing but a dirty rotten cheat!" Hester went on.

Graham took a big puff from the pipe and then blew the smoke in Hester's face.

"That's it! I've had it with you!" Hester yelled, throwing her cards down. She reached out and grabbed Graham by his hair, and just as they were about to fight like wild barbarians, Ugan walked into the cottage. Hester let go of Graham's hair and the three children stood up, looking very surprised.

"Well, well! I wasn't expecting company, but even so, I must say that I'm glad to see I have guests," Ugan said.

The children looked at each other, and then Davina said, "Aren't you even upset that we broke into your house?"

"Upset? How could I be upset at the sight of three lovely children as yourselves. An old chap like me rarely gets such fine company," Ugan said, while hanging his cloak on a wall hook.

Graham hid the smoking pipe behind his back, but Davina and Hester gave him dirty looks because of the smoke and stink it was putting out.

Ugan also noticed the smoke seeping up from behind Graham's back and said, "Oh, I see that you've found my pipe."

Graham's freckled face went tomato red with embarrassment, and he became tongue-tied.

"Well, I'm glad you're enjoying it," Ugan continued.

Once again the three children looked oddly at each other because of Ugan's reaction to the pipe.

"You hardly look human. What are you?" Hester asked.

"I am a dwarf, and my name is Ugan." Ugan offered his hand to Graham. Graham thinking Ugan to be strange, hardly touched his hand and when he did, he pulled it away quickly.

"Welcome to the land of Bernovem," Ugan said. Ugan took each girl by her hand and placed a kiss on it.

Hester gave Davina another weird look at this gesture. "We want to know how we got here," Hester said, her snootiness rising up once again.

Ugan didn't know how to answer, so he thought quickly and made something up. "You see, children, you may not realize how very fortunate you are," he said. "You have been chosen by the most honorable Queen Sentiz of Bernovem to visit her in her beautiful palace, where you will be treated as royalty." Ugan hoped this would entice them.

Davina's and Hester's faces lit up, but Graham looked very suspicious.

"When do we get to go?" Davina asked excitedly.

"We must leave at once, for the sooner we get there, the sooner your pampering will begin," Ugan answered, rubbing his hands together.

Graham did not quite believe what Ugan was offering them. "How do we know we can trust you?" he asked apprehensively.

Ugan thought hard for a moment and then said, "You know, I can tell you are a very smart young man, with much concern for your friends' and your own safety, and this tells a lot about you. I must tell you that Her Majesty is longing for such a nice boy as yourself that she can spoil as she did her own son, whom I'm sad to say"— Ugan lowered his head as if from great sorrow—"has passed on."

Graham's suspicious look suddenly changed to an annoying grin. Hester stomped her foot hard on Graham's toe to let him know that he'd better not ruin this once in a lifetime opportunity.

"Ouch!" Graham yelled. Not only did his toe hurt, but he'd also burnt his finger on the hot pipe. As he did so, he stepped backwards and hit the top of his head on the underneath of the fireplace mantel, causing three books to fall off, one of them being the Book of Prophecy. The three children began to bicker among themselves and so paid no attention as the book lay open on the floor—with their names on the open page.

Ugan snatched it up quickly, and as he did so, he could see the word "*zelbocks*" very faintly appearing, and then the word "*pillage*," and then his brother's name, "*Rumalock*". He quickly glanced out the window to see eight zelbocks coming out of the forest, carrying torches.

"We really must leave now!" he said urgently.

"We're more than ready," Hester said, grabbing Graham by the arm.

Ugan put on his cloak and tucked the Book of Prophecy inside it. Then he led the three children out the back door and down a path to the forest. A few minutes into their journey, they smelled smoke, and when they turned around, they saw Rumalock's cottage lit up in flames. Now Ugan realized the meaning of the last words he saw appear on the page in the Book of Prophecy.

- 13 -

Camping under the Stars

Kristina and Werrien were in the second day of their journey, and everything was going quite smoothly; even the rain had let up.

"It's going to get dark soon, so we'll need to stop and set up camp for the night," Werrien said to Kristina.

Kristina noticed a smooth spot on the ground not far off in the distance. "Look, there's a good spot over there," she suggested, pointing toward it.

"Good eye," Werrien said.

Kristina liked the fact that she and Werrien were getting along better, and she was starting to see that he had a nice side to him. They got off Taysha, and Werrien led her to a shady area under a large tree. Then he and Kristina went to look for wood to build a fire. While they were looking, they could hear Taysha talking.

"Watch where you're going! I almost stepped on you!" she said.

"Well, excuse me, Madam, but I don't see very well, not to mention that I have no idea where I am," a huffy voice replied.

Kristina and Werrien both stopped what they were doing to

listen. Then they went a little closer to Taysha to see who she was talking to.

Kristina's mouth dropped open in surprise. "Raymond? Is that you?" She walked quickly toward her beloved pet rat.

"Yes, it's me, and am I glad to see you!" Raymond said.

"Werrien, look! This is my pet rat, Raymond," she said excitedly. She picked Raymond up and kissed him on his head.

"Your pet rat? I haven't seen one of those in years," Werrien said, walking toward them to get a better look. He reached out to stroke Raymond's head. "He's a lot smaller than the ones that used to live in Bernovem."

"What do you mean, *used* to?" Kristina asked.

"There used to be rats in Bernovem, until Queen Sentiz had them all exterminated," Werrien said.

When Raymond heard this he crawled in Kristina's sleeve to hide.

"Why'd she do that?" Kristina asked.

"No one really knows, but if you ask me, I think it's because she just plain hates them, probably because they were so useful to the dwarfs and gnomes."

"Raymond's my best friend, but as for—"

Raymond poked his head out of Kristina's sleeve and interrupted her. "Hey! I know what you were going to say. You think that I'm not useful."

"No, Raymond, that's not what I meant," Kristina said, patting him on his little head.

"Well, I sure hope not," Raymond, said.

"You know that you're my best friend," Kristina continued.

"And that's a useful thing to be," Raymond said as he crawled back in her sleeve.

"Yes, of course it is, Raymond," Kristina reassured him.

Werrien went back to looking for wood to build the fire, and noticing he was gone, Kristina quickly joined him. "Anyhow, you were saying that the rats were useful to the dwarfs and gnomes? In what way?" Kristina asked him.

"It's not that interesting; besides, we really need to get a fire built."

"Actually, I found it quite interesting."

As they gathered wood together, Werrien went on. "Well, for instance, the rats could carry large bags of fairy blossom on their backs, which was very helpful when the dwarfs and gnomes harvested the flowers in large quantities. The rats would carry the fairy blossoms to the city, where it would be sold by the bushel in the marketplace. It was a great source of income for the dwarfs and gnomes."

"Were you alive during those days?" Kristina asked.

"I was very young, about three years old," Werrien answered.

Raymond poked his head out of Kristina's sleeve and said, "I hate to interrupt this lesson in history, but would you happen to have a little morsel for me to eat? I'm very hungry."

Kristina opened the food bag and pulled out a few crumbs of bread and gave them to Raymond. "I can hardly believe that Raymond can talk," she said to Werrien.

"I can't believe animals don't talk where you're from," Werrien said.

"It would make headline news if they did."

"That's odd. I couldn't imagine a world without talking animals." Werrien arranged the wood into a teepee-shape at their campsite and then lit the fire.

Evening set in, along with a thick fog. The two children sat by the crackling fire, eating the soup that Leacha had prepared for them. When they were finished, Werrien took the Magic Warble out of his pocket and swirled it around on the palm of his hand.

"Do you know how much farther we'll have to travel to get it to where it needs to be placed?" Kristina asked.

"If all goes as planned, I'd say we'll reach the city of Salas by evening tomorrow. From there, it should take us about a half a day to reach the bottom of Mount Bernovem. Then we'll climb as far as Taysha can climb. After that, I'll send her home on her own, and we'll travel the rest of the way on foot to the very top of the mountain."

"Why can't Taysha come?" Kristina asked.

"It's too steep for her. I'm just hoping we'll be able to make it.

74

I haven't told you yet, but it's a very treacherous climb. Nobody I know of has climbed to the top of Mount Bernovem—that is, at least since Queen Sentiz took over."

As Werrien stared at the Magic Warble, its rich dark-purple color swirled around inside it and changed into blue. "Hold out your hand," he said. Kristina held her hand out, and he dropped the ball onto her palm. "Thanks for letting me carry it," Werrien said. "It's been an honor for me to hold on to something that will finally bring peace and justice to our land and allow my mother, Lafinia, the true Queen of Bernovem, to be able to reign again."

"Lafinia—that's a beautiful name. What about your father? Where is he?" Kristina asked.

"I really don't know where he is or if he is even still alive. All I was told by my mother was that he and my uncle Corin—he's my father's brother—had to go on a long journey. They never returned, and so we figured that they must have been killed."

"I'm so sorry," Kristina said as she placed the Magic Warble back in her pocket.

They rolled out their sleeping mats and they lay on them under the bright stars. Kristina couldn't help but notice that the moon in the sky seemed much different than the moon at home. It was much larger, and its color was a pearly white.

"Werrien," she said.

"Yeah?"

"Where is your mother?"

"She's imprisoned in the top of a tower."

"Has anyone tried to rescue her?" Kristina asked.

"There have been many attempts, but so far they have all failed. You see, the tower is surrounded by the shark-infested Citnalta Sea. Her room is at the top of the tower and has only one small, barred window."

"It sounds like a very lonely place," Kristina said.

Werrien didn't respond.

"You must really miss her."

"I used to think that I'd never see her again, but now that the Magic Warble has come, I have hope."

They gazed up at the moonlit sky, both silent for a while. Then Kristina broke the silence, saying, "Werrien, I was wondering if you could tell me a little more about the Magic Warble?"

Werrien rolled on his side to face her. "When it is put back in its resting place, the spell that has allowed Sentiz to reign as sovereign queen over Bernovem will be lifted—at least, that is what the believers believe."

"Who are the believers?" Kristina asked.

"The ones who have held to the belief that the Magic Warble will return someday."

"Are there many nonbelievers?"

"Actually, there seem to be more of them than believers. It started out the other way around, where there were more believers, but over time, many gave up hope and became nonbelievers," Werrien said.

"What do the nonbelievers believe?" Kristina asked.

"They have accepted the horrible Sentiz as their sovereign queen, and they've been brainwashed to believe that the Magic Warble is just a fable," Werrien answered. Then he changed the subject. "Anyhow, tell me about where you are from. Is it much different than Bernovem?"

"In some ways it is, and in some ways not," Kristina answered.

"How is it different?" Werrien asked.

"Well, for instance, we don't have dwarfs, gnomes, fairies, or talking animals."

"Wow, that must be weird," Werrien said.

"And another thing, my world is much more modernized. We have motorized cars, trains, and airplanes, as well as computers and cell phones. Bernovem seems to be at least a century or more behind the time in my world," Kristina said.

Werrien yawned and closed his eyes. Kristina could see that he was growing very tired so she reached out and gently shook him. "Werrien," she said.

"Yeah?" he answered.

She sat up and took the Magic Warble out of her pocket. "Werrien, I want you to carry the Magic Warble."

"Why?" Werrien asked.

"I feel it will be safer with you, and besides, I would like you to have the honor of carrying it to where it needs to go," she said.

Werrien smiled. "You'd do that for me?"

"Just don't let it go to your head." Then she handed it back to him, and they went to sleep.

- 14 -

The Guests Arrive

While Ugan was filling his canteen with water at the Indra River, Davina, Hester, and Graham sat on a washed-up log on the riverbank.

"We're tired of walking! How much longer until we get to this so-called queen's palace?" Hester nagged Ugan.

"Now, now, patience, my dear. It's not much farther, and once you arrive, you'll have so much fun that you won't even remember how long the walk was," Ugan answered.

He actually was thinking that he couldn't wait to get the brats to the palace to meet her ladyship, "Sentiz the Horrible."

"This hiking stuff is really a boring drag. I sure wish I was home, where I could be playing video games," Graham griped as he flung dirt from a stick toward Hester.

The dirt hit Hester on her cheek. She quickly grabbed the stick away from Graham and was about to hit him with it. "You lousy, filthy—"

"Lovely children," Ugan interrupted as he finished tightening the lid on his canteen. "Save all that energy for the fun and games at the palace. Look at your friend. Why don't you follow her example?" He pointed to Davina, who was calmly gazing out at the Indra River and picking her nose. "She seems to be having a nice time."

Hester threw the stick on the ground and said, "Can we just get going? This walk is taking way too long."

Ugan started walking back to the forest and the three children followed him. They passed through the fairy colony, and they were fascinated by the very tall trees.

"Wow, I've never seen such gigantic trees in all my life," Davina said.

Then, suddenly, three fairies came from out of nowhere and zoomed around Graham's head, like bees around a flower. Graham ducked and waved his hands around as if they were attacking him. The fairies laughed and continued to torment him.

Davina, who was always game to whack at something, grabbed a branch off the ground. "Don't worry. I'll get the little pests. I'm not afraid of bees," she said, swinging the branch at the fairies. But it was Graham she almost hit in the head.

"Hey, watch my head!" Graham yelled.

The fairies were too fast for Davina and flew away without as much as a scratch on them.

"Those were the largest bees I've ever seen," Graham said to Ugan.

"They're not bees at all; they're fairies," Ugan replied.

"Fairies? Like the ones in little-kid stories?" Graham asked excitedly.

"There called 'fairy tales,' dumbo," Hester said sharply.

Graham's face broke into an annoying grin. He looked at Ugan and said, "Do you happen to have a jar or something? I'm gonna catch some of them and take them home. Then I'll charge people to see them, and I'll get filthy rich."

"Why, yes," Ugan replied. "We have just the sort of jar you'd need, but it is at the palace, so why don't we hurry along so we can get there? Then we can look for that jar."

If he didn't get back to the palace soon, he knew that the queen would punish him for taking too long.

~~~

Meanwhile, at the palace, Queen Sentiz sat at her ornate table, once again looking into the magic crystal. Her loyal counselor, the old Sir Rupert was at her side, now in a wheelchair because of his failing health.

"Can you see them?" she asked impatiently.

"Patience, my lady, they will appear shortly," Sir Rupert said.

Queen Sentiz got out of her chair and started pacing the floor. "Why hasn't that nincompoop dwarf returned yet?"

"Quick, my lady, come look," Sir Rupert said.

Queen Sentiz hurried back to the crystal to look inside it. "Where are they?" she asked.

Sir Rupert pointed his bony finger between the tall trees in the forest, and Queen Sentiz rubbed her hands together with satisfaction.

"Oh, yes, there are the little dumplings. I can hardly wait for their arrival," she said, a wicked smile appearing across her gaunt face. But then her expression changed to an insecure worried look, and she began nervously tapping her long red nails on the table.

"What is it, my lady? Is something distressing you?" Sir Rupert asked.

"I'm wondering where that good-for-nothing son of mine

is. Make the magic crystal do its thing again, so I can see his whereabouts," she said.

"As you wish," Sir Rupert responded. He closed his eyes and waved his bony fingers around the crystal, but just as he was about to begin his chant, the itch in his throat came back. Queen Sentiz glared down at him with ice-cold eyes as he tried desperately to hold in his cough. Thankfully, the itch went away, and he was able to continue on with his chant. The crystal lit up, and it began to spin again. Its colors swirled around the room. Then, once again, they formed a tornado-like funnel over the crystal and, just as before, were suddenly sucked back inside it. Prince Ramon appeared in the crystal, sitting in a field against a fallen tree, with his horse standing by his side.

"What is he doing?" the queen asked Sir Rupert.

"It looks to me, my lady, like the prince is whittling wood."

"*Whittling wood*? Why that lazy—"

"Someone is coming from off in the distance," Sir Rupert interrupted. "Look, my lady." He pointed his finger for her to see, but before she could see who it was, Sir Rupert's nagging itch came back in his throat. His face turned lobster red and he began to sweat. He tried to hold back his cough, but it was no use and he let out such a loud hack that it knocked the crystal over. Then it turned dark and teetered back and forth on its side.

Queen Sentiz was furious, and in her rage she stomped over to the door and flung it wide open. Two dwarfs were standing at attention right outside.

"*Take him!*" she yelled, pointing toward Sir Rupert.

They ran into the room and quickly rolled Sir Rupert's wheelchair out. The queen slammed the door shut behind them. She could hear Sir Rupert coughing as he was being rolled away down the long hallway to his bedroom. She stormed back over to the table, took a deep breath, and then calmly sat down. She stood the crystal up and, just as Sir Rupert had, waved her hands around it, but nothing happened. Her anger began to bubble up inside her, but she managed to calm herself. She tried for a second time to wake up the crystal, but again, nothing happened. Furious, she grabbed hold of the edge of the table and dug her nails into the wood. Then

81

she grabbed the crystal in both hands and held it over her head, as if she was going to smash it on the table. But before she could do it, a soft knock came at the door. She took a deep breath to calm herself and then gently laid the crystal down on the table. "Enter!" she yelled.

It was one of the dwarfs. "Your Majesty, Ugan has arrived with the three children," he said.

"How wonderful," she purred. "Where are they?"

"They have just entered the palace garden," the dwarf answered.

"Very good. I will have time to freshen up before they enter the palace."

The dwarf bowed and then left the room.

Queen Sentiz quickly went to her vanity mirror and applied white powder to her already pale complexion. Then she put on her blood-red lipstick, (a concentrated mixture of fairy blossom mixed with the blood of slave fairies that had died from being overworked). She brushed her hair and admired her reflection in the mirror.

Another knock came at her door.

"Enter!" she said cheerfully.

The same dwarf opened the door again. "The children have arrived and are waiting in the atrium for you, Your Majesty."

She smiled one more time at herself in her mirror. Then she blew herself a kiss and got up to meet her guests. Little did they know they actually were her victims.

- 15 -

Captured

Kristina, Werrien, and Raymond slept peacefully under the stars, but unfortunately, not far off, things were not quite so peaceful. Queen Sentiz's zelbocks had split up into bands and were scouring the land in all directions. One of the bands was not aware that it was not far off from where the two children lay sleeping. Their fire torches lit up the dark, damp forest as they carefully looked for any clues. Werrien had done his best to cover up all of Taysha's tracks, but unfortunately there was one that was left behind.

The lead zelbock of one of the bands noticed something white hanging from a tree branch, so he stopped and dismounted his horse. "Look here," he said in a gruff voice.

The rest of the band brought their attention to where he stood, holding a few strands of white horse tail in his hand. He sniffed them and said, "This is not one of our horses; it must be the boy's horse." A wicked smirk filled his grotesque face.

"They're not far off," another zelbock said.

The leader got back on his horse and quietly led his crew onward. They rode under the tree where Roage, the raven, and his fellow mates were perched, sleeping. One of the ravens woke from the sound of the horses passing under them. He pecked at Roage to wake him.

"Can't I get any sleep?" Roage snapped.

"Sorry, Roage, but a band of zelbocks just passed under us," the other raven said.

"Ah, you're just dreaming. Go back to sleep," Roage said.

"No, I saw them with my own eyes," the other raven insisted.

"All right, I'll go take a look," Roage said. He flew off to see for himself, and it wasn't long before he was back. "It's the zelbocks, all right, and they're traveling in bands. I have no idea what they're searching for, but we can't take any chances. We must notify the fairies at once," he said.

"Would you like me to go to tell them?" another raven asked.

"No! I'll warn them. You all stay here and keep watch for anything else that might look fishy," Roage said. Then away he flew, in search of the fairy colony.

~ ~ ~

While Kristina and Werrien slept peacefully under the stars, the zelbocks grew closer and closer to where they lay. The leader of the zelbocks stopped again and suspiciously sniffed the air. "I smell the remains of a fire," he said. They were now less than an hour away from the two children.

Meanwhile, Roage was flying through the dark forest in search of the fairy colony, and he was having a hard time seeing in the dark, so he'd stop occasionally to perch on a tree branch to figure out what direction to take. Finally, while in flight, he heard the trickling of a brook, and he knew he was near. Fairies always lived by brooks, where they had access to clean water for daily living. Their homes were high in the tall trees, in holes made by woodpeckers.

Roage flew amid the trees until he found the tallest and largest one, where Oreades, King of the Fairies lived. Roage landed on one of the branches and then hopped his way up to the highest branch at the top of the tree, where there was a very large bulge in the trunk. Inside was King Oreades's home. He found the tiny door in the bulge and pecked on it. There was no response, so he pecked on it a second time. He waited patiently and then a light shone through a tiny stained-glass window in the door. The door opened, and King Oreades, dressed in shimmering royal blue, stood in the doorway, holding a tiny lantern.

Roage bowed and said, "Sorry to wake you, Your Highness, but we have seen a band of zelbocks passing through the forest."

King Oreades's face went pale, for he knew that this could only mean something bad was about to happen. "They must know that the Magic Warble has returned," he said.

"The Magic Warble has returned?" Roage said, taken by surprise.

"I will wake my daughter at once and have her go to warn the children," the king said. King Oreades said farewell to Roage and watched through his window until Roage disappeared into the dark forest. Then he went to his daughter's bedroom and held his lantern over her bed. "Clover," he said.

Clover sat up and rubbed her eyes.

"You must leave at once to warn Werrien and the girl that zelbocks are in the forest, searching for them.

"I was afraid that this would happen. Werrien would be better off to deliver the Magic Warble by himself. That girl will only get him caught," Clover said disdainfully.

"Do I detect a bit of jealousy?" King Oreades asked.

Clover didn't respond.

"I expect more from you, Clover. Remember, you are a fairy princess, and it is your duty to be kind and help all in need. But that is not how you are behaving."

"I'd best be going," Clover said, getting out of bed and heading for the door.

King Oreades watched again through the window, this time as his daughter flew away into the dark forest.

Looper, who had been listening from his bed, wanted to go with Clover, but he knew his father wouldn't let him go out so late in the night. He waited for him to go back to bed and when he was sure the king was sleeping, he snuck out of the house to catch up with his sister.

While flying threw the forest, Clover heard strange noises, like owls hooting, frogs croaking, and spooky hissing sounds. She had never before left her house so late at night to go into the forest. Being alone in the deep, dark woods was a lot different than just going a few trees away from her own to visit a fellow fairy—and it was much scarier.

She suddenly heard a weird noise very close to her, and so she quickly flew up to a tree branch to hide. Standing very still, she glanced about the dark forest. She could feel her heart pounding hard in her chest, so she took a deep breath to calm herself. Soon after, she decided that what she had heard was probably nothing to worry about, so she decided to carry on her search for Werrien and Kristina. But just as she was about to leave the branch, she suddenly felt something cold, wet, and stringy tickling her on the back. She jumped around and at the same time, something jumped down from above and onto the branch where she was standing—and it growled. Clover quickly broke a small twig off the tree and held it out in front of herself, like a sword.

"It's just me, silly!" Looper said, beginning to laugh.

"I should whip your behind with this branch!" Clover said angrily.

"Calm down, Sis. I just didn't want you to have to go all alone, so I caught up with you."

"Aren't you sweet," Clover sneered.

Looper looked over Clover's shoulder and saw a light coming through the trees ahead of them. "Clover, we must hide quickly!"

"If you don't stop playing pranks on me, I'll—" Clover was interrupted by the sound of something coming toward them. Looper quickly pulled her close to the tree's trunk, and the two of them stood straight as pins against it. A band of zelbocks walked under the tree. The leader stopped his horse and looked around suspiciously.

"We're very close to the two children," he said.

It was an eerie feeling for Clover and Looper as the zelbocks stood beneath them.

Finally, the leader said, "Move on," and the band of zelbocks moved onward.

"That was a close one," Clover said.

"Yeah! Aren't you glad I snuck out of the house? You'd probably have been caught by the zelbocks and brought to Queen Sentiz's palace, where you'd spend the rest of your days as a slave fairy," Looper said.

"Looper, you're lucky that I don't have time to argue with you. We have to beat the zelbocks to Werrien—or else," Clover said.

"Or else what?" Looper asked.

"Or else the zelbocks will surely capture him, and maybe even kill him, and then they'll take the Magic Warble and destroy it." Clover said.

"And what do you think they'll do with Kristina?" Looper asked.

"Oh, yeah, her," Clover said disdainfully. "I suppose they'll do the same to her."

The two of them jumped off the branch and flew as fast as they could through the dark forest until they were very close behind the zelbocks.

"What are we going to do if we don't get to Werrien and Kristina first?" Looper whispered.

"That can't happen. We just have to get to him—I mean, them—before the zelbocks do," Clover said.

The band of zelbocks stopped again. "We are very near. I can smell them," the leader said.

"Look between those trees. There they are!" another zelbock said.

The leader grinned, revealing his rotten, spike-like teeth. "Our mission is almost accomplished," he said. Then he laughed in a horrible way.

"What are we going to do, Clover? They've found them!" Looper cried.

"We'll have to get to them before the zelbocks do," Clover said.

"We'll never make it."

"We must," Clover insisted.

She pulled her brother by the arm to head in a different direction. The fairies flew as fast as they could through the trees to try to beat the zelbocks to where Werrien and Kristina lay sleeping. But they were too late—the zelbocks had already arrived.

The leader stopped his horse and quickly dismounted. Werrien heard the sound and woke up. He stood up and attempted to draw his knife, but the zelbock was faster than he was—it threw a burlap sack over Werrien's head. Taysha reared up at the zelbocks in an attempt to stop them, but they whipped her, and she ran off.

Werrien tried to fight his way out of the sack, but when two more zelbocks joined in, Werrien was outnumbered. They carried him to the leader's horse, but Looper, having arrived only a few seconds after the zelbocks, flew over to Kristina, who was hiding with Raymond behind a tree.

"Quick! Follow me," he whispered.

Kristina followed Looper, but a zelbock noticed her.

"Grab the girl! She's trying to escape!" he yelled to another zelbock.

The zelbock grabbed Kristina and carried her to his horse. She kicked at him and pounded him with her fist, but the zelbock was much stronger than she was. Then, just as he was about to throw her onto the back of his horse, Raymond crawled out of Kristina's leather vest and bit the zelbock, hard, on his hand. The zelbock dropped Kristina, and she ran with Raymond as fast as she could into the forest.

"After her!" the zelbock shouted.

Three more zelbocks chased after her, but Looper guided her to a hiding place inside a thorn brush.

"Quick! Hide in here," he said, showing her a small hole in the bush that was just big enough for her to crawl into.

She crawled inside the tangled thorn bush, trying to avoid the large, sharp thorns that stuck out at her from all directions. When she was inside, she sat very still, trying not to breathe too hard, but after being chased by the zelbocks, she was practically out of breath.

The zelbocks searched for her and came very close to finding her. They even stood right beside the thorn bush where she was hiding. As they sniffed the air, she sat very still. They were so close that she could see their ugly greenish-brown feet with their long, cracked yellow toenails. It felt like an eternity, but sitting still in the thorn bush paid off—the zelbocks finally decided to leave.

- 16 -

Leaving the Forest

As the zelbocks were leaving, Kristina could feel the heat from their torches as they passed by her. The leader suddenly yelled, "Halt!" The horse that was carrying Werrien stopped right beside the thorn bush where Kristina was huddled, and its zelbock rider got off to check if the sack in which they'd placed Werrien was tied down securely. Kristina was so close to the sack that she could have reached out and touched it. But that would have meant doom for Werrien and her, and she felt hopeless as the zelbock leader mounted his horse and rode away.

After she was sure they were gone, she crawled out of the prickly thorn bush. The air was still as she stood in the dark forest, with only Raymond for company. But that was about to change.

Like a flash of lightning, Clover flew down from a nearby tree branch. "Hurry! There's no time to waste!" she said urgently. "We must get you and the Magic Warble to the top of Mount Bernovem before Queen Sentiz tortures Werrien—or maybe even kills him!" She expected Kristina to follow her, but Kristina stood still, not knowing what to say or do. When Clover noticed that she wasn't following her, she flew back and stopped abruptly in midair, very close to Kristina's face. "What's the matter with you? Why won't you come?" she asked, irritated.

"There's somewhat of a slight problem," Kristina answered.
Clover put her hands on her hips. "And what might that be?"

"I…don't have the Magic Warble."

Clover clenched her fists angrily at her sides. "You lost the Magic
Warble? I knew it! I just knew you would fumble this mission," she
ranted. Then she turned around and began to fly away.

"Wait a minute!" Kristina yelled after her. Clover didn't turn
around to acknowledge her, so Kristina yelled, "I gave it to Werrien!"

Like a speeding bullet, Clover flew back to her. "You gave *what*
to Werrien?" she asked.

"The Magic Warble," Kristina answered.

"Why?" Clover asked.

"Because I wanted him carry it."

"Well, isn't that sweet?" Clover taunted her. "Now look what
you've done. You ruined any chance of Bernovem gaining back
its freedom."

"Well, it wouldn't have mattered anyway, because I have no way
of knowing where I need to bring it," Kristina said, feeling flustered.

In the midst of their conversation, Looper flew up to them. "I know where they're taking Werrien. We must hurry and follow them!" he panted.

"Where?" Clover asked.

"To a horrible prison in the city of Salas," Looper said.

"How do you know?" Clover asked.

"I followed the zelbocks, and I overheard them discussing it," Looper said.

"If our father knew you were out here, following zelbocks, you wouldn't be allowed out of the colony for the rest of your childhood years," Clover said.

"Look, Sis! If not for me, you won't be able to find Werrien in time, and the zelbocks will surely deliver him into the hands of Queen Sentiz."

Clover sneered at Looper and said, "If you wouldn't talk so much, we could already be on our way."

The fairies flew ahead of Kristina, lighting the way.

"It'll still be a ways before we're out of this forest," Looper said.

Then, as if from nowhere, they could hear the sound of something running toward them.

"Quick! Take cover! Something's chasing us!" Looper said.

The fairies flew up to a high branch in a tree, but Kristina couldn't find a place to hide, so she began to run back in the direction from which they had just come. She ran as fast as she could, with Raymond clinging to her for dear life. Whatever it was that was chasing her was quickly gaining ground on her.

Was this going to be the end of her life? Did she survive the arrows of the mysterious black-cloaked figure, and then almost drowning in the raging Indra River, only to be murdered by a disgusting foul creature like the zelbock? The thought of this was so horrifying that tears began to stream down her face. She was trying her hardest not to give up, but the cramp was back in her side, and the more she ran, the more it intensified, like a sharp knife piercing her. She soon couldn't run any farther, and so she stopped behind a large tree to catch her breath. As she leaned against the tree, she could hear whatever was chasing her had stopped dead in its tracks—on the other side of the tree. It, too, was breathing heavily from the chase.

Raymond poked his head out of Kristina's vest and whispered, "Well, if we have to go, at least we'll go together."

"Thanks, Raymond. That really makes me feel better," Kristina whispered.

Raymond crawled back inside her vest. Kristina closed her eyes, as whatever had been chasing her slowly came around to her side of the tree. She could feel its warm, moist breath on her face.

"Open your eyes," it said.

Kristina opened one eye, and then the other. To her surprise, standing in front of her was Taysha, and at her side were Clover and Looper, giggling.

"Taysha! Why didn't you say that it was you?" Kristina asked the beautiful white mare.

"You should know by now that the quieter we are in these woods, the better. We can't take the risk of your getting caught by the zelbocks," Taysha answered.

"Well, I guess you have a good point, but you scared me almost to death," Kristina said. She reached her arms around Taysha's neck and gave her a hug.

"We must hurry. There's no time to waste. Get on my back," Taysha said.

Raymond poked his head out of Kristina's vest again. "We're going to ride on her again? How can you be sure she won't rub us off against a tree—or something even worse? I surely don't trust her," he said.

"Don't be so rude, Raymond," Kristina said.

"She almost stepped on me," Raymond said.

Taysha snorted at Raymond, and he ducked back down into Kristina's vest. This was the first time that Kristina rode Taysha on her own, and everything was going quite smoothly until they came across a large fallen tree that was blocking their way. All around the tree were overgrown thorn bushes.

"How are we going to get around this?" Kristina asked.

"You're just going to have to hold on!" Taysha said.

Kristina grabbed hold of Taysha's mane and with that, Taysha leaped high in the air and over the tree. Kristina slid sideways a little but didn't fall off.

"Wow! That was actually quite fun," she said.

As the group traveled on, the darkness started to fade and the early-morning light set in. "Look, we're almost out of the forest," Looper said, pointing toward the east.

"And it's a good thing," Clover said to Looper, "because we'll have to get home before father wakes and sees that you've left the colony."

"Do you really have to go?" Kristina asked Looper.

"I'm afraid so," Looper said sadly.

"How am I to know how to get to the city of Salas?" Kristina asked him.

"It's easy; you head south until you come to the Citnalta Sea. Then follow the cliffs and bluffs east, along the sea, until you see a small cottage off to your left. Then head north, over the hills, until you come to a dwarfs' burial ground. At that point, you will head east, and then you will run into the city of Salas," Looper said.

After Looper finished explaining the directions to Kristina, they said good-bye, and Kristina headed out of the forest. She would miss Looper's company; as for Clover, maybe not as much.

- 17 -

Delicious Cream Puffs

Eagerly waiting to meet Queen Sentiz, Davina, Hester, and
Graham sat in the lavish atrium. They were gazing up at
all the exotic plants when the door opened and one of the
queen's servants, a gnome, entered the room. He was carrying a
shimmering golden tray, and upon it sat a large mound of powdered
cream puffs. The children's eyes lit up as the gnome, dressed like
a court jester, walked up to them with the tray.

"Cream puffs, anyone?" he asked, placing the tray on a table
in front of the three children.

Without even saying "Yes, please"—or anything else, for that
matter—Davina, Hester, and Graham started digging into the
sugary confections. As they devoured the treats, the servant gnome
stood silent, like a soldier on guard.

"Well, are you going to put on a show for us?" Graham asked
him, with his mouth stuffed full.

The gnome didn't answer or even seem to listen to him. Graham
looked at Davina and Hester and shrugged his shoulders. The three
of them ate and ate, until there was only one cream puff left on the
tray. Hester didn't want it; her stomach was so full that she said she
thought that she might burst. She leaned back on the couch rubbing

her full belly, while Davina and Graham both grabbed at the last snowball-like morsel.

"You had more than me. You hog!" Davina complained to Graham.

Graham looked at Davina's wide girth and replied, "Yeah, but you definitely don't need another one."

Davina grinned and suggested, "I tell you what—why don't we split it?"

With his mouth still full, Graham shrugged his shoulders. "Okay, I'll go for that."

Davina picked up the last cream puff, but instead of breaking it in two, she placed it between her thumb and index finger and squished it. Out squirted gooey cream, all over Graham's face.

Graham's eyes grew wide, and he clenched his teeth. "Why you overgrown, good-for-nothing stuffed turkey!" he yelled.

Davina's small eyes grew to the size of nickels behind her thick glasses. She picked up the tray and held it over her head. Trying to hit Graham on the head, she smashed it down. But he was quicker than she was, and he ducked out of the way. The tray came down on the table with a loud smash. Davina, in her temper tantrum, began backing Graham into a corner.

Hester, who was feeling very sick now, sat slumped on the couch, staring up at the queen's large portrait on the wall. She began to see double, and then she felt the room start to spin. "Hey, guys, could you knock it off? I'm not feeling very well," she said. Her hands began to feel very itchy, and then her nails suddenly grew longer and pointier. Hair began to grow on her hands and everywhere else on her body. As she opened her mouth to scream, her two front teeth grew three times as long—and then she turned into a beaver.

Davina and Graham stopped fighting and glanced over at Hester. Then they looked back at each other, and each saw about four of the other.

"I think I'd better sit down," Davina said.

Davina walked toward an armchair, but as she was walking, her steps suddenly turned into hops, and in midair she turned into a bullfrog. She hopped onto the chair and turned around to face Graham, croaking loudly at him. Graham, who had been hiding from Davina behind a large tropical plant, stuck his face through the palms. As he did, his nose grew longer and whiskers grew out from the sides of it. Then he turned into a weasel and fell into the plant's pot.

The door to the parlor slowly opened, and Queen Sentiz stepped into the room, smiling at each creature. "Welcome, little critters. I'm so glad you could make it to my palace for such a pleasurable stay."

Hester thumped her large flat tail on the couch. Davina's throat filled with air like a balloon, and then she let out a load croak. Graham poked his pointy nose out of the pot, sniffed the air, and let out a high-pitched squeak.

The queen yelled for Ugan, who was usually right outside the door to any room, but this time, he did not answer. She yelled a second time, louder and more harshly. When he still didn't respond, she began to get very angry. She was just about to storm through the door to find him when she heard the familiar jingling of the bells on his hat. The door opened slowly, and Ugan, in his court jester outfit, walked into the parlor and bowed to her.

"Where were you? You know you are always to be right out side the door," she snarled.

"I was sewing on a bell that had fallen off my hat, my sweet queen," Ugan replied nervously.

He actually had been hiding the Book of Prophecy that he had taken from Rumalock's cottage, because he didn't want the queen to know that he had it.

Queen Sentiz stood over him like a tall monster, suspiciously glaring down at him. Then, like a snake lashing out at its prey, she grabbed the hat off his head, and one by one, ripped off seven of the eight bells that hung from it and threw them across the room. "You may as well sew the rest on again, since they were all loose," she said, grinning down at him. Ugan tried to retrieve the bells, but the queen stepped on his foot, so that he couldn't. "In your spare time, that is," she added.

What spare time? Ugan thought. Every stinking, waking minute of his day was spent waiting on her.

"I expect to see them sewed on properly, by six in the morning, tomorrow," she said.

"Yes, my lady," Ugan answered.

Then she took her large foot off of his small one. "Take these varmints to the dungeon, where they will await their lovely ride to Treachery Island," she said.

"Right away, my lady," Ugan responded.

~~~

Later that evening, as Sir Rupert lay asleep, his face gravely pale, Queen Sentiz came to sit by his side. It wasn't very long before his loud snoring began to irritate her.

"Ugan!" she shouted, her shrill voice startling the frail old man, but not waking him.

Sir Rupert's door cracked open, and Ugan poked his head inside the room. "Yes my lady," he answered.

"Get this old coot to the meeting room at once!"

"But my lady ..." Ugan had started to protest.

"Don't you 'but' me," she said.

"As you wish, my queen," he answered somberly.

Queen Sentiz stormed out of the bedroom, leaving Ugan to lift Sir Rupert into his wheelchair by himself. After grueling effort, he finally managed to get the old man into his wheelchair. Then he rolled him back down the long hallway to the meeting room and knocked softly on the large door.

"Enter," the queen yelled. She was already at the table, waiting for them, with the crystal in front of her. "What took you so long?" she barked.

"I think Sir Rupert's health is failing rapidly, my precious queen," Ugan said.

"That's nonsense," the queen said, slamming her fist down onto the table. "Hurry and lift him into the chair here at the table. I must look in the crystal to see what that wretched boy and girl are up to."

Ugan desperately tried to lift Sir Rupert from his wheelchair, but he wasn't able to do it. "He's barely conscious, my lady, and he is very heavy," Ugan said.

"Get out of the way, you feeble weakling," Queen Sentiz said, pushing Ugan to the floor. Then, with ease, she lifted Sir Rupert into the chair herself.

Sir Rupert, due to his deteriorating health, thought it was mealtime. "Yes, I'll take cream in my tea, thank you," he said. And with those words, he lay his head down on the table—and passed away.

"Wake up, you lazy old man. I need to know where those little troublemakers are," the queen griped, not realizing that he was dead. Of course, Sir Rupert didn't respond. "Don't you know that if I don't get the Magic Warble and destroy it, it will be the end of my reign as sovereign queen?"

"I'm sorry to say it," Ugan said softly, "but I do think Sir Rupert is no longer with us, my dear queen."

"Oh, you do think, do you?" she roared.

"Yes, my queen," Ugan responded.

"Stop thinking, and get up here and make this stupid piece of glass work!" she screamed, lifting Ugan up by his beard and plopping him down in the chair in front of the crystal. "You've eavesdropped enough to know how it works."

With shaking hands, Ugan stood the crystal upright, but he didn't know what to do next.

"Hurry, stupid dwarf. I don't have all day. Wave your hands around it," the queen demanded, glaring at him with her ice-cold eyes.

"Oh, of course, my lady, of course. How foolish of me," Ugan said. He waved his hands around the crystal.

"Now do the magic chant," she ordered.

"The magic chant?" Ugan asked timidly.

"You don't know the magic chant?" the queen hissed.

"I'm so sorry, but I'm afraid not," Ugan answered.

With that, Queen Sentiz completely lost her temper. She picked up the crystal, and, in her anger, held it over Ugan's head, ready to hurl it down on him.

"Is this part of the procedure, my queen?" Ugan stuttered.

"It is about to be!" Queen Sentiz growled.

"Wait! Please, my lady! I know of another way for you to know where they are," Ugan said, while holding his arms over his head to protect himself.

Queen Sentiz looked at him suspiciously through squinted eyes. "This better be good," she said.

"Would you be as kind as to lower the crystal, so it doesn't fall on my head?" Ugan asked faintly.

The queen dropped the crystal on the floor, right beside him, and it shattered into what seemed like a million pieces.

"May I go and get something?" he asked.

"You'd better be back within five minutes," the queen said, grabbing a five-minute timepiece off the table.

"Yes, my lady," Ugan said. He bowed to her and left the room. While heading down the winding staircase, Ugan felt once again like a failure. He pictured the look of satisfaction that Queen Sentiz would have on her face when he handed the Book of Prophecy to her.

18

Off to Treachery Island

Kristina rode Taysha over the vast green plains and hills until she came to the cliffs, where Looper said she would meet the Citnalta Sea. She stared out over the rough gray waters. There was no land in sight, other than a very small distant island off to the south. Taysha noticed the island, and she turned away from the sea.

"Is there something the matter?" Kristina asked her.

"I just can't stand to look at that place," Taysha replied.

"What place?" Kristina asked.

"Treachery Island. It gives me the creeps."

"The name even sounds creepy to me," Raymond said, poking his head out of Kristina's vest.

"Is Treachery Island the horrible place where Queen Lafinia, Werrien's mother, is being held prisoner?" Kristina asked.

"It most definitely is. We must not waste any more time, because Werrien will most likely be heading there very soon as well," Taysha said.

The trio continued on their journey along the cliffs and bluffs, heading eastward until they could see the small cottage that Looper had mentioned. Near it, a gnome man and a gnome woman were working with hoes in a vegetable garden. When they caught sight of Kristina riding Taysha, they put down their hoes. Then the man picked up a basket, and the woman and he both ran toward them.

"I think they want to give us something," Taysha said to Kristina.

"Should we trust them?" Kristina asked.

"My instinct tells me they are friendly," Taysha answered. She trotted toward the gnome couple.

"Do not worry; we are believers," the gnome woman said with labored breath.

"Please accept this gift from us," the gnome man said, holding out the basket full of fresh vegetables and fruit.

"How do you know us?" Kristina asked.

"Word is getting around among the believers," the gnome man said.

"Thank you for the food. It comes at a perfect time, for our supply is getting low," Kristina said.

The gnome woman took Kristina's hand in hers and said, "Bless you, child, for you are the one chosen to restore Bernovem."

Kristina felt a lump in her throat after hearing these words. Then the gnome woman kissed her hand, and they said good-bye. As Kristina rode away, the couple shouted after them, "Long live Queen Lafinia!"

Meanwhile, back at Queen Sentiz's palace, Ugan stood outside the ornate door of the meeting room, this time with the Book of Prophecy. He thought that instead of being the one chosen to save Bernovem, he would be the one known throughout history for ruining any chance of Bernovem's becoming free again. The words *"Ugan the Traitor"* popped up in his mind, and in his imagination, he could see a large crowd of fellow dwarfs and gnomes chanting the words. Then another thought came to his mind: *What if I just turned around and ran?* He did have an escape route for a time such as this. All he would have to do is run down to the kitchen and then into the broom closet. Once in there, he would remove a few loose bricks from the wall and then crawl through an opening that led to the palace vegetable garden. Once outside, he'd crawl through the vegetable garden until he came to the palace wall. At that point he would move a garden statue of the queen, which he had placed on top of a small tunnel he had dug. Then he would crawl through and under the wall to his freedom. Once out of the palace garden, he'd hide at a fellow dwarf's house until Bernovem was restored to its original way.

It all seemed simple enough, but as he contemplated these ideas, he began to realize that he'd already had the chance to escape when he went to get the three children from Rumalock's cottage, but he hadn't taken it. *I'm just too much of a coward*, he thought.

Queen Sentiz suddenly yelled his name, as she usually did when she wanted him to enter into the room. He hesitated for a few seconds, and then she yelled again, even louder, "Your five minutes are almost up!"

He could still try running away and have a chance of being known throughout history for saving the Book of Prophecy. *Oh, how good it would feel to be known for at least one honorable deed,* he thought. But his heart began to pound, and self-doubt quickly crept into his mind, and he became fearful. It was no use; he just didn't have the courage to escape. Now, he knew his fate had been sealed, and with a shaky hand, he turned the golden knob of the large door. As he entered the room, Queen Sentiz was sitting in her usual place at the table, drumming her long red nails on the table. When she noticed the prophecy book held in his arms, a wicked smile came to her face.

"What do we have here?" she asked.

Ugan walked over to her and bowed down on one knee. Then he held the book out to her. She snatched it out of his hands and stared down at its cover, which read *Bernovem's Great Book of Prophecy.* She began to laugh hysterically. "Very good, very good," she crooned. Then she grabbed Ugan by his beard. "I always new you would betray your own people. You're nothing but a spineless jellyfish. Now, get up and go bury the old man outside the palace wall. When you're done, load the three animals into the boat."

"But my lady, don't you think Sir Rupert deserves a proper burial in the palace graveyard?" Ugan asked timidly.

Queen Sentiz let go of his beard. "Why should he get a proper burial, when he couldn't even stay alive long enough to find out the whereabouts of that dirty little peasant boy and that good-for-nothing girl?" She brought her attention back to the book and opened it to its last written page. She ran her fingernail along the words until she came to the name "*Werrien.*" The last sentence on the page read "*Prince Werrien has been captured and is imprisoned in the city of Salas.*" She began to laugh insanely. Then she glanced back down at the page. "Oh, look, more writing is popping up." She clapped her hands delightedly. "It says that the girl Kristina is heading to the city of Salas in hope of rescuing Prince Werrien." She looked at Ugan with a mock pout. "Poor little fool doesn't realize how heavily guarded that prison is. She'll be captured in no time."

She patted Ugan atop his hat. "Thanks to you, my faithful little coward, the two little mongrels don't stand a chance now of delivering the Magic Warble to its so-called resting place. And they thought they could defeat the infamous Queen Sentiz." She laughed obnoxiously once more, but then stopped suddenly. "Why are you still standing around here when you've got plenty of work to do?"

"Yes, my dearest queen," Ugan said. Then he bowed and left the room.

As the queen sat looking through the Book of Prophecy like an excited child with a new Christmas gift, a black raven cawed loudly outside her window. She got up to close the shutters. "Get out of here, you horrible black varmint," she ranted, slamming the window shutters.

Little did she know that it was Roage and that he had been listening in on her conversation with Ugan.

~ ~ ~

Ugan buried Sir Rupert outside the palace wall, as two of the queen's zelbocks stood on guard, watching him. When he had finished, he laid a handful of fairy blossoms on top of the old man's grave. As he stood there silently, paying his last respects, he thought of how Sir Rupert and he were not so different. They both lived for a wicked queen, even though she was an impostor. Due to lack of courage and a lust for riches, they didn't attempt to change their situations. Now, one of them was dead and not even allowed a proper burial.

Will this be my fate as well? Ugan thought, as he left the gravesite to get the animals that had been the three children. He carried the animals in three small cages onto the queen's boat.

Soon after, the queen arrived at the boat, carrying the prophecy book and singing, "Victorious I am! Victorious I am! The brats be captured just in time, so Bernovem will be mine. *Mine, mine, mine, mine!*"

Ugan helped the unusually gleeful queen onto the boat and then untied it from the rocky shoreline. As they drifted away from the rocks, the sky started to cloud over and the wind brushed over the water, causing the boat to totter. A raindrop fell on Ugan's nose. "Looks like the weather's turning for the worse," he said.

"Stop your belly-aching and start rowing, before these creatures turn back into children," the queen replied.

With that, Ugan started to row the boat toward Treachery Island.

19

The Graveyard

Twilight was setting in as Kristina and Taysha neared the dwarf graveyard that Looper had mentioned. Heavy dark clouds rolled across the sky, and the wind started to pick up, blowing the fallen leaves around the tombstones.

"It looks like a storm is approaching," Taysha said.

Raymond poked his head out of Kristina's vest, and the wind came directly at him, blowing his whiskers against the sides of his face. "I hate storms! Can't you pick up the pace a little so we can get out of here?" he asked Taysha.

"If the ride's not good enough for you, I can always stop and let you off. Maybe you could run faster yourself," Taysha answered.

"I suppose I'll just have to tough it out," Raymond said, feeling sorry for himself. He went back inside the vest to take cover.

"It is eerie, passing by a graveyard in this stormy weather," Kristina said.

"You can thank Queen Sentiz for that. Before she came to power, Bernovem only had one graveyard for the gnomes and dwarfs, but now, due to the shortage of fairy blossom, the gnomes and dwarfs don't live long, so there are many graveyards scattered throughout the land," Taysha said.

Kristina thought of Leacha giving away her last bit of fairy blossom and hoped that she was still alive. The wind picked up even more, and thunder pounded the atmosphere. Then lightning struck right in front of one of the tombstones.

"Did you see that?" Kristina asked Taysha.

"What? The lightning? It's very common in our land," Taysha said.

"No, I saw something run from behind that tombstone over there, to that tombstone over there," Kristina said, pointing at where she saw.

Taysha looked toward the tombstone. "I don't see anything," she said.

But then, whatever it was ran again to hide behind another tombstone. "Did you see it that time?" Kristina asked.

"No, but we'd better get out of here, in case it's one of the queen's zelbocks," Taysha said, and she quickly picked up her pace to a gallop.

"Hey, don't take off so suddenly! You didn't give me a chance to hold on," Kristina said, sliding to the right side of Taysha.

Taysha came to an abrupt stop, and Kristina fell to the ground. Then Taysha turned to face her. "I'm sorry, but it could be a zelbock in the graveyard. I told you before, when it starts to get dark, that's the time you'll most likely see one of them. They are always out at night, trying to find anything that they think looks suspicious," she said.

"It sounds like someone I know back at home," Kristina said, remembering Davina, who was always suspicious of her.

"We'd better get out of here—and fast," Taysha said.

"No! Let's wait until it's dark. That way we'll have a better chance of not being seen," Kristina said, jumping to her feet.

A drop of rain fell on her head and then a few more followed.

"Look, over to your right—there's a large tree over there. We can take cover under it," Taysha said, and she began heading toward it.

As Kristina followed Taysha, the rain began to pour down and thunder roared in the sky again. Kristina waited for the lightning to follow. When it struck, she poked her head around the tree, checking if anything was lurking in the graveyard. When another bolt of lightning flashed across the sky, the suspicious character ran from behind one tombstone to another, just like it had before.

"I think it's a dwarf, and it seemed to be limping," Kristina said.

Raymond poked his head out of her vest. "I must say, I think the horse had a good idea when she said we should get out of here."

"It seems to be trying to hide from us," Kristina said.

"I say we leave now, while it's running in the other direction. It could be going to tell someone of our whereabouts," Taysha said.

"But what if it is a dwarf or gnome, and what if it's hurt, and it thinks that we're Queen Sentiz's spies?" Kristina asked.

"We can't take any chances," Taysha said.

Kristina paused for a moment and then replied, "I'm sorry to say, Taysha, that I think this time your instinct is wrong. If it is a dwarf or gnome that's hurt, we need to try to help."

"I suppose you're right, but what can you do to help? We can't take him with us. It would only slow us down, and then we'd most likely be captured by the zelbocks," Taysha said.

"We won't have to take him," Kristina said.

"Then you can't help whoever it is, and besides without fairy blossom, the poor soul won't survive long, no matter what you do," Taysha said.

Kristina paused again and then said, "I have some fairy blossom."

"How can that be? We haven't come across any growing," Taysha said.

"I never told Werrien or you," Kristina said, "but Leacha gave some to me, before we left on our journey."

"Why would she give you her fairy blossom when she needs it herself, in order to survive?" Taysha asked.

"She wanted me to have it in case one of us was injured on our journey. We haven't used any so far, so if it is an injured dwarf or gnome behind that tombstone, I'm sure that I could spare a little." Kristina reached into her pocket to get the fairy blossom.

"Well, do what you feel is best," Taysha answered.

"Wait here, then. I'll be back as soon as possible," Kristina said.

She was just about to run over to the graveyard when Raymond poked his head out of her vest and said, "Would you mind if I stayed here with the horse? I'm really not one for graveyards."

Kristina smiled at Raymond. "You mean you'd rather stay with Taysha? All right." She took Raymond out of her vest and placed him on Taysha's back. Then without looking back, she ran off toward the graveyard.

"Wait! Wait! Please don't leave me here on top of this large, unpredictable beast!" Raymond yelled.

But Kristina didn't respond; she figured it was about time that Raymond got out of his comfort zone.

Taysha was annoyed at Raymond for calling her an unpredictable beast, so she shook vigorously. This frightened Raymond half out of his wits, and he held on for dear life.

The rain poured down on Kristina as she opened the rusty gate that led to the graveyard. It reminded her of the gate in front of her own house, except that it made a creepy creak when it opened. Just as she walked through the gate, a loud thunder clap startled her, and she drew out the knife that Werrien had given her. When she arrived at the tombstone, lightning flashed across the sky again, revealing the suspicious character. To Kristina's surprise, she recognized who it was. They both looked each other in the eyes and at the same time said the other's name.

"Rumalock!" Kristina said.

"Kristina!" Rumalock said. "If I'd known it was you, I wouldn't have hidden behind this tombstone."

"And If I'd known it was you, I wouldn't have drawn out this knife," Kristina said.

Rumalock looked surprised. "Where did you get that?" he asked.

"It was given to me by a boy named Werrien," Kristina said.

"So you did meet up with him," Rumalock said, as if to himself.

"Remember you told me that I might get help along my journey? Well, you were right, because I met up with Werrien. Anyhow, it's so good to see you, Rumalock. I have so much to tell you," Kristina said. She was going to explain all that had happened to her, but then she noticed that Rumalock looked unwell. He leaned his head against the tombstone, seeming to not have much energy. "What happened to you?" she asked.

"I was returning home from collecting fairy blossoms when a

band of zelbocks caught sight of me. They arrested me and took all the fairy blossoms that I had collected. Then they tied my hands together behind my back, and tied me with another rope to the back of one of their horses. They led me to where my house used to stand." He paused for a few seconds as tears welled up in his old eyes.

"What do you mean, *used to* stand?" Kristina asked.

"It's no longer there. They burned it to the ground, along with all my belongings, including the only prophecy book in Bernovem." Kristina felt very sad as Rumalock continued. "They dumped out the sack of fairy blossoms that I had worked so hard to collect and told me that it was a crime to collect the blossoms in such large quantities. Then they burned them. After that, they led me away, and I had to walk and walk, sometimes being dragged when I was too exhausted to move as quickly as they wanted. They took me to the city of Salas, and as we entered it, all the dwarfs and gnomes, who were going about their usual business, stopped dead in their tracks. They watched in awe as I was lead by the zelbocks through the main street. Then the zelbocks brought me to the city prison, where they threw me in a cell. I was there for two days, and was told I would be leaving for Treachery Island on the third morning. I felt hopeless, for there was no way of escaping—a zelbock posted in front of my cell made sure of that. Feeling weak and weary, I fell asleep on the hard concrete floor. Then I started dreaming of the horrible place, Treachery Island. It was a terrible dream, in which the wicked Queen Sentiz was dragging me by my beard to a damp, cold cell. As we approached it, I could see that there was no floor in it, just bars, and beneath the bars, vicious sea monsters were snapping their jaws at anything that dangled even an inch below the bars. The queen was just about to throw me into the cell, but then I woke up, and to my surprise, fluttering above me and tugging on my beard, was Clover—bless her heart. She said she thought I'd never wake up—I was so glad to see her," Rumalock said, a glitter of hope sparkling in his watery eyes.

"How did she get past the zelbock on guard?" Kristina asked.

"He had fallen asleep, and so she managed to pull the key out of his hand. After that, she dragged the key as close to my cell as possible, but because it was the same size as Clover, she couldn't lift it off the ground, so she flew threw the bars and woke me. Then I stuck my arm through the bars and grabbed the key."

"Didn't the zelbock wake up?"

"No, thank goodness. He was snoring so loudly that he didn't hear as I reached my arm through the bars and tried to put the key in the lock."

"So you unlocked the cell door?"

"I almost had it, but then I dropped the key, and the zelbock flinched, but he didn't wake up. So I tried once more, and that time, I was successful. I pushed the large barred door open and made my escape."

"What happened to Clover?" Kristina asked.

"She led me out of the prison. Then she said she had some business to take care of, and that is when we parted."

More lightning flashed across the sky, revealing Rumalock's wrists. They were wrapped in cloths that were soaked in blood.

"What happened to your wrists?" Kristina asked.

"The ropes that were tied around them cut into them as I was being dragged behind the zelbock's horse," Rumalock answered.

"Mind if I take a look?" Kristina asked. "Maybe I can help."

"That's very kind of you, but without the magic fairy blossom, there's really nothing you can do." Rumalock sat down and leaned against the tombstone. His strength was fading fast. "I'm just glad that I escaped the prison and a most assured horrible existence or even death at Treachery Island. At least now I have peace in my heart, knowing that the Magic Warble has returned. After it is delivered to its final resting place, Bernovem will be restored back to its original way. So now I can pass away, near my beloved Knopsie. May she rest in peace." His eyes began to close.

Lightning flashed across the sky once more, illuminating the tombstone, and Kristina read the inscription that was written on it: "*Knopsie Hoblestock, Wife of Rumalock Hoblestock.*" Kristina looked back at Rumalock, who looked like he might fall over and die right there.

"Wait! Hold on!" she said. She took his left hand and gently removed the cloth that was tied around his wrist. Then she removed the other cloth from his other wrist. In the dark, it was very hard to see the extent of the damage that the ropes had caused. "Hold your wrists out into the rain," she said.

With the little strength he had left, Rumalock held his bloodied wrists up to the rain and the blood rinsed away. With trembling hands, Kristina took fairy blossom from the small pouch. She pinched about a third of it between her fingers and dropped it onto her other palm. Holding her open palm up to the rain, she let it fill with rainwater and squished the soaked fairy blossom onto Rumalock's wrists—they healed instantly.

Rumalock's eyes suddenly opened and had a vibrant glow. He glanced down at his healed wrists and said, "Bless you, child. You have saved my life." Then he stood up with renewed strength. "I wish that I had some way to repay you, but I'm sorry, everything was taken from me."

"There is one thing you could do for me," Kristina said.

"Name it, and I will do it for you," Rumalock said.

Kristina opened the little pouch and took about half of what was left of the fairy blossom and wrapped it in a napkin. She handed the napkin to Rumalock. "Could you please take this little bit of fairy blossom to an elderly gnome lady? I'm sorry that I don't have much information about her, other than that her name is Leacha and she lives in the bottom of a large tree in the forest."

Rumalock tried to recall who she was.

"She is Werrien's guardian, if that helps any."

"You mean Prince Werrien, Queen Lafinia's son, the true prince of Bernovem?" Rumalock asked, surprised.

"Yes, don't you remember my mentioning him to you a few minutes ago?" Kristina asked.

"I'm sorry; I guess the intense pain made me forget. Anyhow, however did you meet him? Did the fairies introduce you?"

"Yes, you could say that," Kristina answered.

"I certainly do know Leacha and the boy as well. It will be nice to see her."

"That will be great if you could deliver the fairy blossom and pay her a visit at the same time," Kristina said.

"Yes, that would be wonderful," Rumalock said.

"There's something else that I need to tell you," Kristina said.

"What is it, child?" Rumalock asked.

"Werrien was captured by the zelbocks two days ago and brought to a prison in the city of Salas. Do you think it could be the same place that you were in?"

"There is only one prison in the city of Salas, so it must be the same place." Rumalock said.

"How much farther is it from here?" Kristina asked.

"If you leave now, you should be able to make it before sunrise," Rumalock said.

"Then I'd best be going." Kristina said.

"One more little thing—may I look at the Magic Warble one more time? It will give me more strength," Rumalock said.

"Oh, sorry, Rumalock, but I gave it to Werrien. I know that I probably shouldn't have but—"

"Then you really need to hurry to him," Rumalock interrupted. As Kristina ran back toward the tree where Taysha and Raymond were taking cover, Rumalock called out to her. "Hurry, child! Werrien will most assuredly be on his way to Treachery Island at the crack of dawn tomorrow.

113

20

Sir Rupert's Best Potion

While Ugan rowed the boat, Queen Sentiz sat on her purple velvet pillow as she looked through her telescope. She panned the land they had left, looking for any sign of Kristina. The problem was, she could only see along the cliff's edge and the lower shoreline. Kristina and Taysha were much farther inland at this time. The wind started picking up and a large raindrop hit the lens of her telescope.

"Can't you row any faster?" she blurted out to Ugan.

Even though it was very hard for him, Ugan managed a fake smile as he tried to row faster in the dark choppy water. Hester, the beaver; Davina, the bullfrog; and Graham, the weasel, were in their cages, sliding from one side of the boat to the other. Ugan felt sorry for them, and so he stopped rowing for a brief moment to place a heavy rope beside their cages to stop them from sliding.

Queen Sentiz rolled her eyes at him in disgust and then looked back into her telescope at the dark, dancing waters ahead of her. "Aha!" she yelled suddenly, startling Ugan so that he momentarily dropped the oars. "There it is that wonderful place, Treachery Island. Oh, how I love visiting it," she said gleefully. She collapsed her telescope once more and rubbed her long, bony hands together. "Not much longer, and you'll be in your new home," she said to the three animals. Davina croaked at her remark, and Hester beat her big, flat tail on the bottom of the cage. The queen noticed the weasel's head was changing back into Graham's head. Soon after that, the weasel's whole body changed back into Graham's body, and it burst through the cage, breaking it. Graham was back to normal and lying on the wet bottom of the boat. He was unconscious but starting to come to. He rubbed his eyes and then stared up at the hazy figure of Queen Sentiz. Even though her image was distorted, she somehow looked very beautiful to him. He mumbled something about the cream puffs.

"The potion in the cream puffs was supposed to last longer than this," the queen said angrily.

Graham shut one eye to try to focus, but it didn't help. The swaying of the boat was making his stomach sick, so he sat up. "I think that I'm going to get sick," he said, his freckled face as white as a sheet.

"Now, now, dear, I have just the thing for you," the queen said soothingly. She reached into her pocket and pulled out a small box made of abalone shell. She clicked opened its latch with her fingernail. As the lid sprang up, a puff of pink, green, and purple smoke swirled out. Graham shook his head again, trying to comprehend what was going on. "I have a lovely candy that will settle your stomach," the queen said, taking out a pink, green, and purple swirled candy. "Now open your mouth," she continued.

Even though he felt sick, Graham was mesmerized by the queen. He closed his eyes and opened his mouth. She dropped the candy onto his tongue. Its flavor was so intense and delicious, bursting with lime, grape, and strawberry flavors, all combined together. It sizzled and popped as it began to dissolve on his tongue.

As he finished it, he said, "Um! That was so good. I want anoth—" And that was when he changed back into a weasel. The candy had been laced with the same potion that had been in the cream puffs.

"Didn't your mother ever tell you, 'never accept candy from a stranger'?" the queen said slyly. She picked him up by the scruff of his neck and put him in the cage with the beaver.

As they continued along the dancing sea, the wind grew stronger, coming toward them from the south. This made it even harder for Ugan to row, and to make matters even worse, the weather was getting stormier by the minute. A bolt of lightning flashed across the sky, followed by the usual roar of thunder. The swelling waves made it feel more like a carnival ride than a boat ride.

"Put the canopy up, you idiot!" the queen bellowed to Ugan, while trying to smooth her tangled, windblown hair.

Ugan struggled with the canopy, and the rain plunged down at full force. The fierce wind blew steadily at him, and the queen sat with the Book of Prophecy clenched tightly to her bosom. Up, down, and side to side, the boat bobbed in the wild sea.

Ugan was back at the oars, rowing toward the small island. The place where he sat was not covered by the canopy, so the drenching rain poured down on him, soaking his clothes and chilling him to the bone. Luckily the animals were covered, but even so, the rain had now accumulated about two inches on the bottom of the boat.

"My feet are wet. Start scooping the water out, you lazy fool," the queen yelled at him.

Ugan stopped rowing and picked up a bucket that was near him. He stood up in the ankle-deep water and began scooping it up and dumping it overboard. As he scooped, the boat tottered back and forth. This made it very hard for him to stand, and after every time that he dumped water over the side, he would have to grab the side of the boat to steady himself. The winds blew even harder, and the rain came in just as fast as he was able to dump it out of the boat.

"Work faster, dwarf!" the queen commanded from her plush pillow.

Ugan worked as fast as he could to dump the water overboard, and when he looked over the edge, he could see many sharks swarming around the perimeter of the boat. The rain began to taper off, and he decided that scooping up the water one more time would be sufficient. Then he'd get back to rowing and try to get away from the sharks. Every bone and muscle in his body ached from being in the icy wind and rain, and his fingers were almost totally numb.

He scooped the last bit of rainwater and was about to throw it into the sea, when his foot got caught in a rope on the bottom of the boat. The boat swayed to one side and then to the other, and he fell forward over its right side. With his foot caught in the rope, he dangled, just inches above the dark, twisting sea.

"*Help!*" he yelled franticly as a shark's fin brushed against his face.

Queen Sentiz got up off her pillow and glared down at Ugan over the side of the boat. She seemed to enjoy watching him dangle in fear. Two sharks jumped up, angrily snapping at each other, no more than a foot away from his head.

The queen laughed wickedly. "Do you want to come up?" she asked.

"Please, my most gracious queen, don't let me die," Ugan

begged.

"Well, I could row myself," she said, looking toward the sky. "But I don't think I will. I don't want to break a nail." She grabbed the rope and pulled Ugan back into the boat. "Now get back to the oars, and don't let it happen again, or you'll be making some shark a tasty feast," she said, tugging on his beard.

As they neared the island, fog enveloped them that was as thick as pea soup. Ugan lit a lantern and hung it on a hook attached to a pole in the back of the boat. He continued rowing toward a cave in the rocky side of the island. Once inside the cave, Ugan noticed it was cold and damp and a musty smell lingered in the air. *If this isn't hell*, Ugan thought, *there isn't any other place that could be more like it.* A chill ran down his spine, just thinking about it. As the oars stirred up the water, the only sound that could be heard was the moisture dripping off the cave walls, and the only source of light to pierce through the darkness was that of the lantern. A bat that had been hanging on the cave wall awoke and flew straight toward the boat. It swooped down at Ugan's head, but he ducked and was able to get out of its way. Then it flew in the direction of the cave's entrance.

The queen was looking through the Book of Prophecy and was so enthralled with it that she didn't seem to notice the bat. She began to laugh, startling Ugan to the point that his heart began to palpitate.

"Oh, how wonderful! It says that Ramon is waiting for the arrival of Kristina," she said. "He and his troop of zelbocks are at the Salas city prison." The light from the lantern gave a green tinge to her pale complexion. Ugan tried to smile, but the most he could do was slightly lift one corner of his mouth. "I guess you'll have to get the penthouse suites ready for her and the boy's arrival tomorrow morning," she went on, laughing insanely again, which made Ugan cringe.

They finally reached the end of the cave, and Ugan brought the boat to a stop next to a ladder that was hanging from a trap door in the roof of the cave. Near the ladder hung a large brass bell. Ugan reached for the rope hanging from it and rang it. The gonging was so load that it echoed off the cave walls. A light shone down, and a large iron-barred crate with two zelbocks crouched on top of it was lowered down into the boat. The two disgusting creatures jumped off of the crate and one of them, who had a key hanging around its neck, opened a lock hanging from a rusty chain. It pulled the large chain from the crate, and opened the crate's lid. The two zelbocks carried the two cages with the animals in them to the crate, opened it, and dumped the animals into it. The zelbock with the key put the large chain back around the crate and locked it up. Then it rang the bell, and the two of them jumped back on top of the crate. Two other zelbocks, who were waiting up above, slowly pulled the crate back up. As it ascended, the beaver turned back into Hester, and then Davina and Graham turned back into themselves as well. Hester sat up and looked at Queen Sentiz through the bars of the crate.

"I must say, that potion was one of Sir Rupert's best inventions," the queen said, just before the crate disappeared out of her sight.

- 21 -

Salas

It was almost midnight when Kristina, Taysha, and Raymond neared Salas. They had come to the top of a hill that overlooked the sleeping city below. The clouds had cleared and the mother-of-pearl moon shone brightly in the dark sky. A calmness lingered in the air as they gazed up at the twinkling stars above them. They were arranged so differently than the ones Kristina was used to seeing out of her bedroom window, and for a brief moment, she felt homesick.

Raymond sniffed at the cool breeze. "A fellow could get used to a place like this," he said, looking up at the moonlit sky.

"I have to agree with you. It is very lovely here, but I'm just sad that the wicked queen has taken so much freedom away from the inhabitants of the land," Kristina said.

While they stood gazing at the stars, someone wearing a long hooded cloak came running up the hillside toward them. Taysha reared up on her hind legs. Raymond disappeared back into the vest, and Kristina held on tight to Taysha's mane.

"What is it now, Taysha?" Kristina asked, not yet seeing the cloaked figure.

Taysha didn't answer but turned and ran in the opposite direction.

"Wait! Please, wait! I come in peace," the cloaked figured called out, from about halfway down the hillside.

Taysha stopped and turned around to face the mysterious stranger, and Kristina took notice of it for the first time. The cloaked figure removed its hood to reveal that it was young gnome man.

"Please, don't be alarmed and run away. I have a message for you," he said, slightly winded from running up the hillside.

"How can we be sure you're telling the truth?" Kristina yelled.

"It's from Prince Werrien," the gnome yelled back.

"What do you think, Taysha? Should we trust him?" Kristina asked the mare.

"If he is telling the truth, it may be very important," Taysha replied.

Raymond poked his head out of the vest. "I say we don't trust him and stick to our original plan."

Kristina thought for a moment and then replied, "Raymond, we don't have an original plan, or really any plan, for that matter. I say we trust him."

Raymond shook his head in disagreement and then disappeared back into her vest. Taysha trotted down the hillside toward the gnome. When they were about twenty-five feet away from him, he fell down on his knees with both hands clasped above his head. "Bless you, chosen one. You have finally come to restore Bernovem," he said. He got up, walked over to Taysha, and stared up at Kristina with large, bulging eyes and a wide grin on his face. "My name is Retzel. It is such an honor to meet you," he said, still grinning from ear to ear.

"Thank you," Kristina said, feeling slightly awkward.

"In the city, we believers can't show our joy publicly, so we have secret meetings, where we can express ourselves and celebrate your coming, as well as the return of the Magic Warble," he went on.

"Thank you for such an honor. I will do everything I can to deliver the Magic Warble to its resting place," Kristina said. By her outward appearance she seemed brave, but on the inside, she was just a scared child, not knowing what to do or expect next.

"I work at the prison in the city of Salas. I deliver the food rations to the prisoners," Retzel went on, the excitement clear in his voice.

"Have you seen Werrien?" Kristina asked.

"*Prince* Werrien," Retzel corrected.

"Oh, yes, of course, Prince Werrien," Kristina said. Even though he was a prince, to her he was just a regular boy. "Is he okay? I mean, they haven't hurt him, have they?"

"I'm sorry to say that they did whip him several times," Retzel said sadly.

Kristina felt her stomach sink. She couldn't imagine her newfound friend being whipped.

Raymond poked his head out of the vest and said, "Those dirty rotten creatures. When I get hold of the one that did it, I'll bite its ugly, pointy ears off."

Retzel looked oddly at Raymond. "What kind of an animal are you?" he asked.

Raymond raised his nose in the air and answered, "I am a rat and, I'm proud to say, a fancy rat, for that matter. That is what the pet shop sign read, when I resided there."

"We haven't had rats in Bernovem in..." Retzel paused a moment to think, and then continued. "Well, I'm not quite sure how long. Most gnomes and dwarfs had at least one or two per household. They were really good-natured and polite and, you could say, one of a gnome's best friends."

"Werrien told us a little about the rats and also how that horrible queen was responsible for their extinction," Kristina said.

"What a nice little fellow," Retzel said, petting Raymond on his head. He glanced up at Kristina.

"They were trying to make Werrien tell where the Magic Warble is," he went on.

"Did he give it to them?" Kristina asked.

"Why, I don't think so," Retzel said, putting his finger to his mouth and looking puzzled. "Does he have it?" He tickled Raymond under his chin.

"Yes, I gave it to him to hold, not long before he was captured by the zelbocks," Kristina said.

Retzel was so fascinated with Raymond that he seemed to have forgotten about the message he was to give.

"Did you say you had a message for me?" Kristina asked.

"A message," Retzel repeated, seeming a little confused.

"Yes, isn't that why you came to find us?" Kristina asked.

"Oh, yes, of course, the message," Retzel said, bringing his attention back to her. "Werrien knows that you are coming to rescue him, so he wanted to warn you to not go to the back side of the prison, because there will be zelbocks hiding there, waiting for you. Instead, you are to go to the east side, where his cell window is. He said he can give you further instructions when you get to that point." Retzel went back to petting Raymond.

"Is there anything else I need to know?" Kristina asked.

"I think that's about all," Retzel said, looking back up at her with his large protruding eyes and a slightly annoying grin. "I must hurry back." He put his hood back up over his head, said good-bye, and ran down the hillside toward the city.

Kristina rode Taysha down the hillside, the same way that Retzel had left, and they continued under the moonlit sky toward the city.

"He sure was a nice fellow. I haven't had that much attention since I've been here," Raymond said.

"I'm sorry that you feel deprived Raymond, but it's not like I've had a lot of time to spend playing with you since we've been here," Kristina said.

"I'm not sure that I trust him," Taysha said.

"I know *I* don't trust *you*," Raymond said, "especially when I'm left alone on your back."

"I meant Retzel," Taysha said.

"What do you mean?" Kristina asked.

"There was something creepy about him," Taysha went on.

"I found him to be quite nice," Kristina said.

"Maybe you're just a little jealous that I got all the attention and you didn't," Raymond said to Taysha.

"No! It has nothing to do with that. It's just the strange look he had on his face, and those protruding eyes," Taysha said.

"Well, one should never judge by appearances," Raymond said.

"Hey, look, guys, straight ahead," Kristina said.

Taysha and Raymond stopped arguing to look ahead toward an elaborate iron gate not far off in the distance. Arched across the top of it was lettering that read "Salas," and arched under that, more lettering read "A City Dedicated to Her Majesty."

124

- 22 -

Salas Prison

All was very quiet as the three approached the city gates; not a single soul was to be found. The closer they got, the taller and wider the gates seemed to grow, and when they finally stood under the enormous archway, they noticed the many details in the ironwork. Its archway was a depiction of two trees bending toward each other to form the arch, and at the base of the trees, there were vines twisting around the bottom of the trunks, entwining them all the way up to the tips of each and every branch. It gave the impression that the vines were choking the life from the trees. The gate itself was in bad condition, broken in sections and rusting. While standing under the archway, Kristina couldn't help but notice a large statue standing directly ahead of her. It was an enormous replica of Queen Sentiz that stood over twenty-five feet tall. It stared down with eyes that seemed to be glaring right into her eyes, and it sent a chill down her spine. In the statue's right hand was a tall scepter, and at its top was a cobra snake's head. Its mouth was wide open, revealing two sharp fangs. In the other hand, she held a scale of measurement, in which the left scale outweighed the right one entirely.

"Is that statue a replica of who I think it is?" Kristina asked Taysha.

"If you're thinking Queen Sentiz, then you're right," Taysha answered.

"She looks so powerful," Kristina said.

"That's her whole intention," Taysha responded.

The three continued on past the statue and down the main street of the city—Queen Sentiz Street. Rundown shops lined its sides, along with empty fruit and vegetable stands. As they walked along it, Taysha's hooves clacked loudly on the cobblestone road.

"I think we'd better get off this street and onto softer ground," Kristina said.

They headed for a dirt alleyway, and just as they turned its corner, a window in one of the buildings lit up. A dwarf in a nightdress poked his head out of the window to see where the noise was coming from. Luckily, Kristina and Taysha were already down the alley and out of sight.

The alleyway was very dark and they couldn't see anything as they walked, but the darkness didn't prevent them from hearing a horrible blood-curdling screech, followed by a loud clanking noise. It frightened Taysha and she bucked.

"Wow, Taysha!" Kristina whispered.

"What was that?" Taysha asked.

"I don't know," Kristina said.

From the left side of the alley just ahead of them, two bright yellow, glowing eyes appeared, and a few seconds later they heard a loud screeching sound.

"Why don't you watch where you're stepping?" a voice said from below Taysha.

"She's getting quite good at that," Raymond said.

"It's a cat," Kristina said.

The cat began to run away.

"Wait! We're really sorry," Kristina cried out after it.

The cat stopped and looked back, its eyes gleaming.

"We wondered if you might be able to help us," Kristina said.

"Why should I?" the cat asked.

"I can pay you," Kristina said.

"Money is of no use to me," the cat said as it turned around and began to walk away.

"Wait, please! I have some cheese," Kristina said.

The cat slowly turned around and sauntered back toward them. "I will do it, for the cheese and some fairy blossom," the cat said.

Kristina thought of how Werrien had been beaten and was now sitting in a cold prison cell. He would most likely need the fairy blossom in order to have the strength to escape. "I can give you the cheese, but I can't give you any fairy blossom," Kristina said.

"Well, then, the deal's off," the cat said, turning once again to leave.

"Okay, I guess that I can spare a little," Kristina said.

The cat walked back toward them once again, and Kristina jumped down off Taysha and opened the food sack. She took out what was left of the cheese that Leacha had given her. Then she opened the little sack of fairy blossom to see that there was about one tablespoon left. She divided it in half and then wrapped one part in a napkin. Then she placed the cheese on the ground in front of the cat. The cat gobbled up the cheese so fast that Kristina wondered if it hadn't eaten in weeks.

"Now give me the fairy blossom," it said while licking its paws.

"First, you need to lead us to the prison, and then I will give it to you," Kristina replied.

The cat didn't answer but turned and started to walk away.

"Okay, have it your way," Kristina said, placing the napkin on the ground. Once again, the cat turned around. Then it ran toward the folded napkin and picked it up with its mouth. It turned and ran away, this time not stopping when Kristina called after him.

"Now what are we going to do?" Kristina wailed. "We have no idea how to get to the prison, and there's not a soul around who can help us."

"We'll just have to keep searching until we find it ourselves," Taysha said.

The three continued on through the city's dark alleyways, and when they got to the end of each one, they would stop and look down the street to see if there was any sign of the prison. After searching for what seemed to be a couple of hours, they began to worry that they would never find it.

"The sun will be rising very soon, and if we don't find the prison before sunrise, we probably won't see Werrien again," Taysha said sadly.

After they had been down what seemed to be every street and alleyway, Taysha stopped walking.

"Why are you stopping?" Kristina asked her.

"Let's face it: we've been down every possible street and alley, and we haven't found the prison."

"We can't just give up," Kristina said.

"I don't know where else to look," Taysha said. No sooner were the words out of her mouth than the glowing yellow eyes appeared again from behind a garbage can.

"Follow me," the cat's voice commanded as it started down the alley ahead of them.

"Where were you? We had a deal! You promised to help us, but then you left us for more than two hours," Kristina said.

"You should know by now that you can never trust a cat," Raymond said.

"I had business to take care of, so either follow me now, or I'll leave for good," the mysterious cat said, and then it trotted ahead of them.

The cat led them out of the very dark alley and across a street. Then it crossed over to another street and jumped over a fence into what seemed to be someone's backyard.

It trotted over to a gate and rubbed up against it. Taysha followed and pushed the gate open with her nose. Then she went into the backyard.

"Why did you lead us here?" Kristina asked the cat.

"This is the prison warden's backyard, and we need to go through it in order to get to the prison," the cat said.

There was another gate at the back of the yard, and the cat pranced over to it and squeezed underneath it. Taysha approached the gate, and Kristina noticed that it was chained and locked to the fence.

"How are we supposed to get through this gate when it's locked?" she asked the cat.

"I told you that I would lead you to the prison, but I didn't say it would be an easy road," the cat said, looking back at her with its fiery eyes.

"I'm just going to have to jump over it," Taysha said.

"Maybe there is another way around," Raymond said, but before he could go back inside Kristina's vest, Taysha was already in midair, jumping over the gate.

The cat ran ahead of them, down a pathway leading into the wooded forest. Taysha followed behind it, winding to the left and the right for what seemed to be a very long time. The prison finally appeared ahead of them. It was huge, with barred windows, and in front of it, a row of torches lit up the darkness. Two zelbocks stood at attention, guarding it. The cat stopped and looked back at Kristina. Then without saying a word, it ran off the path and into the thick of the woods.

"The cat's taking off again. Now how are we supposed to get past those zelbocks?" Kristina asked.

From within the woods, they heard the cat say, "Follow me."

Taysha turned toward its voice, and Kristina was able to see the familiar glowing eyes peering out from between the trees ahead of her. Once again Taysha followed the cat, — off the groomed path and into the woods. Leaves and fallen branches crunched and snapped under her hooves. One of the zelbocks seemed to hear the noise, and it looked suspiciously into the woods. The cat stopped and stood silent.

"I know these woods like the back of my paw. You must watch where you go, and only go where I lead you. If you don't and they see you, you don't stand a chance of escaping. Now follow directly behind me to avoid the hidden traps. Remember, one wrong move, and you'll most likely fall into one," the cat said.

Trying to stay directly in its trail, Taysha cautiously followed the cat until it stopped again. It looked side to side and then up and down.

"What's the matter?" Kristina asked it.

"There's a trap here, and I'm contemplating how to go around it," the cat answered. Finally, it decided to go to the right of it, and Taysha carefully followed. Soon after, they came to a very tall fence topped with swirling barbed wire. They could see the back of the prison beyond the fence.

"Please stop!" Kristina said to the cat. The cat turned to look back at her. "I was told not to go to the back of the prison, because there are zelbocks waiting for me there. Instead, I should go to the east side, where Werrien's cell is," Kristina said.

"I will run on ahead and check to see if this is true," the cat said.

While the cat ran toward the prison, Taysha stood very still, trying not to make any noise. The woods were spooky to Kristina— she could hear all kinds of strange noises. She tried to keep calm by closing her eyes and imagining herself somewhere else, and even though it was only a few minutes, it felt like an eternity before the cat finally returned.

"I checked the backside of the prison, and there was nobody there, so I went to the east side. There seemed to be no one there either, but as I turned to leave, I heard some rustling in the nearby bushes, so I turned around and approached the bushes, pretending to be a pesky cat, looking for food. That is when I heard the voices. There seemed to be many of them, in hiding, waiting for someone."

"I knew we shouldn't have trusted that weird little gnome, Retzel," Taysha, said.

They stood wondering what to do. Kristina looked toward the prison, and saw that the sun was rising up over the rooftop. "What do you suggest we do?" she asked the cat, but there was no response—the cat was gone.

- 23 -

A Wild Fantasy Dream?

Hester screamed as the zelbocks lifted the crate onto a horse-drawn wagon. Her scream was so loud that it instantly woke up Graham and Davina, who had been very groggy from the potion. The zelbocks paid no attention to them but went about their business.

"What's the matter with you two? Can't you see that something horrible is happening to us?" Hester said, snapping her fingers in front of Graham's and Davina's faces to try to make them more aware of their surroundings.

Graham shook his head, trying to focus. "Do you think this is part of the special treatment that the weird little guy was talking about?" he asked.

"It may be special treatment to you, but it's definitely not up to my standards," Hester said.

"I have a crushing headache," Davina said, rubbing her temples to ease the pain.

"That's the least of your worries. Take a look around you," Hester said.

Davina looked through her Coke-bottle glasses and noticed the bars that surrounded them. Then she noticed the dark, damp stone

131

walls with dimly lit torches aligning them.

"It feels like we're back in the Dark Ages," Graham said.

"Where do you think they're taking us?" Davina asked.

"I don't know, but this is definitely not the royal treatment we were promised," Hester said, looking through the bars toward the zelbocks. "Hey, you up there! Where are you taking us? And why did you put us in this horrible crate?"

One of the zelbocks turned around and looked straight at her, but because of the darkness, it was hard to see its hideous face, other than its glowing red eyes.

"Well? Where are you taking us?" Hester demanded.

The zelbock didn't answer but turned back around.

"Do you have any idea who you're dealing with?" Hester yelled again, this time rattling the bars that held them captive.

"I'm really cold," Davina said, looking down at her damp nightgown. "How'd we get wet?"

"I don't know, but I'll tell you what's really weird. I was dreaming that I was on a boat, and this beautiful woman gave me a candy. It was the best candy that I'd ever tasted. Then I lay down in a pool of water," Graham said.

"Yeah, and then what?" Hester asked.

"I don't know, but maybe it's got something to do with how we got wet," Graham said.

"Oh, sure, we all got wet because of your fantasy dream," Davina said, rolling her eyes in disbelief.

"Why don't you grow up, Graham? This isn't a time for silly stories," Hester said.

The wagon turned a corner and continued down another tunnel with prison cells aligning both sides of it. The three children sat up on their knees and stared out at the cells as they passed by them. At one point, a bony hand reached through one of the cell bars. "Fairy blossom," a parched voice called out.

As they continued past more cells, they heard groaning, moaning, and even insane laughter.

"I demand you stop at once and let us out!" Hester shouted to the zelbocks. But there was no response. "You won't get away with this, once my parents hear about how you're treating us!"

Graham pulled at Hester's nightgown and said, "Hester, your parents can do nothing for you here."

"You keep your mouth shut, Graham Kepler!" Hester shouted, pushing him away. Just as she was about to yell again, the wagon suddenly stopped. "See? They did listen to me," she said, looking down at Graham.

The two zelbocks approached the crate, but it was still too dark to see their gruesome faces. Hester smoothed her hair back as she got ready to discuss matters with them. The zelbocks hopped up, one on each side of the wagon. One of them unlocked the barred crate. They lifted its lid off and stared down into it. Graham and Davina crouched inside, with their knees held tightly to their chests, but Hester stood up confidently and held out her hand, as if she wanted to be helped out of the crate.

"You really should look into a good mouthwash," she said, waving her other hand in front of her nose.

Once again the zelbocks didn't pay attention to her.

"Well, aren't you going to help me out of this dreadful crate?" she asked impatiently.

The zelbock closest to her grabbed her around her waist and threw her over its shoulder. "Hey, the only one who's ever carried me like that was my father, and that was only once, when I was four. Now put me down," she said, kicking her feet.

The zelbock didn't respond but jumped down off the wagon and began carrying her down the tunnel. The other zelbock stood on guard, watching over Davina and Graham, who were afraid to move a muscle. As it stared down at them, breathing heavily, the two sat staring up at its large belly moving in and out, and they could smell its foul breath. It was so putrid that Graham slowly brought his hand to his nose to plug it; soon after, Davina plugged her nose as well. Finally, the other zelbock hopped back up on the wagon.

"Where's my cousin?" Graham asked it in a small voice.

"Don't you worry. You'll soon be joining her," the zelbock answered in a deep guttural voice. Then a grin came across its face, revealing its rotten teeth. The two zelbocks grabbed Davina and Graham and threw them over their shoulders. They hopped down off the cart and carried the two children deep into the tunnel. Davina and Graham kicked and punched as they were carried past the insane prisoners staring out of their cells. After a short walk, the zelbocks finally stopped in front of a cell, where another zelbock stood on guard in front of it. It opened the cell door, and the two other zelbocks walked inside, with Davina and Graham still kicking and punching. Hester was already in the cell, sitting in the corner with her knees drawn up tightly to her chest, the same way the other two had sat inside the crate. The zelbocks dumped Graham and Davina onto the cold concrete floor. Then the zelbocks walked out of the cell and locked the barred door behind them.

After they left, Graham and Davina got up and quickly went to the bars to watch the zelbocks disappear down the dark tunnel. Davina fell to her knees and began to cry bitterly, and she pounded her fists on the floor. She looked up at Graham and then over at Hester, and with her face all red and covered in tears, she said, "Why did I listen to you brats? We were perfectly fine in that little cottage." Then her frustration turned to anger. "But no, it wasn't good enough for you!" She stood up, clenched her fists tightly by her side, and walked over to Hester. Her long, greasy black braids were hanging in front of her face. "Now look at the mess you got me into!" she yelled.

"Please don't spit on me," Hester replied in a calm yet angry tone.

That seemed to enrage Davina even more, but Graham interrupted. "Uh, Davina, it was actually me who didn't want to go with the weird little guy. You and Hester were all for it, as I recall." Then in a higher, mocking voice, he went on, "'Oh, come on, Graham, you'd better not ruin this for us.' If there's one thing I've learned, it's to never leave the decision making up to a female."

With a blank look on her face, Davina turned to face Graham. Then, like an angry lioness, she pounced on him and began hitting him and pulling his hair. Graham kicked and screamed in a muffled voice, until Hester interrupted.

"Stop fighting! I hear something," she said, but Davina didn't stop. "I mean it!" she said again, this time getting up and tugging at Davina's nightgown. "Listen, do you hear it?" she asked.

Davina stood up. Her glasses were steamed up and sitting crooked on her nose. Graham stood up as well. His hair was sticking out like a hedgehog from Davina's pulling it. He stood under a small barred window, which was about five feet above his head. He jumped up to try to grab the bars, but he couldn't reach them.

"Get out of my way," Davina said, pushing him to the side. She tried to jump up herself, but she could only jump half as high as Graham.

"Davina, I don't think its going to happen," Graham said.

Davina stopped jumping and turned around to face Graham. She placed her hands on her hips, and her eyes were squinted into two very small black-eyed peas. "What's not going to happen?" she asked.

"You, reaching that window. You're just to darn fat to jump that high," Graham said bluntly.

"You must be a sucker for punishment," Davina said, lunging forward to grab him by his nightshirt. This time, she didn't succeed because Hester stepped in between them.

"Would you two stop fighting and grow up!" she yelled.

Graham and Davina looked dumbfounded at Hester.

"And what do you suppose we do?" Davina asked.

"Well, why don't you give Graham a boost up, so he can look out the window?" Hester said.

Davina looked at Graham suspiciously.

"You are the strongest of us all," Hester went on.

Davina finally cracked a slight smile and said, "That sure is the truth." Then she walked over to the wall and stood under the window. "Well, hurry up. We don't have all day," she said to Graham.

Graham shook his head. *Women! It is just so weird how they can switch moods so suddenly,* he thought.

Davina lifted Graham just high enough so that his eyes could see out the window.

"Well, what do you see?" Hester asked impatiently.

"Not much, just a bunch of waves," he said.

Davina was just about to let him down when he said, "No, wait! I see something else."

"Well, what is it?" Hester asked.

"Spit it out. I can't hold you up all day," Davina said, her voice straining.

"Hold on—it went behind a wave," Graham said.

The two girls rolled their eyes impatiently.

"There it is!" Graham said excitedly. "It's that same boat and lady that were in my dream!"

Davina unclasped her hands, causing Graham to fall to the ground. The two girls stood over him, staring down at him.

"We told you, Graham—we don't want to hear about your stupid fantasy dream," Davina said. Suddenly, she croaked like a bullfrog.

24

Overboard

The lantern swung from side to side, making it hard for Queen Sentiz to read the prophecy book.

"Speed it up, you numbskull! Do you think I want to be out here all day?" she yelled from beneath her dry canopy. She sat huddled under a thick bear stole, sipping on a steaming-hot cup of fairy-blossom tea.

Ugan's arms ached as he strained to keep the large rowboat on course in the pouring rain. Oh, how he wished he could change places with the queen, if even for a brief moment in his meager life.

The queen took another sip of her tea, and then, almost spilling it, yelled excitedly, "They've arrived at the prison!"

When Ugan didn't respond to her sudden glee, she yelled even louder, "Did you not hear me, stupid dwarf?"

"I'm sorry, my lady, but the rain is so heavy that I can neither hear you well nor see you well," Ugan yelled back to her.

"You are just getting too old and feeble. I'll have to get a replacement for you as soon as possible," the queen said. She got off her plush pillow and walked toward the front of the boat. It swayed to and fro, over a large swelling wave, and she suddenly lost her balance and fell headfirst over the side of the boat and into the cold, dark sea. Ugan dropped the oars and jumped up. He looked all around at the waters surrounding the boat, but Queen Sentiz was nowhere to be found. *Could she have drowned so quickly?* he wondered. A lump came into his throat, and he actually felt somewhat scared without her. Then he thought of how she had said that he was old and feeble, and that she would replace him. He tried to push that thought out of his mind and instead think of a fond memory of her, but he just couldn't recall any. Soon after, his fear began to fade and it was as if a large load had been lifted off his shoulders. He looked one more time into the dark waves that surrounded the boat, but there was no sign of her queenship, not even a piece of her clothing floating on the waves.

Being quite convinced that she must have drowned, he went to the rear of the boat and quickly guzzled the remainder of the fairy-blossom tea she had left in her cup. Instantly, he felt a surge of warm energy flow through his veins. He glanced down and noticed the Book of Prophecy was on the bottom of the boat. It was open, with its pages blowing in the wind. He picked it up and quickly turned to the last written page. He ran his finger down the words, until he came to the name *Clover*.

"Clover? Where have I heard that name before," he asked himself. He continued reading: "*Clover, the fairy princess, was captured at the Salas Prison.*" Why did that name seem so familiar?

A memory suddenly popped into his mind of a visit to Rumalock's house on a beautiful sunny day. His brother was busy taking his clothes off the line while a spunky little fairy buzzed around his head, teasing him. Rumalock laughed as she poked at him and tickled his ears. Rumalock later told Ugan that this was his special little friend Clover. Yes, this must be the fairy that the book indicated was captured. He noticed more writing popping onto the page, which read: "*At Salas Prison, zelbocks wait in hiding, for the human child Kristina to fall into their trap.*"

Ugan closed the book and tucked it under the queen's pillow. He went back to the oars and began to row as fast as he could, and even though it was cold and windy and the rain poured down on him, it was not nearly as bad as having Queen Sentiz ridicule him and dictate orders to him. No, the weather didn't bother him one bit, now that he had a chance to change his destiny. Oh, yes, he would be known throughout history as *Ugan the Brave*, instead of *Ugan the Traitor*. This was the happiest moment in his life.

Now that the queen has drowned, I must go as quickly as possible to Salas Prison and find that imbecile Ramon, Ugan thought. *I will tell him that he is needed at the palace at once—Mommy's orders! Then I will inform him that I am to relieve him of the burden of escorting the boy Werrien to Treachery Island. He's so lazy, he'll be glad to let me take the boy, but of course, I will release Werrien, so he and the girl can deliver the Magic Warble to its resting place. Oh, I hope the legend of the Magic Warble is true. The next thing I will do is release Clover, so she can tell Rumalock the great deed I have done. Yes I shall be known throughout history as Ugan the Brave, the Great Deliverer.*

Ugan pictured himself in the future, sitting with his grandchildren by a cozy fire, sipping fairy-blossom tea and thumbing through the great Book of Prophecy. His grandchildren would be enthralled with his heroic stories, and they would ask, "Is that really you, Grandpa? Did you really help save Bernovem from that horrible Sentiz?" And he would answer, "Yes, dear children, if it hadn't been for my great bravery, you two possibly wouldn't even be here today." Oh, what joyous thoughts these were to entertain.

But if Ugan had looked behind the boat, his thoughts would have been very different—because he would have seen that Queen Sentiz hadn't drowned after all. Tired, cold, and madder then a nest of angry hornets, she bobbed up and down in the rolling waves, as she swam along behind him. *Wait until I get my hands on that retched dwarf. Why, I'll boil him alive and feed him to the zelbocks,* she thought.

Ugan finally reached the rocky shore of Bernovem, and as he hurried to tie the boat to the dock, he noticed a raven flying above him in the rainy sky. It was Roage.

"Miserable creature," Ugan grumbled as he nervously secured the boat to the dock. Tucking the prophecy book under his coat, he ran up the path that led to the palace, and like a hawk tracking its prey, Roage glided in the sky above him. Ugan's heart began to pound when he noticed that the raven was following him. All had been going so well, but now, he was afraid that he might be attacked by the vicious ravens again. He ran faster to try and get away from Roage, but Roage flew faster and kept right up with him. Then Roage flew ahead of Ugan and disappeared into the forest.

Phew! That was a close call, Ugan thought as he stopped to catch his breath.

But then Roage flew back out of the forest and landed on the ground right in front of Ugan. Clutching the prophecy book to his chest, Ugan began to take steps backwards. He recognized Roage from the time the raven had stolen his lunch bag.

"It's you, the horrible raven who viciously attacked me," he said. Then he tripped on a rock and fell flat on his bottom. Roage hopped toward him and Ugan shuffled backwards on his bottom.

"No, no, please don't hurt me again," he said.

"How could I possibly hurt you? You're much bigger and stronger than one raven," Roage said.

Ugan looked up at the sky to see if there were more ravens flying above him, but there were none, so he rose to his feet and felt around his belt for his slingshot.

"I don't think you'll want to do that," Roage said, "for I have important information for you."

"Oh, really? Do you think I'm going to believe you, after what you did to me?" Ugan said, while assembling a stone in his slingshot. He aimed it right between Roage's eyes, but just as he was about to shoot, Roage interrupted his concentration by saying, "Queen Sentiz is alive."

Ugan chuckled nervously. "Good try, but there's no way she could survive in that rough water."

"Oh, but how you misjudge her, and I would have thought that out of anyone, you would know her the best," Roage said.

Suddenly an image came into Ugan's mind. It was of Queen Sentiz frolicking in her swimming pool back at the palace. "I guess she is a pretty good swimmer," he said, letting the stone fall out of the slingshot. Then he fell to his knees and began to weep.

"My life is ruined!" he cried.

"What do you mean? You never had a life to begin with," Roage said.

"Why don't you just get out of here and let me await my horrible fate on my own," Ugan said.

"I have seen how you are treated by the queen, so I have decided to help you," Roage said.

Ugan looked up at the raven with a glimmer of hope in his eyes. "You have?" he said. But then his look turned suspicious. "Why should I believe you, when you practically tried to kill me?"

"At this point, I don't see that you have any other choice," Roage replied.

Ugan's look of suspicion faded away. "You're right. You may be my only hope."

"Then we'd better get moving," Roage said.

"Oh, it's no use. As soon as the queen knows I'm gone, she'll summon her army of zelbocks to hunt me down. We don't stand a chance," Ugan said.

"Well, then, that's the risk that you'll have to take. Now follow me, for I wouldn't doubt that the queen is on dry land as we speak," Roage said.

Roage's hunch was right, because as they headed for the forest, the soaking-wet queen had been listening from behind a nearby tree and had heard all of their conversation.

25

A Call for War

Azelbock was driving a horse-drawn cart, with Werrien in a crate on the back of it. He snapped his whip to set the horses into motion.

"Look," Kristina said, pointing to a figure coming into view.

"It's Retzel!" Taysha said.

A zelbock handed Retzel a small sack and then patted him on his back.

"Why that dirty liar, and to think I fell for his kind words," Raymond said.

Retzel ran toward the fence and when he reached it, he crawled through a hole in the bottom of it.

"Where do you think he's going?" Kristina asked Taysha.

"I don't know, but we'd better catch up with him and find out," Taysha said.

As they headed to where Retzel crawled through the hole in the fence, they could see zelbocks coming out of the prison. It was daylight, and they had to take extra precautions so as not to be seen. They walked through the thickest parts of the forest, keeping the fence always in view, and even though they tried their best to avoid possible hidden traps, Taysha almost stepped in one. They suddenly heard a loud *snap*, and a leg-hold trap, big enough to sever an elephant's foot, slammed shut. Its large, sharp, spike-like teeth skimmed the back of Taysha's hoof and ripped off some of the hairs from the back of it. She reared up, and Kristina had to hold on tight with her legs. She managed to stay on just fine, but Raymond, who had crawled out of her vest, went flying through the air. He turned circles in the air, and his eyes were squeezed shut.

"Oh, please, don't let this be the place that I breathe my last breath, dear God! But if it is, please don't let me splatter," he prayed.

Then, scrunching up his little nose, he prepared to hit the cold, hard ground. But to his surprise, where he landed was not cold or hard at all. It was rather warm and soft. He opened his eyes and stared right into Retzel's bulging eyes. Raymond let out a frightful squeal. Kristina quickly dismounted Taysha, and then both she and Taysha pressed Retzel against the tree where he had been sitting, waiting for them to pass. Without hesitation, Kristina went down on one knee and drew out the knife that Werrien had given her. Surprising even herself by what she was about to do, she pushed Raymond out of the way and held the knife very close to Retzel's throat. "Why did you betray Werrien and lie to us?"

Retzel's eyes grew so large that they looked like they might pop out of his head. "I...I had no...no choice," he stammered.

"I should have guessed you'd come up with such an answer," Kristina said.

"Please, you must believe me! I have a sick child who is in desperate need of fairy blossom and must have a large amount every day, just to stay alive. I could never find enough myself, so I must work for Queen Sentiz as her spy in order for her to supply me with enough," Retzel said.

"Why should I believe you, when you lied so well the first time we met?" Before Retzel could answer, Kristina felt a little tug on her pant leg. She looked down to see that it was Raymond. "Not now, Raymond! Can't you see that I'm busy?" she said. Raymond tugged again on her. "Raymond if you don't—" It was then she saw that her rat was pointing to something between the trees. With the knife still close to Retzel's throat, Kristina looked up to see a young gnome woman, who was holding a bundled-up blanket close to her bosom. A faint cry came from the bundle, followed by a gurgling cough. Kristina looked at the gnome woman's sad face. Then she looked up at Taysha.

"You'd best put the knife down," Taysha said softly.

"First, I must know if the Magic Warble is safe," Kristina said.

"I had to tell them that Prince Werrien had it," Retzel confessed. "That was part the information I was sent to get when I met you outside the city."

Kristina pushed the cold knife against his throat. "So now they have the Magic Warble also? You have not only delivered the fate of Bernovem into Queen Sentiz's hands, but you have made it so that I will never be able to return home to my family!"

"Please, have mercy on me, for Queen Sentiz has said that she would have my family tortured and killed, and then banish me to Treachery Island for the rest of my life, if I didn't follow her orders. I am willing to give up my life, but I can't bear to have my wife and child tortured and killed," Retzel said as tears welled like puddles in his big eyes.

Even though Retzel had caused so much trouble, Kristina couldn't help but feel sorry for him. She put the knife away and stood up. "Okay, I will spare your life, but only if you take me to Werrien," she said.

"I will do anything you want, but please promise me that my family will be safe," Retzel said.

Kristina looked at Retzel's wife and helpless child. Unfortunately, she knew that this was something she couldn't promise. Before she could answer Retzel, Roage flew up to them and landed on the ground. He tilted his head from side to side as he looked at each one of them. When he looked at Kristina, he said, "Greetings, chosen one. It is an honor to finally meet you."

"Who are you, and what do you want?" Kristina asked. She'd learned to be leery of trusting anyone new.

"My name is Roage, and I have important information about Prince Werrien."

"I see, and I suppose you would like to give me directions as to where I may find him," she said, assuming she was being tricked again.

"Yes, that is exactly right," Roage said.

"And then I suppose when I arrive at this destination, there will be zelbocks in hiding, ready to jump out and warmly greet me," she scoffed.

"This is partially true," Roage said.

"Oh, I see! The part that I must have gotten wrong—would that happen to be the greeting from the zelbocks? Maybe it won't be warm," she said, angrily.

"The reason I have come is to tell you that Werrien and the Magic Warble are presently on their way to the top of Mount Bernovem. When they reach the top, Queen Sentiz will have her son, Ramon, destroy the Magic Warble and then kill Werrien," Roage said.

"Is this true?" Kristina asked Retzel.

Retzel lowered his head in shame. "Yes, I'm afraid so."

"Well, then, we must leave at once to rescue Werrien. Would you please tell us the quickest way to him?" Kristina asked Roage.

Once again Roage tilted his head from side to side as he looked at everyone. "I'm sorry to say that you don't stand a chance against the zelbocks. The queen has called up most of her army to follow the party that is taking Werrien and the Magic Warble to the top of the rugged mountain."

"We have to rescue Werrien and the Magic Warble," Kristina said. She began to walk away, expecting that at least Taysha and Raymond would follow her. But when she turned around, she saw that everyone was standing still and staring at her. "Well? Are you coming?" she asked in a frustrated voice.

"You might as well ask us to commit suicide right now," Raymond said. "At least then we would avoid such a horrid death as being captured and tortured by the zelbocks."

Kristina felt her stomach turn as fear tried to overcome her as well. *Look at you!* the spirit of fear seemed to tell her. *Do you think that you—a little girl, a horse, and rat—can defeat an army of zelbocks? You might as well hand yourselves over and save everyone the hassle and embarrassment.*

"I will not give up and let Werrien die!" Kristina yelled toward the sky. Then she looked at the others. "If you won't come with me, then I'll go alone." She turned and began to walk away, but before she got very far, Roage flew over her head and landed on the ground in front of her. "Don't try and stop me! I won't change my mind," she said to him.

"Because you have shown such great courage, I have decided to help you. I will notify all the believing gnomes and dwarfs in our land, and we will rise up our own army. We will fight against Queen Sentiz and her zelbocks," Roage said.

Then Taysha, Raymond, and Retzel all said, "And you can count on us to be the first to enlist."

26

Two Escapes Are Better than One

It was raining heavily at the base of the mountain, so Prince Ramon ordered the zelbocks escorting Werrien to stop for the evening. The harsh weather conditions would make it too treacherous to carry on in the dark, and so the plan was to continue on at first light.

Werrien was imprisoned in a barred crate and had no shelter from the cold rain. From where he sat, drenched and shivering, he could see the zelbocks gathered around a roaring fire, drinking fairy-blossom wine in celebration of their so-called victory of finding the Magic Warble. Their insane laughter echoed through the forest as they crashed their large wooden mugs together in victory toasts. Not far from the fire, set up snug and cozy for the night in his luxurious tent, was Ramon, and in his possession was the Magic Warble. He lay sprawled out on his bed, drunk from the fermented fairy-blossom wine. He tossed the Magic Warble into air and then caught it, over and over, as if it were nothing more then a toy ball. Its swirling colors were changing again, from all the shades of green to a vibrant yellow.

"It is quite a pity that you've waited so long and traveled so far, only to have your beautiful colors smashed to itsy-bitsy pieces.

There were times when I was a child that I secretly wished that I'd be the one to place you on your final resting place. Oh, what glory and honor I thought I would receive. But I was just a foolish lad, not realizing that being the destroyer of the Magic Warble was my true destiny—and a far greater honor!" Beside his bed was a small birdcage on a table. Inside the cage was a tiny prisoner: Clover. Prince Ramon placed the Magic Warble on the bed beside him and then turned on his side to face her. "If only you were my size, I would make you my bride," he said, slurring his words.

"Lucky for me, then, that I'm not your size. But if I were, you wouldn't have been able to capture me," Clover said angrily.

"Oh, is that so? You think you're so tough, do you?" Ramon picked up his horsewhip that lay beside the birdcage. He stuck it through the cage wires and began haphazardly poking it at Clover. "Is it true that if I touch your wings you won't be able to fly again?" he asked between hiccups.

Clover didn't answer; she was to busy dodging his forceful pokes.

Finally, Ramon stopped poking her to guzzle more of his wine, spilling it down the sides of his cheeks. Then he lay back on his bed and began to laugh insanely and kick his legs in the air. A few seconds later, he stopped and became limp, leaving the whip stuck in the cage. His goblet of wine fell out of his hand and spilled onto the bed, and in a drunken stupor, he began snoring loudly.

Clover stood at the back of the cage with her tiny fists clenched tightly around the wires. Her heart was pattering faster than the beat of a humming-bird wings in flight. She glanced up to where the whip was stuck through the cage wires. The poking Ramon had been doing had caused the wires to bend outward, making a slightly bigger space between them. Clover looked up at the gap, and at that instant, she felt hope flood over her.

Could it be big enough for me to escape? she thought. She jumped on top of the whip, and like a gymnast on a balance beam, she carefully walked up to the hole. It was big enough for her to get through, but the problem was her wings. They were too large to fit through without getting damaged. She grabbed hold of the bars, and with all her strength, she tried to pry them apart a little more.

They would not budge. She rested a moment and then tried once more, but this time when she let go, she lost her balance. She fell from the whip and landed with a thump on the bottom of the cage. She stood up again and grabbed hold of the whip, but as she did so, Ramon sleepily reached up and grabbed the end of it. He pulled it out of the cage with Clover hanging on to it. She closed her eyes and folded her wings back in the best way that she could. To her surprise, she slipped right through the hole.

Then Ramon rolled over with his whip in hand and flung her into the air. She opened her eyes to find her wings in perfect condition. She looked down at Ramon, who was lying on his stomach on top of the Magic Warble. He burped loudly and dropped the whip to the floor.

"Disgusting creature," Clover said as she flew out of the tent. Once she was outside, she took a deep breath of the cold, fresh air. Just ahead of her was the roaring fire and the drunken zelbocks, who still were celebrating around it. The fire gave off enough light for her to see the crate that held Werrien. She flew as fast as she could toward it, hoping not to be noticed by the zelbocks. They were so drunk that they wouldn't have noticed her anyway, or for that matter, even cared if they did. When she arrived at the cage, she found Werrien, soaking wet, sitting with his head down between his knees. She flew quietly through the bars and landed on his shoulder. Thinking it was a zelbock reaching out for him; Werrien flinched and pulled away from her.

"Werrien, it's me, Clover," she said.

Feeling a little disoriented from lack of food and sleep, Werrien lifted his head slowly. "Clover! How did you escape?" he asked.

"Ramon got obnoxiously drunk and then passed out. If you ask me, the guy's more then a few bricks short of a load. Anyhow we must act quickly to get you out of here while the zelbocks are celebrating, because once they sober up, we don't stand a chance," she said.

"It's no use. I've been trying all night to figure a way out of here. What I need is a saw to cut through these bars," Werrien said.

Clover flew over to the heavy lock that hung from a chain, securing the door to the crate. She reached inside the lock's keyhole.

Werrien could hear it clanking as she fiddled with it. He had
tried for hours to open it and thought she'd do no better. "Clover, I
really appreciate your effort, but you'd be better off to find a gnome
or dwarf and ask if either of them could come to me with a saw.
At least then—" But before he could finish his thought, the lock
suddenly fell off and landed with a thud on the soft ground. "Clover,
where did you learn to pick locks?" Werrien asked, full of awe.

"Werrien, don't you know my purpose as a fairy?" Clover said
proudly.

"To help those in need is the fairy's creed," they said in unison.

As she spoke the creed, Clover's conscience reminded her of
how mean she had been to Kristina. But she quickly disregarded
it, for it was not the place or time to be thinking of her. She had to
get Werrien away from the zelbocks—and the sooner the better.

Werrien reached his hand through the bars and removed the
lock from the latch. Then he pushed the door open and jumped
out. The wet ground under his feet had never felt so good. "Okay,
let's go get the Magic Warble," he said, while rubbing his ice cold
hands together.

"That's not going to be possible," Clover said.

"What do you mean, not possible? I know Ramon has it, and I know he's in his tent, so let's go get it." Werrien started walking towards Ramon's tent.

"But Werrien, Ramon is much older, bigger, and stronger than you," Clover said, feeling a little embarrassed for pointing out the fact.

"I'm not scared of Ramon. Besides, you said he was passed-out drunk. If I don't take this opportunity now, I might as well get back in that crate and await my death. It will be better than spending the rest of my life in hiding, knowing I was the one who had the Magic Warble and then had it taken away by the zelbocks, who in turn handed it over to that spoiled brat of a false prince," Werrien said. He began walking even faster toward the tent, so Clover flew ahead of him.

She stopped in midair, in front of his face. "There's another thing: Ramon is lying on top of the Magic Warble. You'd have to wake him to get it out from under him."

"I guess I'll just have to take that chance," Werrien said, brushing her out of his way with the back of his hand. Werrien passed by the fire pit, which had died down to a small pile of glowing coals. The zelbocks, who had drunk their fill of fairy-blossom wine, sat slumped over around it, snoring loudly, like a chorus of fog horns. As Werrien approached Ramon's tent, he could see the flickering light of a candle. He peeked between the ties that fastened the door flaps together. Ramon was lying with his back toward the opening, snoring so loudly that the tent walls were vibrating.

"Werrien, do you really think you should go in there? We could escape so easily right now and be home in no time," Clover pleaded.

Werrien gave no reply. Instead, he untied the door flaps of the tent and stepped inside.

27

A Close Encounter with Her Majesty

W hile staring out her carriage window, an ever so slight smile came across Queen Sentiz's blood-red lips. She would soon be arriving at Ramon's base camp, along with her entourage of servant dwarfs, gnomes, and zelbocks. The plan was to set up camp for the night and then leave at the crack of dawn to head up Mount Bernovem. Once at the top of the mountain, the ceremony would begin.

All was falling neatly into place, and going just as she desired. The Magic Warble was in Ramon's possession. The boy Werrien was captured, and even a meddling fairy, who just happened to be the Fairy King's daughter, had been caught. *What a glorious day—and one to remember*, the queen thought. She would have the pleasure of watching her son, Ramon, destroy the Magic Warble, and she would make sure that Werrien had a front row seat for the event. Then, after the Magic Warble was destroyed, she would have Werrien killed.

As she marveled in these thoughts, a sudden flashback came into her mind and her smile changed into an ice-cold glare of insecurity. She envisioned herself clutching the Book of Prophecy and then toppling headfirst into the dark, rough sea. Her stomach turned as she stared blankly out the carriage window, envisioning the book slipping through her arms.

"Gone! Gone forever," she winced and dragged her long red nails down the sides of her pale, gaunt face in anguish.

Even though she had dropped the book onto the boat's bottom when she slipped and fell, she thought that she had taken it overboard with her. *Oh, how I want that book!* she though. *It would have helped me foresee all that is going to happen in Bernovem and how well Ramon is handling being in charge at the camp.* For a brief moment, a tiny bit of appreciation crept into her cold heart, and she actually felt a little proud of her son for having everything in order. *This is the first time he has accomplished much of anything,* she thought.

The carriage finally came to a halt and a few moments later, the queen's door swung open. She extended her bony arm, and a zelbock helped her out of the carriage. They had arrived at the base camp, but it was definitely not what Queen Sentiz had expected. Everything was very still and quiet, except for a few pops in the dying fire.

"Why is my son not here to greet me?" she bellowed.

The zelbock didn't have a clue, so he remained silent—a well-learned discipline when being spoken to by Her Majesty.

"This is preposterous!" she continued. She pushed the zelbock out of her way and began stomping angrily toward Ramon's tent. She passed by the embers of the bonfire, but because of the darkness, she didn't notice the sleeping zelbocks. Clover sat on one of the door ties of Ramon's tent, waiting for Werrien, who was busy searching under the drunken so-called prince for the Magic Warble. He hadn't been in the tent for more than a few minutes when Clover caught sight of Queen Sentiz marching angrily toward it. Clover stuck her little head and arms through the crack in the door flap and began gesturing with her hands for Werrien to come out, but he only shook his head and tried to shoo her away.

Of all times to bother me, she's picked the worst, he thought. *And besides, I don't need to listen to her negativity. I know she wants to tell me it isn't worth risking my life over.*

But Clover persisted by waving her hands over her head. Werrien looked up again to see her drag her finger across her throat. She was trying to let him know that trouble was coming, but he took the gesture to mean, "Cut it out and let's get out of here." He placed his arm between the drunken Ramon and the bed and felt around for the Magic Warble. When he finally located it, he slowly pulled his arm out. Ramon didn't even stop his obnoxious snoring, although he did smack his lips and burp loudly, right in Werrien's face, which caused Werrien to hold his breath from the stench. Now all he had to do was make it safely out of the camp and find Kristina. After that, the two would head up Mount Bernovem, and Kristina could place the Magic Warble in its resting place. Then the spell would be lifted, and Queen Sentiz would no longer be queen. It all sounded so easy, but when Werrien stood up and looked toward the tent door, he saw eight long red nails, four on each side of the door flaps, about to pull the flaps aside.

"Watch out!" he yelled to Clover, who in turn jumped off the tie knot just as the dagger-like nails viciously ripped the tent door open. A cold wind blew in, followed by silence. Clover was blown up into a corner of the tent by the strong wind. Werrien felt a lump rise in his throat as he gazed up at Queen Sentiz in the doorway. Her immense figure cast a dark shadow over his entire body. She stared down at him with dark, ice-cold eyes. Werrien's heart began to pound fast. *There has to be a way out of this situation*, he thought. But he had no weapon to defend himself, and with Queen Sentiz standing in the entrance to the tent, there was not much of a chance in making a run for the tent door. Hopelessness tried to invade his mind, but he didn't let it in. He just knew that no matter what, he must not give in to the evil queen.

It was so quiet that he could hear the smooth rhythm of Clover's wings flapping in the upper corner of the tent. Then Queen Sentiz finally broke the eerie silence. "You must be the boy Werrien," she said calmly, revealing her two large front teeth and a wicked smile.

Werrien stood silent.

"What's the matter, boy? Did a dwarf cut out your tongue?"

Werrien still said nothing.

"*Answer me!*" she thundered.

"Why do you ask, when you already know who I am?" Werrien finally said.

"Don't sass me, peasant boy. I know why you're in here. You're nothing more than a little thief. Now, reveal what you are hiding behind your back!"

"You're the thief and a cowardly liar," Werrien retorted, "and your son is nothing but a drunken fool."

Queen Sentiz looked over at Ramon, still passed out on his bed, and she drew in a large breath of air through her flared nostrils. Her eyes grew twice their size, for she hadn't taken notice of him up until this point.

A drop of sweat fell from Werrien's forehead. Even though he was being brave, he felt like a scared rabbit being cornered by a bloodthirsty wolf.

The queen reached into her fur stole, pulled out a small purple bottle, and carefully removed its lid. "My, what youthful skin you have, and such a flawless complexion," she crooned. Then she took the bottle, tipped it slightly, and dripped a single drop of its contents onto the rug on the tent floor. As the drop hit the rug, Werrien could hear it sizzle, and he looked down to see it had burned a hole through the tent flooring and into the earth below. When it stopped sizzling, there was a three-inch hole in the ground. "I would hate to have to pour this over your lovely head of sandy-blond hair," she said, her evil smile growing more immense. "Now, hand over what you're hiding behind your back, and I'll put this lovely potion away," she said softly.

Werrien looked up at Clover, who was gesturing something again with her hands. Werrien nodded, although he wasn't sure what Clover was trying to tell him. Queen Sentiz began to walk toward Werrien, but before she could reach him, Clover flew at her like a flying arrow. The fairy grabbed hold of the queen's raven-black hair and, like a whirlwind, wound it tightly around her head, covering her eyes.

Queen Sentiz was taken by such surprise that she dropped the potion. Like a soldier fleeing a grenade, Werrien dodged around her and made it safely out of the tent, with Clover right behind him. The spilled potion was so strong that the whole tent lit up and shook violently. It even woke Ramon. He sat straight up in his bed to see a giant crater right beside it. Still drunk and not knowing what to think, he scratched his head and let out a very loud burp.

"Ramon!" Queen Sentiz yelled at the top of her lungs from inside the crater.

Although the loud shaking of the tent hadn't fazed the sleeping zelbocks outside, the blood-curdling scream of Queen Sentiz brought them to their feet.

- 28 -

Help from Above

After Ramon pulled her out of the large crater, Queen Sentiz screamed at the top of her lungs: "*The boy has escaped with the Magic Warble!*"

Inside the tent, now sober but with a nasty headache, Ramon hurried to dress himself, and he hopped around, pulling his socks on. The queen was so furious with him for getting drunk and letting Werrien escape with the Magic Warble that she picked up his horsewhip and began whipping him with it.

"You good-for-nothing imbecile! I can't believe you are even related to me!" She backed him up until he fell into to the large hole. "If you don't get the Magic Warble and that boy back, I'll have you banished to Treachery Island, where you can sit and rot for the rest of your miserable days!"

He looked up into her flared nostrils and cowered at the bottom of the hole.

While Queen Sentiz was busy scolding Ramon, Werrien was also busy—he was planning his next move, trying to find his way out of the base camp. He ran as fast as he could through the camp, dodging between tents and anything big enough to hide behind, so as not to be noticed by the zelbocks, who were now aware that he had escaped. They were swarming the place, looking everywhere for him. At one point, Werrien stopped to rest for a moment behind a tent, and while catching his breath and wiping his brow, he could see the silhouette of a zelbock through the tent's wall. It picked up a spiked flail and headed for the tent door. Werrien knew he couldn't rest long, so he scoped out his surroundings, planning where to run next. Just as he was about to take off, the zelbock's dark shadow appeared in front of him. He could feel as well as smell its stinky breath on the back of his neck. He turned around slowly and saw a zelbock holding a war club, directly over his head. It smiled wickedly, revealing its broken-glass-like teeth. Then with all its might, it violently smashed the war club down toward Werrien.

Werrien was too quick and agile and was able to duck out of the way, allowing the war club to smash down beside him in the moist ground. The zelbock's wicked smile changed into an angry, frustrated look. Then it pulled the war club out of the ground, ripping a large amount of the earth and grass up with it.

Werrien began running again. Now that he had been seen, there wouldn't be any more stopping, no matter how breathless he got. He ran straight through the camp, passing tents, fire pits, and heavy artillery, until he finally made it to a clearing. The mother-of-pearl moon illuminated the land ahead of him, making the forest visible across a flat plain. He continued to run toward the forest, but the zelbocks quickly mounted their horses and charged after him. He glanced back—there were at least fifty of them, all with lit torches and weapons. Sharp pains shot down his aching legs as the last bit of adrenaline empowered him to run even faster. No one knew the woods as well as he did, and if he could make it that far, then he was sure he could lose the zelbocks, at least for the time being. But the zelbocks were quickly gaining ground on him, and he could hear their horses' hooves pounding the ground. They began shooting arrows at him, barely missing him. He knew that he could not outrun their military horses. His energy began fading even more—he hadn't had more than water and a small piece of stale bread in the last few days. He closed his eyes briefly and hoped that his body would not give up on him. As he did so, a memory of his father flashed into his mind.

"Some day, you will be King of Bernovem, and whatever you have to face, no matter how trying, you must be strong and never let your people down. You must never give up at fighting the good fight."

"Never give up" now echoed in his mind. He opened his eyes and looked up to the sky, and to his surprise, he saw hundreds of ravens flying out of the forest. There were so many of them that they blocked the light of the moon, making it hard to see. The ravens flew speedily toward the zelbocks, and once above them, began dropping grenades on them that the dwarfs and gnomes had made. Werrien could smell the strong odor and smoke from the blasts as the grenades plummeted to the ground. It ignited a spark of hope inside him and his father's words flashed through his mind once again: *"Some day, you will be King of Bernovem."*

Werrien stood along the forest's edge, catching his breath. He could see the surviving zelbocks retreating back to the camp. The ones that were hit by the grenades lay scattered along the smoking ground.

All was quiet now except for the sound of the rain that had begun falling again. Lightning flashed across the sky, and at that very same moment, Werrien felt the Magic Warble warm up within his pocket. He took it out and held it in the palm of his hand. Its color began to change again. The vibrant yellow was turning into a brilliant orange right before his eyes. He was happy to have it back in his possession, but now he needed to find Kristina. He placed it back in his pocket and began to make his way into the forest. He couldn't see anything as he entered the thick woods—it was too dense for the moonlight to shine through the trees.

He didn't have anything to light his way, so even though he knew the woods well, it would take too long to feel his way through the darkness. He thought for a moment and then an idea popped into his head. He would use the Magic Warble to light the way. Once again, he took it out of his pocket and held it out in front of him. It gave off just enough light for him to see about twenty feet ahead. Now, at least he could see which direction he needed to go to get to the place where Kristina and he had camped. From there, he could try to find her or Taysha's tracks. If he traveled fast enough, he figured he could make it there within the hour—at least that's what he hoped.

He hadn't traveled very far when he heard rustling in the treetops above him. He held the Magic Warble above his head and looked up to see what was making the noise. When he couldn't see anything, he continued on, but after a few steps he heard the rustling again. He spun around quickly. "Who's up there?" he said sternly. He shined the Magic Warble up into the tree.

"It's probably not a good idea to have that out in the open," a voice said.

"Who are you?" he asked again.

"Roage," the voice answered.

"What do you want?" Werrien asked.

Roage didn't answer but instead asked, "Did you like how my comrades defended you out on the plain?"

"That was your doing?" Werrien responded.

"I know that you are the true prince of Bernovem."

"I don't know what to say other than thank you for saving my life."

"There is no need to say anything else, for I know time is running out."

"What do you mean, time is running out?" Werrien asked.

"The Magic Warble has gone through all of its colors, except for one: red. When it does turn red, which will not be too long from now, it will start to lose its powers. Before that happens, Kristina must place it in resting place in order for the spell to be broken," Roage said.

"I still have to find Kristina, and then we have to climb the mountain and find its resting place. How can we do all of that before it turns red?" Werrien asked.

"There is a way, but you must follow my instructions precisely," Roage said.

"What do you want me to do?" Werrien asked.

"You must travel a little farther northwest, until you come to a certain tree with a soft spot in its trunk. Push in on it with your shoulder, for behind it, hidden inside the tree, is a golden case. Take it out, and put the Magic Warble inside it. This case will protect it from changing color, until you open it again," Roage said.

"But there are so many trees in the forest. How will I know which tree it will be in?" Werrien asked.

"Search carefully, and you will find it," Roage said.

"But what if I don't?" Werrien went on.

Suddenly another raven could be heard cawing from off in the distance.

"I'm sorry, but I must go," Roage said. And before Werrien could respond, Roage flew off.

29

The Golden Case

Werrien decided to put his trust in Roage, and so he headed northwest through the dark, wet forest. And even though he knew it wasn't wise to have the Magic Warble out in the open, it was all he had with him to light the way. He kept searching and searching for the tree with the soft spot that Roage had told him to find, but he couldn't find it, and time was passing quickly.

Could it be that it was so small that he'd missed it? What if he was going in an entirely different direction than Kristina was going? These doubtful thoughts were making him wonder if it would have been better to have stuck with his original plan of going back to the place where Kristina and he had camped out.

As he traveled farther and farther in the opposite direction from which he had first intended to go, he became more and more doubtful of what Roage had told him. Then the Magic Warble suddenly surged with heat again, and its light orange color changed to a dark orange. It was giving the sure sign that time was running out. This just added to Werrien's anxiety, and so he decided he would check fifty more trees, and if he still hadn't found the soft spot, he'd revert to his original plan of going back to the campsite.

At least he'd have a better chance of finding Kristina by following her tracks. He counted the trees, thoroughly checking each one, and when he got to the thirty-seventh one and there was still no soft spot in its bark, he got so frustrated and angry that he decided to not check any more. He turned around, but just as he did so, he heard noises coming from up above in a nearby tree. He shined the Magic Warble toward the noise, and in return, six large, glowing eyes glared down at him. It was a family of snowy white owls—a father, a mother, and baby. The father owl hooted loudly and then said, "We thank you for all you are doing, and our thoughts are with you, Prince Werrien. God speed to you."

It was that little note of appreciation that gave Werrien the fortitude to carry on, and so he went on searching for the tree that Roage had told him to find. He came to the forty-ninth tree and finally, the fiftieth tree, and still there was no sign of the soft spot. He stuck with his decision and turned southwest. But then a very strange thing happened; the Magic Warble heated up again, but not like it had the other times. No, this time was like the very first time he had touched it, when it got so scorching hot that he couldn't hold on to it. He dropped it and shook his hand from the burning pain. Then the Magic Warble suddenly began to roll back in the direction from which he had just come, rolling back *up* a slope and to the tree just ahead of the fiftieth tree. It came to a dead stop in front of what would have been the fifty-first tree. *What a curious thing*, Werrien thought. *Could the Magic Warble be trying to tell me something? Does it have a mind of its own?* He ran the palm of his hand over the tree's rough surface, the same as he had with all the others. Lo and behold, he felt it—the soft spot. He pushed in on it, and a chunk of the bark fell back into the tree. A bright light shone out from the hole, causing him to squint. He peered into the hole and saw the golden case that Roage had told him he would find. *That raven really knows his stuff*, he thought.

He reached inside and took the case out of the tree. Then he picked up the Magic Warble, which had cooled down significantly, and placed it inside the case. At that very moment, a swift wind blew at him and stirred up the leaves on the ground. It swirled upward, and when it was just above his head, he heard a deep voice say in a low whisper, *"You must have faith."*

Werrien stood silent for a moment as a memory flashed through his mind. It was again of his father, King Warren, and a time when the king had crossed over a fallen tree straddling the raging Indra River. When he had gotten to the other side, he held out his hand and told Werrien to come, but Werrien was scared and apprehensive. That is when his father said those exact words: *"You must have faith, son."* Werrien had crossed over the tree, but when he neared the end, he slipped and began to fall. His father grabbed hold of him, and with his strong hands brought his son to safety at the other side of the river.

With his eyes still shut, Werrien tried to savor the moment, but the wind suddenly died and the memory along with it. He opened his eyes and stared down at the Magic Warble, with its vibrant orange color swirling throughout it. Then he closed the lid of the golden case, and at the same time that it clicked shut, thunder roared in the sky, followed by a flash of lightning. Now that the Magic Warble was safely in the case, a blanket of darkness enveloped Werrien. He was wet, cold, and extremely hungry, but worst of all, he couldn't see anything. It was a totally helpless feeling, and he fought against doubt as well as fear, which were trying to pry their way into his mind again. The only way he kept them out was by saying the words, "I will have faith." He repeated these words as he leaned his back against the tree, weary and exhausted.

The dark forest was very quiet except for the pitter-patter of the rain falling on its many tree branches. The soothing sound calmed Werrien's nerves and made his eyelids very heavy, and he began to nod off. *Just a few minutes of sleep will make me feel so much better,* he thought. But just as he began to drift off, he was awakened by the sound of branches snapping. He opened his eyes to see a light flickering through the trees, just west of him. Then a few moments later, a dark figure emerged from between the trees, carrying a lantern. Werrien carefully slipped the golden case between his back and the tree. The mysterious figure walked toward him, with the lantern creaking as it swung from side to side. Even with the light from the lantern, Werrien couldn't make out whether it was a gnome, dwarf, human, or even a zelbock, for that matter. It passed

166

by the tree, seeming not to notice him, but he could see its smoke-like breath. Then there was a strange silence, followed a few more footsteps. The steps stopped suddenly on the opposite side of the tree, and the mysterious figure came to his side of the tree.

"Rumalock?" Werrien said, his voice full of surprise as well as relief.

"Hello, Werrien! I am so relieved that I found you. I have been commissioned to lead you to Kristina."

"Was it Roage that sent you?" Werrien asked.

"Yes, it was. Do you have the Magic Warble?" Rumalock asked.

"Yes," Werrien answered.

"Then come with me. I will take you to Kristina." Rumalock began to walk away briskly.

Werrien followed as Rumalock led him through the forest with his dimly lit lantern lighting the way. "Where are you taking me?" Werrien asked.

"It's best not to discuss it now. Could be spies out here. Anyhow we'll be where we need to be very soon." Rumalock's mood seemed serious and his pace quickened.

Werrien kept quiet as he followed Rumalock north through the dark and damp woods, always keeping a sharp eye for any signs of the enemy. He had known Rumalock for most of his life, and he trusted him, but the anticipation of not knowing where he was being led or what the plans were was giving him an anxious feeling in his stomach. To add to his anxiety, the golden case, tucked inside his shirt, was warming up and cooling down, constantly reminding him of the task that lay ahead.

Rumalock changed his course and headed west in the direction of the Indra River. When they arrived at its bank, the two boarded a raft. Werrien sat down on the raft and held the lantern. Its fragile flame was their only source of light. Werrien wondered where Rumalock was taking him, but he dared not question him. The old dwarf was far too busy steering the raft across the rough waters. One wrong move and they could topple over and be swallowed by the raging river.

By the time they reached the opposite shore, the rain had tapered off, and in its place came a cool breeze, carrying with it the scent of smoke. Not too far into their walk, they could hear the crackling and popping of wood burning, and soon after, they heard hammering, along with voices conversing.

"It's not much farther," Rumalock said. He climbed up a steep hillside and when he reached the top, he turned around and held out his hand to Werrien. Werrien grabbed hold of it, and as Rumalock pulled him up, his firm grip brought back the memory of his father's strong hand, gripping his own and pulling him up the same hillside. Then he remembered his father having a premonition of a place where dwarf, gnome, animal, and human believers would gather together to prepare for a great battle that would change the destiny of Bernovem.

At the top of the hill, they could see a clearing in the woods, and in the midst of it, a roaring bonfire. Gathered around the fire were many gnomes as well as dwarfs, busily making weapons. Two young girl gnomes, about Werrien's age, one with brunette hair and the other with blond, sat on a fallen tree, sewing garments. When they caught sight of Werrien walking toward the fire, the blond whispered something to the brunette, and then they both giggled. They dropped what they were doing and ran excitedly to him, each taking him by one of his hands.

"Prince Werrien, come and sit, and we will give you something to eat," the brunette said.

Werrien was more than happy to take her offer. Nearby was a large cauldron on top of some glowing coals. The blond gnome girl ladled a bowl of hot soup out of the cauldron and handed it to Werrien. He took it with both hands and thanked her, and she smiled at him bashfully, her round cheeks blushing in the light of the fire. He was so hungry that he could have eaten the soup in a couple of gulps. The brunette gnome girl handed him a chunk of bread, which was delicious. "I've just baked it," she told him. The last time he had tasted bread like that was when he was a little boy, and the cook at the palace had baked it fresh. While he was eating, Looper flew up behind him and landed on his shoulder.

"It's about time you showed up," Looper joked.

Werrien nodded, as his mouth was full, and as he did, the golden case warmed up against his skin, bringing him once again to the reality of his mission. "I need to find Kristina. Is she here?"

"Well, not exactly, but I've come to bring you to her. Come on—follow me," Looper said, jumping off his shoulder. He looped around a few times in the air and then headed northwest into the forest. Werrien followed him, feeling much better now that he had eaten.

The sound of the gnomes and dwarfs working around the fire began to grow distant, and the sound of raging water in the Indra River grew louder.

"Where are we going?" Werrien asked.

Looper flew up to his ear and whispered, "I'm not supposed to talk in these parts of the woods. Rumalock's orders."

Werrien understood and so he kept quiet.

After walking a long while, they finally came to a cliff overlooking the Indra River. Werrien stood at its edge to look down at the turbulent water. Looper stayed back a distance, for fear of being swept away by the wind. The strong gusts of cool wind blew a fine mist in Werrien's face, and it reminded him of when Kristina and he had jumped off the cliff similar to this one. *That girl is pretty brave*, he thought. He realized then that he actually did miss her.

"Come on, Werrien. We need to keep moving," Looper yelled from behind him, clinging on to a tree branch so as not to be blown away by the rough winds.

Werrien wiped the mist from his face and turned to follow Looper. They traveled on in silence until Looper finally stopped and landed on the ground. Then he began picking up the leaves and moving them from where he stood.

"What are you doing?" Werrien asked.

"Could you help me move the leaves and dirt from this spot?" Looper asked.

Werrien got down on his hands and knees and began helping Looper. As he was digging, his finger hit something sharp. "Ouch!" He lifted his hand, shaking it. He had gotten a wood sliver under his nail.

"Yes! It is the right place. I was so nervous that I might not be able to find it again," Looper said excitedly.

169

"Glad I could be of help," Werrien said, pulling the long sliver from underneath his nail. The sliver had come from a hidden door in the ground, with a round iron ring attached to it.

"Pull on the ring to lift up the door. It's very heavy, but if you can get it up about two inches, I can slip through the crack," Looper said.

Werrien bent over and grabbed the ring. He began to pull hard on it, and he managed to lift the door about an inch. But then he dropped it. "This thing weighs a ton. I don't think I can lift it more then an inch, even if I wanted to," he said.

Just after he spoke, Roage flew toward them and landed on a nearby tree branch. "May I be of some assistance to you?" he asked Werrien.

"I'd like that, Roage, but I don't think you'll be able to lift it, either," Werrien said.

"Look behind this tree I'm in. At its base there is a rope buried under the leaves," Roage said.

Werrien found the rope.

"You must hurry; for there is a band of zelbocks headed this way, and they'll be here within a few minutes," Roage continued.

Werrien took the rope and placed it through the iron ring. Then he threw the ends of it over a sturdy tree branch and began to pull on it as hard as he could. The door lifted up, but then his hands suddenly slipped from the rope, and the door dropped and slammed shut again. Using all his strength, he pulled on it again and managed to lift it slightly higher than the last time.

"It's big enough for me to get through," Looper said.

"Then go quickly! I don't think I can hold it much longer," Werrien replied, his voice straining.

Looper cautiously went in, and just as he disappeared, Werrien dropped the rope and the door slammed down.

"They will have to come quickly for you, or else you will surely be caught again by the zelbocks," Roage said to Werrien.

Werrien was still not sure what was going on, or even what the door in the ground was for. "Who will have to come for me?" he asked.

But before Roage could answer, the door in the ground suddenly lifted up, and Rumalock stuck his head out. "Ah! Werrien! You have made it. Come down inside," he said.

Werrien took the rope off the tree, placed it back where he had found it, and started to cover it up again.

"Just leave it and go," Roage said impatiently. "You can't afford to be caught again."

Werrien went into the underground after Rumalock, and the door slammed shut after him. Roage quickly buried the rope and covered the door with the leaves. He had just finished when the zelbocks approached.

One of them caught sight of him and shot an arrow at him. It caught the end of his wing and pulled out a few feathers. It landed in the earth, no more than a quarter-inch from the covered door. Roage let out a shrill caw and flew off.

30

Flaming Arrows

After the door in the ground shut, Rumalock climbed down an old wooden ladder, and Werrien followed after him. Above them, they could hear the pounding of the zelbocks' horses' hooves as they trampled over the hidden door.

The underground was cold, and it smelled of damp earth. Rumalock began to walk north, toward a dark tunnel. He carried the same lantern that Werrien had held on the raft ride earlier that evening, and again, it was their only source of light.

"Where are you taking me?" Werrien asked Rumalock.

"Just follow me," Rumalock replied, leading the way through a tunnel that was just tall enough for him to fit through. Werrien had to duck as he walked, for he was at least a head and a half taller than Rumalock. The farther they traveled, the thicker the silence became, and Werrien began to feel somewhat claustrophobic. Finally, they reached a wall, and Rumalock turned left. They walked on farther yet, until a light could be seen coming from a room up ahead. Sitting in the middle of the room were Ugan, Retzel, and Kristina, and on Retzel's shoulder sat Raymond. The four of them were sitting around a table, looking at a map. Clover sat on the edge of the table, swinging her legs to and fro, looking not the least bit interested in the whole situation. When they heard Rumalock and Werrien approaching, they stopped talking.

"Werrien!" Kristina yelled excitedly, jumping up and running toward him. She wrapped her arms around him and gave him a big hug. "It's so good to see you," she said, squeezing him tight. As she did so, the Magic Warble heated up the golden case, tucked inside Werrien's shirt. It became very hot, causing her to jump back quickly.

"It's nice to see you, too," Werrien replied, feeling a little awkward.

"Now, children, I am going to help you the best that I can, but we must get straight to business. As you are well aware, Queen Sentiz and her zelbocks are after you," Rumalock said. He placed his lantern in the middle of the table between two large dripping candles. Kristina sat back down in her chair, and Retzel quickly pulled out a chair for Werrien to sit in.

"I have sent a spy into the queen's camp to find out the direction they will be heading," Rumalock said. He brought everyone's attention back to the map. "The queen's army will be heading northeast. Then, at about this point," he said, pointing to the map, "they will head east, to get to the far north side of the mountain." He dragged his finger a short distance and then stopped and said, "They will climb the mountain at precisely this spot."

"That's the way I was planning to go. It is the only place I know of that one can climb up the mountain. As a matter of fact, there is no other way," Werrien said.

"Over the past several years, I have searched the mountain's base for another way up, and I have found one more spot. Here!" Rumalock said, pointing his finger a little more west on the map. "It's a little risky, but it can be climbed, at this spot."

Werrien looked closely at the spot on the map. "Funny, I've been around the base of the mountain a few times, and I've never noticed a place there where the mountain could be climbed," he said.

"Trust me; it's there. Would you bring out the Magic Warble?" Rumalock asked Werrien.

Werrien reached inside his shirt and took out the golden case, but as he was about to place it on the table, it got so very hot that he had to drop it. It slid across the table and stopped in front of Kristina.

"Well, at least we know it's in there. I will explain to you the safest and fastest way for you to get to this spot at the mountain's base, without running into the queen's army," Rumalock said.

"Oh, how I dread seeing those horrible zelbocks," Raymond chimed in.

Ugan, who had been sitting quietly up until this point, decided to speak up. "There's something I'd like to give to you, my brother." He reached into his coat, pulled out the Book of Prophecy, and slid it across the table toward Rumalock.

Rumalock looked surprised. "My brother, where did you get this?"

"I saved it from burning in the fire at your home," Ugan said.

"That is so noble of you. I wouldn't have thought you to do something so great," Rumalock said.

"It was not a great deed that I did. Actually, I'm no more then a coward. You see I gave it to the queen, but it was not without consequences, for in my spirit I grieved, knowing I had done nothing good in my life. But then, for some reason, I was given a second chance when the queen fell overboard into the sea, and I was able to get back the book. That's when I made a promise to myself that I would return it to you, if it were the last thing I did in my miserable life." Ugan lowered his head in shame.

There was silence for a moment, and a sad expression came to Rumalock's face. "At least you have come this far, my brother," he said softly.

A swift breeze blew into the room and extinguished the two candles. Kristina grabbed hold of them so they wouldn't fall over. At the same time, the Book of Prophecy blew open to the last page that had writing on it. New writing began to scroll across the page as they watched.

"What does it say?" Kristina asked.

All six gathered around the book, and then Werrien read out loud: *"Queen Sentiz and her zelbocks are leaving the base camp to begin their assent up Mount Bernovem in search of Werrien and Kristina."*

174

Clover balanced on top of the golden case, like a circus performer. "Ouch!" she yelled suddenly, jumping off into the air and grabbing both feet in her hands. Everyone turned their attention on her. "It's hot!" she said in an irritated tone.

"I'm sorry to say that there is no more time for discussion," Rumalock said. "We must leave at once!" He closed the Book of Prophecy and tucked it under his arm. Then he picked up the golden case, but it became so hot again that he had to drop it. It fell on the floor and slid under the table. He picked it up, and handed it to Werrien. Then he picked up the lantern and began to walk briskly toward the dark tunnel. Kristina grabbed Raymond and followed him; the others followed after her. When they arrived back at the ladder that led up to the hidden door, Rumalock took a piece of paper out of his pocket and handed it to Werrien. "Here, take this small map. It has your directions from this point on. I have outlined in red the way you should go."

"But I have no weapons to defend us," Werrien said.

"I have taken care of that," Rumalock said as he went behind the ladder. He came back with a bow and a quiver full of arrows.

"That's my bow and my arrows! How did you get these?" Werrien asked.

"Let's just say I have my connections," Rumalock said. "I sharpened your arrowheads myself," he added. Then he turned to Kristina. "My thoughts are with you," He turned to Ugan and

Retzel and said, "I want you two to go with the children."

"What about you?" Kristina asked Rumalock.

"Don't worry about me, child. You have enough to think about." He opened the hidden door, and watched as Werrien, Ugan, Retzel, and, lastly, Kristina climbed up the ladder.

When all of them were outside, Kristina said, "Wait!" She went back down the ladder and threw her arms around Rumalock. "I'm worried that this could be the last time I see you," she said as a tear rolled down her cheek.

"Dear child, I know how you must feel, but I'm sure everything will turn out for the best. Now, you hurry up and get going." Rumalock gave her a pat on her blond head.

Kristina went quickly back up the ladder, and the hidden door slammed shut behind her. But just before it did, Clover slipped through the opening—if she had been even one second later, she would have been squished like a bug. "Couldn't wait just a few seconds longer?" she snapped at Kristina.

"Look, Clover, we don't have time for arguing. Besides, you didn't have to come," Werrien said in Kristina's defense.

Clover's eyes grew wide with embarrassment. *How can he talk to me like that, and especially in front of Kristina? The nerve he has, after I saved him from the wicked queen,* she thought. "I see you won't be needing me anymore," she said haughtily. She wrinkled her nose and stuck her tongue out at Kristina. Then she flew off, as fast as a humming bird.

"Feisty spirit that one has," Retzel said.

"She'll get over it; she always does," Werrien said. Then he turned to Kristina, "Where's Taysha?"

Kristina shook her head sadly. "After Rumalock took me into the underground hideout, we heard a great commotion above us. Rumalock said it must be the zelbocks, searching for me. We stood very quietly at the bottom of the ladder, and when the noise finally stopped, Rumalock said it would be safe for me to check on Taysha. So I went outside again, but I couldn't see her anywhere, and even when I called for her and looked all around, she was no where to be found."

Werrien lowered his head in sadness also.

"I'm so sorry, Werrien," Kristina said.

"She's a smart girl. She'll find her way home," Werrien said. He took the map out of his pocket and began to look it over. "It says we're to head northwest from here. If everything goes as planned, we should have the Magic Warble up the mountain and in its resting place within a day, hopefully."

The four had been walking for about half an hour when Raymond, who had been sitting on Retzel's shoulder, stood up on his hind legs and began to sniff the air.

"What is it, Raymond?" Kristina asked.

"I sense something is coming our way," he said.

They all stopped and stood silent.

"I don't hear anything," Ugan said.

"Sh-h! I think I might hear something," Werrien said. He drew one of his arrows out of his quiver and quickly placed it in his bow. "Quick! Everyone take cover," he said.

Kristina, Ugan, and Retzel, along with Raymond, ran and hid behind the nearby trees. Werrien drew his bow back and was ready to shoot, but just before he let the arrow fly, he heard a soft whinny. "Taysha? Is that you girl?" he asked.

A large figure emerged from among the trees, and Werrien could tell that it was his beloved mare. She went to him and nudged his arm with her head.

"I'm so happy to see that you are well," she said.

Werrien hugged her around her neck. "And I'm so glad to see you are well also," Taysha said.

Their reunion was interrupted by more noise coming from the same area where Taysha had just come from. Werrien raised his bow again, ready to shoot.

"It's okay; I brought a friend," Taysha said.

Then another horse emerged; it was about the same size as Taysha but black in color.

"Oh, great, not another big brute," Raymond said, as they all came out from hiding.

"Lisheng?" Ugan questioned the dark horse.

"Do you know this horse?" Werrien asked Ugan.

"Very well, as a matter of fact," Ugan said. "This is Lisheng, Ramon's horse."

177

"Why have you come here?" Werrien asked Lisheng.

"I have always wanted to escape my horrible owner, but there was never an opportunity. I felt it was only a farfetched dream for me, but today my dream has come true," Lisheng said joyfully.

"For me also, my good friend, but let me ask you—how did you ever manage to get away from Ramon?" Ugan asked.

"Well, you see, Queen Sentiz was in a rage, yelling out orders to the zelbocks. I saw her storm into Ramon's tent. Then he came out with her on his tail. She was shouting at him to saddle me up and ride me ahead of the zelbocks. He was to lead them up the mountain. When he came to the place where I was tied up, I noticed his behavior was very strange—he was hiccupping and staggering, and his breath smelled horrible. Then another odd thing—he'd usually saddle me before untying me, but this time he untied me first and then went to get the saddle. When he left, I noticed the zelbocks were running to and fro, preparing to leave. It was the perfect opportunity for my escape, and escape I did," Lisheng said.

"Well, I guess you couldn't have come at a more opportune time," Werrien said. "We could sure use two horses to speed us along."

"I am honored to be at your service, Prince Werrien," Lisheng said enthusiastically.

Ugan and Retzel mounted Lisheng, and Kristina and Werrien got onto Taysha, but before they proceeded, Werrien took out the map once again to make sure they were heading in the right direction.

"Looks like we're on track," he said.

The horses started to gallop, but it wasn't too far into their journey when they were visited once again by Roage. He flew between the two horses and landed on the ground in front of them. Taysha, startled, reared up on her hind legs.

"Wow, girl! It's all right. He's on our side," Werrien said.

Roage stretched out his wings and cawed loudly, making both horses skittish once more.

"Could you stop trying to scare the horses?" Kristina asked Roage.

Raymond, who was now hiding in Retzel's cape, stuck his head out and said, "Look, raven, I'd like to make it back to my home in one piece, if you don't mind."

"I am confused as to why you are going in this direction," Roage said.

"This is the way the map tells us to go," Werrien responded.

"And if you don't mind, we'd like to get going before its too late, and I become lunch for one of those horrible zelbocks," Raymond added.

"I'm sorry to be the bearer of bad news, but you are heading straight toward the enemy," Roage said.

"That can't be possible. Rumalock gave us his word that we'd be heading in a totally different direction," Kristina said.

"The queen's army is heading northwest, and within a few minutes, you'll be running right into them," Roage said.

"Do you think he's telling the truth?" Kristina asked Werrien.

"At this point, I'm not sure what to believe," Werrien answered.

"Listen, you must not wait any longer. They will be here very soon. Take my word for it," Roage said.

"Which way do you suggest we go?" Werrien asked.

"Head directly west, until you hit the coast, and then follow it north, until you come to the far west side of the base of the mountain. Then you'll—"

Roage was interrupted when a flaming arrow flew past them.

"Quick, Lisheng, head west, as Roage said. I will catch up with you as soon as possible," Werrien said.

No sooner had Lisheng passed through the trees when the trees burst into flames. Roage took to the air. Werrien, Kristina and Taysha, could feel the heat of the blaze as it began spreading from tree to tree, very near to where they stood.

"Pass me an arrow out of my quiver," Werrien said to Kristina. Kristina pulled one out and handed it to him, but as he was placing it in his bow, he noticed that the arrow had no spearhead on it. "I need another arrow—this one's broken," he said.

She pulled another one out and handed it to him, but it also had no arrowhead. "Try another one," Werrien said.

Kristina reached for the third one, but it, too, had no arrowhead. She pulled out more and more until there were no more in the quiver. None of them had arrowheads.

How can this be? Werrien thought.

Then a picture of Rumalock, handing him his quiver, entered his mind, and he remembered the old dwarf's words: *"I sharpened your arrowheads myself."*

Werrien's face went pale white and his heart seemed to sink in his chest. *Rumalock must have done this*, he thought.

The zelbocks were coming into their view, and all Werrien and Kristina had to defend themselves was the knife that Werrien had given to Kristina. It wouldn't be enough. Werrien knew Kristina and he wouldn't stand a chance when fighting the zelbocks.

"We're going to have to go through it," Werrien said.

"Do you mean the fire?" Kristina asked.

But before Werrien could answer, Taysha began to charge at full speed toward the blazing trees.

31

A Change of Plan

Taysha ran through the flames, and Kristina ducked her head behind Werrien's back. Once they were past the fire, Taysha made a dead stop and turned toward the blazing trees.

"Are you all right?" Werrien asked Kristina.

Kristina ran her hands over her hair and her clothes to make sure that she hadn't caught fire. "I'm fine." But just as she answered, three more flaming arrows came whizzing through the blaze, right toward them. "Duck!" Kristina yelled.

They ducked down and the arrows zoomed over their backs and into the trees just ahead of them. The fire spread quickly all around them.

"It looks like we'll have to do it again. Hold on tight!" Werrien said.

Taysha began to gallop toward the burning trees, and this time she didn't stop; instead, she kept running at full speed through the forest.

"Keep your head down. There are too many trees and low branches around this area," Werrien said.

Taysha continued running until Werrien felt they were far enough ahead of the zelbocks. Then he brought her to a jolting halt. All was quiet now except for the sound of a small brook trickling down a slope nearby. Taysha was very hot, and the steam coming off her body could be seen in the cool, crisp air.

"Do you think we've lost them?" Kristina asked.

"I think so, at least for the time being," Werrien answered.

He dismounted Taysha, and Kristina dismounted after him. Then he led Taysha to the brook so she could drink. While Kristina waited, she began to stretch her sore legs.

"It's a good thing we were able to out run them. I can't imagine what they would have done to us this time," she said.

Werrien just stared into the darkness.

"What's the matter?" Kristina asked.

"Don't you realize what's happening?" Werrien said, seeming angered by her calm attitude.

"What? Are you mad because your arrows were so dull?" she asked.

"It figures you'd think something as dumb as that," Werrien snapped.

Kristina didn't reply; he'd embarrassed her with that remark.

"Look, Kristina, I'm sorry to snap at you, but my nerves are really tense at the moment," he said. They were both silent again, and then Werrien asked, "Do you remember Rumalock's telling me that he sharpened my arrowheads himself?"

Kristina shook her head. "No, I'm sorry, but I don't recall."

"Well, I remember it clearly," Werrien said.

"If he had sharpened them, why were they so dull?" Kristina asked.

"They weren't 'dull,' Kristina. They had no arrowhead on them."

"Do you think Rumalock took them off?" Kristina asked.

"I'm afraid so," Werrien said.

"Why would he do such a thing?" Kristina asked.

"I'm sorry to say it, but the only thing I can think of is that he must be working for the queen," Werrien said.

The thought of it made Kristina's heart sink. First Retzel had betrayed them and now Rumalock.

Werrien took the golden case out of his shirt. "Funny, I haven't felt it warm up lately," he said as he opened it. He stared down at it, and a grim look crossed his face. The worst thing that he could have possibly imagined had happened. *"It's gone!"* he cried.

"I can't believe it!" Kristina said. "Why didn't he take it when I first met him? He had every chance then. Why would he wait until now?" Kristina asked.

"Can't you see? The queen needed for you to meet up with me so she could rid of me too. They must have known that the Magic Warble would bring us together!"

"Now I see why Rumalock said, 'You might even get some help along the way.' He knew I would meet up with you," Kristina said.

"Exactly! Have you ever heard the saying 'Why not kill two birds with one stone?'"

"What are we to do now?" Kristina asked.

"We'll have to go back to the underground hideout and get the Magic Warble back from Rumalock," Werrien said.

"What about the zelbocks and the fire?" Kristina asked.

"I don't know. We'll just have to take a chance," Werrien said, as he helped her to get back up on Taysha.

On the way back, they passed by the burned and still-smoldering trees. There was no sign of any zelbocks, and all was quiet when they arrived back at the underground hideout. Werrien dismounted Taysha, and then Kristina took her to hide in the trees.

Werrien went back into the pitch-black underground and though he couldn't see anything, he new that the tunnel was straight ahead. He walked carefully, until he finally felt the cool earthen wall, Then he turned left and continued on until he could see the light coming from the room where they had been earlier. As he walked cautiously toward it, he heard voices.

"Rumalock and Queen Sentiz are already on their way up the mountain. Ramon has the Magic Warble, and is on his way also, with the queen's army."

Werrien went a little closer and could see that it was one of the queen's servant gnomes talking to a zelbock. When he heard them mention Rumalock's name, he felt like someone had dropped a load of rocks in his stomach. It was a heavy blow to his heart, for he had known Rumalock for most of his life and had always thought him to be nothing other than a trustworthy, caring friend.

"Once at the top of the mountain, Ramon will destroy the Magic Warble," the gnome said.

"What about the boy and the girl?" the zelbock asked.

"No worries; it's all taken care of. You see, Rumalock gave Werrien a map that will lead him directly into Ramon's army."

Werrien heard their footsteps coming toward the tunnel, so he turned and quickly went back the way he had come. When he reached the ladder, he hid behind it. A few moments later the gnome and zelbock came out of the tunnel. Then the gnome opened the trap door, and both he and the zelbock went up the ladder and out of the underground.

The trap door slammed shut, and Werrien was left standing in the pitch-black darkness. Many thoughts began to swirl around in his mind, like why Rumalock would betray him, or how he and Kristina were to get the Magic Warble back, now that it had been snatched away for the second time. And what about the Book of Prophecy being in Rumalock's hands? And what about all those gnomes and dwarfs preparing for battle under Rumalock's command? Did they have any idea that Rumalock had betrayed them as well? Werrien wondered if he was kidding himself, thinking that Kristina, a young girl, and he, a not-much-older teen, could actually accomplish this dangerous task of delivering the Magic Warble. The load of worry began to get very heavy, and he felt things couldn't possibly get any worse. He leaned his head on one of the steps of the ladder and felt very discouraged. Just then, he felt something crawl across his face and onto his hand. He lifted his head up to see a large spider sitting on his hand. It opened its mouth to reveal two large fangs that seemed to be dripping with venom. Werrien knew if he tried to move, the spider would most assuredly bite him, but there was no other choice. He lifted his other hand up very slowly to whack it, but just as he was about to do so, the spider lifted up into the air. He looked up to see the trap door opening above him, and as it did so, the spider's web, which was attached to the trap door, pulled the spider up and into the air. It swung back and forth, toward Werrien's face, but he quickly backed away just as it reached its long legs toward his face, trying to latch on to him.

"Werrien!" Kristina called down from above.

"I'm down here," Werrien called back.

"Are you okay?" she asked.

"I'm much better now," he said, breaking the web and flinging the spider away toward the tunnel. He hurried up the ladder and out into the much-appreciated open air of the forest. Kristina, Ugan, and Retzel were all standing around the trap door when Werrien came out of the underground hideout.

"What are you guys doing here?" Werrien asked.

"When you didn't come to meet us, we got worried and decided to come back and look for you," Ugan said.

"Did any of you see a gnome and a zelbock come out a few minutes ago?" Werrien asked.

"Yes," Kristina said.

"Did they see you?" Werrien asked.

"No, I don't think so. We were hidden pretty well," Kristina said.

"Which way did they go?" Werrien asked.

"They headed northeast," Ugan said.

"I'm sorry to have to tell you this, Ugan, but your brother Rumalock has stolen the Magic Warble," Werrien said.

Ugan's face went pale, and he looked very sad. "I have always looked up to my brother, and now he does this. I suppose we are both the same, two of kind, sneaky cowards," he said, lowering his head in shame.

Retzel put his arm around Ugan. "If it's any consolation, I feel just as much a coward as you."

"Well, I must say one thing—at least you two realized and confessed your faults," Kristina said.

"I'm going to have to change our plans," Werrien said. He went to get Taysha, who was still hidden behind the trees with Lisheng. Ugan followed to get Lisheng. Then they all mounted the horses.

"Where are we going, Prince Werrien?" Retzel asked.

"I'll explain later," Werrien said as he led them eastward through the forest.

Taysha galloped at full speed, with Lisheng right at her tail, and once again Kristina kept her head down low behind Werrien's back to avoid the many tree branches. After a while, the smell of smoke and the sound of voices filled the air again. Taysha and Lisheng slowed down, and Kristina lifted her head up to see that Werrien had led them back to the place where the gnomes and the dwarfs were preparing for battle.

Looper, surprised to see them back, flew toward them. "What's going on? Aren't you supposed to be on your way up Mount Bernovem?" he asked.

Werrien ignored Looper's question and rode Taysha toward the gnomes and dwarfs, who were now busy dressing in their battle attire. "May I have your attention!" he called out. They all fell silent and looked up at Werrien. "I'm sorry to say that Rumalock, the one we have all known to be noble and trustworthy, has betrayed us," he said. The gnomes and dwarfs looked to each other, shaking their heads in disbelief. "I know this is very hard to believe, but it is true. He has stolen the Magic Warble, and it is presently on its way up Mount Bernovem, where Ramon is planning to destroy it."

"But how could this be?" one of the gnomes said. "Rumalock is our leader and friend. He told us to meet him at the base of the mountain, to hold back the queen's army."

"Listen, you were planning to defend Kristina and me, and as you can see, we are not on our way up the mountain to deliver the Magic Warble. We're here, before your own eyes," Werrien continued.

The gnomes and dwarfs whispered among themselves, and then the same gnome who had spoken before said, "So what are we to do now?"

"I ask you now to trust in me, for my mother, Lafinia, is the true queen, and I will be king after her," Werrien said, with authority in his voice. The gnomes looked among each other, not knowing what to believe. "Do you wish to be free citizens once again, free to harvest the fairy blossom and prosper as you did once before, or do you prefer to be under Queen Sentiz's power and barely get by?"

"Of course we prefer to be free and prosper, but what you are saying about Rumalock—this is very hard for us to believe," the gnome answered.

"Well, I can't force you to believe me, but just think: why would I, the true future king, want to do you any harm? Has my family done anything other than look out for your best interests?" Werrien asked.

The gnome who spoke before and an older male dwarf whispered to each other. Finally, the gnome said, "We will do as you wish, for we know you are the true Prince of Bernovem, and there has been no peace, justice, or happiness since your mother, Lafinia, has been imprisoned."

"I will do everything in my power to make sure you don't regret your decision," Werrien said.

"So what should we do now?" the gnome asked.

"Follow Kristina and me to the base of Mount Bernovem. Once we are there, we will wait in hiding for Ramon's army. Then, I will take back the Magic Warble from Ramon, and Kristina and I will head up the mountain to deliver it to its resting place."

"And what about us?" a young dwarf man asked.

"You will stay at the base with Ugan and Retzel, and keep Ramon's army from coming after us," Werrien said.

"Prince Werrien?" A softer female voice spoke up from the crowd, and she raised her arm into the air so that Werrien could see her. It was Bronya, the girl gnome who had given him soup to eat earlier that evening. "My sister and I wish to give you and Kristina something," she said.

"What is it?" Werrien asked.

The girls made their way through the crowd toward Taysha, and when they stood in front of her, each laid out on the ground a protective chainmail vest and a warm woolen cape, one for Kristina and one for Werrien.

"Sorry they were not finished earlier," Neela, the blond girl gnome, said.

Werrien and Kristina dismounted Taysha and tried on the vests. They fit perfectly.

"Wow!" Werrien said, looking at Kristina.

"If you don't have anything nice to say, don't say anything at all," Kristina said, expecting Werrien to make a sarcastic remark about the way she looked.

"I was just going to say that you look great," Werrien said.

"You don't look so bad yourself," Kristina said.

Werrien turned to the two gnome girls. "Thank you, Neela and Bronya. I will not forget the kindness you have shown us."

"There is something else," Bronya said. She gestured to Retzel's wife, Mitzi, to come out of the crowd.

Mitzi came toward them carrying two more protective vests, as well as a shiny, round steel container. She laid them on the ground as well. "These are for Retzel and Ugan," she said.

Retzel and Ugan dismounted Lisheng to dress in their vests.

"What is the steel container for?" Kristina asked curiously.

"I made it especially for Raymond, to keep him protected, if the enemy shoots arrows at him," Mitzi said.

"How thoughtful," Kristina said. She took Raymond from Retzel and placed him in it. On the top of the container was a mesh lid that Raymond could push open with his nose to stick his head out. "How do you like it, Raymond?" Kristina asked.

"Well, it's not as comfy and warm as being inside your vest, but I suppose if it will protect me, it will do," his voice echoed out the top of it.

"How does he like it?" Neela asked.

"He likes it just fine," Kristina answered.

"I think we'd better get moving if we want to beat Ramon's army to the base of the mountain," Werrien said.

"How do you suppose we can beat them when Ramon is already on his way," Ugan asked Werrien.

"Well, now that I'm not following Rumalock's directions, I think I might know a shorter and faster way than the way they are going," Werrien said.

Retzel hugged his wife, Mitzi. "Everything will be better soon," he said softly.

All the men gnomes and dwarfs mounted ponies to begin their journey to the base of the mountain. As they rode off, following Werrien and Kristina, their heavy-hearted wives and children stood watching until they disappeared into the forest.

32

The Battle

Werrien, Kristina, the dwarfs and gnomes were all desperately hoping that they'd make it to the base of Mount Bernovem before Ramon's army did. The closer they got, the colder the air grew, and so they stopped briefly to put on the warm capes that the gnome girls had made for them. While doing so, Raymond poked his head out the top of his container to sniff the crisp air, and a snowflake landed on his nose.

"Is this the same stuff I saw falling out your bedroom window?" he asked Kristina.

"Why, yes, it is, Raymond," Kristina answered.

"What is it called?' Raymond asked.

"It's called snow."

The thought of the snow falling outside her bedroom window suddenly saddened Kristina, for it reminded her that if the Magic Warble wasn't brought to its resting place, she and Raymond wouldn't be going home. And even though she had made more friends in Bernovem than she had ever made at home, she couldn't imagine never being able to go back and see her family again. Thinking about it was more chilling than the icy wind blowing in her face.

190

The ground was covered in snow when they arrived at the base of the mountain, and there were no footprints to be seen, nor any other signs that Ramon's army had gotten there before them. Werrien brought Taysha to a halt and then jumped down off her to look for a place where they all could hide and wait for Ramon's army to arrive. As he disappeared into the surrounding forest, Kristina stayed with Taysha and their army of gnomes and dwarfs. She looked up at the moon that was shining brightly. It made the snow on the ground seem like it was covered by millions of tiny diamonds. It was so pretty that she closed her eyes and took a deep breath of the fresh air to savor the moment. But while her eyes were still closed, she suddenly felt the wind swoosh over her head. Taysha reared up, and Kristina opened her eyes to see Roage standing in the snow, a few feet ahead of her.

"The next time you come swooping down to scare the wits out of us; could you at least give us a warning?" Kristina said angrily.

Raymond poked his head out of the top of his container. "Just as I suspected! It's that sneaky bird again. Can't a fellow get a bit of shut-eye without being thrown on his head?" he said.

"If there was time to greet you formally, I would have, but unfortunately there is not. Ramon's army is less than a mile away from here, so you had better start preparing for their arrival," Roage said.

Werrien ran back to them. Then Roage turned to Werrien and said, "Ramon's army will be coming this way in a matter of minutes."

"Thanks for the warning," Werrien said, and he got back on Taysha. He turned her around to face the gnomes and dwarfs. "I have found a place for you to hide. Follow me." He led them to a ravine that was big enough for all of them, as well as their ponies, to hide. Then he jumped down off Taysha and turned to Kristina. "You will have to stay here until I return, and when you see me coming back, be prepared to flee with me." Then he turned to Lisheng. "I'll need you to be standing by Taysha. I will ride you."

"It will be an honor for me," said Lisheng.

Ugan and Retzel dismounted Lisheng.

Then Werrien turned to them. "I'll need you two to be the

leaders of this army. When you see me running back this way, make sure the rest of the gnomes and dwarfs have their bows and arrows ready. Ramon's army will most assuredly be right on my tail. Also, stay down low in the ravine until I run past you. Then give the rest of the gnomes and dwarfs the go-ahead to rise up and launch their arrows." Lastly, he turned to Roage and said, "When I go now, I'll need you to fly ahead of me, and let me know the whereabouts of Ramon. Then, after I take the Magic Warble back from him, fly back to Ugan and Retzel and let them know I am on my way back."

"As you wish," Roage said.

After he gave out the orders, Werrien ran back to the place where Kristina and their army had waited previously for him. He hid behind a tree, and Roage flew off, to see how far off Ramon's army was. Not long after, Roage came back, but before he could report, Werrien heard the sounds of Ramon's army approaching, and shortly after, he saw the fire from their torches.

"Did you see Ramon among them?" Werrien whispered to Roage, who was now sitting in the tree directly above him.

"Yes, he is on a gray horse at the head of his army," Roage said.

"Did you happen to notice whether or not he was carrying the Magic Warble?" Werrien whispered.

"Not exactly, but he was holding a small leather sack on his lap," Roage said.

"Well, I've probably got only one shot at this, so I hope it's in there. Now, I have to figure out a way to get it from him," Werrien said.

"I've got an idea," Roage said.

"Oh, yeah? At this point I'm open to anything," Werrien said.

"Here's what I'm thinking: When Ramon's army is directly in front of us, I'll make noise in the branches. That way, they'll stop and Ramon will come over here to see what it is," said Roage.

"Then what?" Werrien asked.

"I don't know. You'll have to come up with the rest," Roage said.

"I don't have anything better planned, so let's give it a shot, and see what happens," Werrien said.

When Ramon was directly in front of them, Roage began to make a ruckus in the tree. Then Werrien picked up a stone and threw it at Ramon, hitting him in his leg.

Ramon shouted, "Halt!" and his troop came to a standstill. All was silent as he looked around suspiciously, wondering who had thrown the stone at him. Roage shook the branches again and brought Ramon's attention directly to the tree where he was sitting and where Werrien was hiding. "There's someone in the trees over there," Ramon said, pointing to the exact spot they were hiding. "Malodor, get off your horse, and go see what is making the noise," Ramon said.

"Now what are we going to do? He's sending a zelbock to come and look," Werrien said.

"I'll quickly fly somewhere else and make more noise," Roage said.

"Okay, go!" Werrien said.

Roage flew to another tree and began to hop on the branches to make more noise. It caught Ramon's attention again.

"Stop, Malodor! It is coming from over there," Ramon said, pointing to the trees.

Malodor turned and walked toward it, and when he was almost there, Werrien threw another rock at Ramon, this time hitting him on his buttock.

"There are more than one of them," Ramon said, as he began dismounting his horse. Werrien poked his head around the tree to see Ramon coming toward him with the leather sack dangling from his belt.

All Werrien had was a knife that a dwarf had given him. He drew it out and stood very still on the opposite side of the tree. His heart began to pound faster as Ramon neared him. Just as Ramon stepped to the other side of the tree, Werrien quickly reached out with his knife and cut the ties of the leather pouch. Ramon looked down to see the sack drop into Werrien's hands, and before Ramon could reach out to grab him—or the sack—Werrien was on his way, running back toward his army.

With fumbling hands, Ramon reached for his battle horn, and when he finally managed to get it to his lips, he blew on it so hard that his angered face turned dark purple. The zelbocks, who had been preoccupied watching Malodor try to figure out what was in the other tree, turned their attention back to Ramon.

"After him, you idiots!" Ramon yelled furiously. "Can't you see he's getting away with the Magic Warble?"

The zelbock's quickly mounted their horses and charged in Ramon's direction. They ran straight at him, and he fell backwards into a thorn bush, one that he himself had planted years earlier. When his rear end hit the sharp thorns, he let out a shrill scream.

Werrien heard it, but he didn't look back; instead, he looked up to see Roage flying above him. "How far back are the zelbocks?"

he yelled up to him.

"Maybe a few hundred yards," Roage told him.

As the zelbocks grew nearer, Werrien could hear their horses' hooves pounding the forest floor. Finally, the top of the ravine came into view, and Roage flew on ahead to warn the gnomes and the dwarfs that Werrien was almost there.

"Quick, get ready to launch your arrows as Werrien runs past you. The zelbocks are right behind him," Roage called out to them.

Kristina was sitting on Taysha, with Lisheng by her side, when Werrien ran past the ravine and jumped on Lisheng. Then the gnomes and dwarfs launched their arrows, and the zelbocks did the same. After the arrows were used, they went at each other with swords, flails, pikes, and clubs. Kristina and Werrien could hear the eerie cries and screams of the battle behind them, and Werrien wished he could have stayed to help. Still, he knew that Kristina needed his help to deliver the Magic Warble. Eventually, the sound of the battle faded and soon after, they reached the base of the mountain.

~ ~ ~

Queen Sentiz and Rumalock were already at the top of the snow-capped mountain, in a warm tent, waiting for Ramon to deliver the Magic Warble. As the fierce winds tossed the snow outside their tent, Rumalock sat looking through the Book of Prophecy.

"The battle has started," he said to the queen, who sat wrapped in her bear stole, drinking a steaming-hot cup of fairy-blossom tea.

"Wonderful. It's about time that son of mine does something I can be proud of," she said.

More words began to pop onto the page. "Ramon's name is coming up, just as you mention him," Rumalock said, smiling wickedly.

"What does it say?" the queen asked excitedly. Before Rumalock could answer, she stood up. "Wait—I am so smart, let me tell you what it says. Ramon has caught the two wretched hoodlum children and is presently on his way up the mountain to destroy the Magic Warble." She took a sip from her cup, leaving a large amount of red lipstick to run down the sides of it.

"Well, no, it does not say that, Your Majesty. It says Werrien has taken the Magic Warble from Ramon. Then it goes on to say that Ramon fell in one of those thorn bushes you had planted, one he had planted himself, and he is presently trying to pull thorns out of his bottom," Rumalock said, with an uncontrollable chuckle.

The queen fell silent and stared straight ahead. The blood seemed to drain from her already-pale face, and her thin, red lips shriveled up, like she had just sucked on a sour lemon.

"I'm so sorry to have read that Werrien has the Magic Warble," Rumalock said, sensing her tension.

The queen's head didn't move, but her eyes shifted to meet his. "How dare you laugh at this situation," she said through clenched teeth. Then she reached over and ripped the prophecy book away from him. She ran her fingernail down the page to the spot he had just finished reading. More words began to pop up, and when she read them, her nostrils flared, and her eyes looked like they would pop out of her head. "No! This can't be!" she wailed, dropping the book on the floor. Her mood turned to anger again, and she took up her tea mug and violently smashed it on the floor in front of Rumalock. Rumalock quickly scurried to pick up the shattered pieces, while the queen fell back into her chair, taken over by despair. "Oh, what am I to do now?" she cried, dragging her long fingernails down her face, as she usually did when distressed.

"I might have a good idea, my queen," Rumalock said, as he cautiously picked up the prophecy book.

"And what might that be?" the queen asked calmly, while blotting her lipstick with her handkerchief.

"What about the three other children?"

"What about them, you idiot?" the queen snapped. "Isn't it clear to you that they have already been captured?"

"Yes, of course, Your Majesty, but may I ask why is it that you had me bring them here, instead of leaving them in the prison at Treachery Island?" Rumalock asked.

"You dwarfs are so stupid. I had you bring them here in case we needed them to blackmail the girl, if all else fails," the queen hissed.

"Well, that is precisely my point. Don't you think we should do it, now that the other children have taken back the Magic Warble?" Rumalock asked.

Queen Sentiz fell silent again as she soaked in what Rumalock had just said. She twisted up her pale face and drummed her long red nails on her chin. Then she sat up, cleared her throat, and said, "I have a brilliant idea."

"Yes, my lady, and what might that be?" Rumalock asked enthusiastically.

"I have made the decision to have you bring the three children to the spot where the Magic Warble is supposed to be laid, and wait for Werrien's and the girl's arrival."

"Yes, that is exactly what I was meaning to say," Rumalock said, his eyes growing large with enthusiasm.

"Don't try to take credit for my idea!" the queen yelled.

"Of course not, my lady. I could have never come up with such an idea myself," Rumalock said nervously.

"No, you couldn't have, that's for sure," the queen said. She walked over to the entrance of the tent and peeked through the door flaps. After viewing the foul weather outside, she turned around to face Rumalock. "Before I resort to blackmailing them with the other children, I have one more idea up my sleeve," she said.

~ ~ ~

Meanwhile, near the bottom of the mountain, the gnomes and dwarfs finally defeated the zelbocks in battle. They had killed or wounded many of them. The ones that were left standing ended up retreating back to Ramon. When they arrived back to where Ramon had landed in the thorn bush, they found him sitting on his knees with his hands cupped together in front of him.

"I knew you idiots wouldn't be able to defeat them without my leading you," he said.

The zelbocks said nothing in return.

"Well, don't just stand there like great lumps. Get me my canteen!" he ordered.

Malodor went to where Ramon's horse was now happily grazing on forest ferns that had not yet been covered by snow. He untied

Ramon's canteen from the saddle and quickly brought it back to him.

"Open it, you brainless fool," Ramon demanded.

Malodor pulled the cork out of the canteen and then sniffed what was inside it. The fumes of fermented fairy blossom streamed up to his nostrils. Being very thirsty from fighting in the battle, he was about to take a sip of it, but Ramon stopped him.

"Drink that," Ramon warned, "and it will be the last drink you'll ever take." Malodor took the canteen away from his mouth and held it out to Ramon. "Hold it steady," Ramon said. He put his cupped hands over it and dropped something inside it. "Hurry—give me the cork," he barked, holding his hand over its opening.

Malodor handed Ramon the cork and he quickly plugged the canteen with it, but Malodor could hear the sound of something fluttering around inside the canteen.

"You may have gotten away before, little princess, but this time there's no escaping," Ramon said, just before he began to laugh insanely.

- 33 -

The Cliff

As Werrien and Kristina climbed the mountain, the fierce winds grew very strong, and it seemed like even the elements were working against their delivering the Magic Warble. The icy wind even penetrated the thick, wool cloaks they wore. To add to their problems, the mountain was growing steeper and steeper, and even though they had just started their ascent, the horses were having a hard time climbing it.

Werrien brought Lisheng to a stop and then jumped off him. "This is as far as the horses can go. We'll have to travel on foot the rest of the way," he said.

Kristina jumped down from Taysha. Then she untied Raymond's container from the saddle and peeked inside it. Raymond lay curled up, sleeping at the bottom of it. Trying not to wake him, she gently closed the lid. But he heard her and woke up. She peeked inside again. "How can you possibly sleep in this freezing cold weather?" she asked him.

"It's called hibernation," Raymond responded, while yawning.

"Oh, yes, of course, I'll try not to bother you anymore," Kristina said.

"Thanks," Raymond said, as he lay back down to sleep.

She closed the lid once again, and it made her feel a little better, knowing that Raymond wasn't feeling the effect of the cold as she was.

After gathering their small amount of food supplies, Werrien told Taysha and Lisheng to go back down the mountain to join the gnomes and dwarfs. They said good-bye, and then Werrien and Kristina watched as the horses disappeared down the mountain and into the wind-driven snow.

They turned and began to climb the mountain on foot. They climbed for what seemed hours, with the wind blowing the snow into their faces. It made it hard for them to see anything, except for white and the occasional rock or tree branch sticking up out of the snow.

"I'm really starting to feel weird, not being able to see anything other than whiteness," Kristina yelled to Werrien.

"I feel the same, but we have to keep going. It shouldn't be too much farther before we reach the top," Werrien yelled back.

He really had no idea how much longer it would take them to actually reach the top, but he felt if he told Kristina that, she wouldn't be able to make it. The mountain grew even steeper, and the snow got even deeper as they trudged upward on ever-so-tired legs.

"Could we stop and rest for a moment?" Kristina asked, feeling out of breath.

"Let's go a little farther," Werrien suggested, but Kristina's foot suddenly slipped on some slick ice below the snow's surface and she fell. Werrien grabbed hold of her cloak, but his hands were so cold and numb that it slipped through his fingers, and she went tumbling down the mountain. Once again, Werrien felt that familiar ache in the pit of his stomach, as he watched Kristina disappear into the pure-white atmosphere. He called out to her, but there was no answer, and so he began to descend the mountain. He soon found out that going down was no easier then climbing up. Then, his foot hit some ice as well, and he slipped and fell, but he was fortunate not to tumble down the mountain as Kristina had.

"Kristina! Kristina!" he called again, but there was still no answer. *What am I to do now?* he thought. The mountain was so vast, and with the snow blowing in his face, the odds of finding her were slim. After descending almost a quarter of the way back down the mountain, he stopped for a moment to rest, and as he stood in the wind and snow, contemplating what to do next, he felt the Magic Warble heat up inside his shirt. Then lightning flashed in the sky above him, followed by a very strong wind that almost knocked him over. He heard a voice in the wind say, "Look up the mountain, to your left." He looked up and saw something very small, bounding toward him over the snow. As it drew nearer, he could see that it was Raymond.

"Raymond! Am I glad to see you," he said.

"And I to see you," Raymond replied.

"Is Kristina okay?" Werrien asked.

"Yes, but for how long, I can't be sure. You must come quickly," Raymond said.

Werrien followed Raymond a short way back up the mountain to a cliff. Near the edge of it was Raymond's container. Werrien quickly went over to the cliff's edge and saw Kristina hanging from a tree branch. More than fifty feet lay below her, and there was only a chunk of rock sticking out of the mountain for her to land on, if she were to fall.

"Werrien! I don't think I can hold on much longer!" Kristina yelled, as a strong wind blew against her, causing her to sway to and fro.

"Try to stay calm!" Werrien yelled back. He lay on his stomach and reached his hand down toward her. "Grab hold of my hand," he said.

Kristina tried to reach his hand, but it was too far away from her. "It's no use! I can't reach it!" she cried.

Once again the wind blew her outward from the cliff. Werrien stood up to take off his cloak. While doing so he heard a familiar caw in the sky above him, and he looked up to see Roage soaring on the strong winds. "Roage!" he called out.

Roage began to descend toward him. Werrien lay at the cliff's edge again and hung his cloak over it for Kristina to grab. The wind blew her away from the cloak and then back toward it. She reached out to grab it, but again, the wind blew the cloak one way and her the other way. After one more try, she finally grabbed hold of it. Then Werrien pulled her up to the cliff's edge, but just as she made it up, the golden case slipped out of his shirt and rolled over the edge of the cliff.

Werrien's face went as pale as the snow as he watched the golden case tumble away from him. *"No-o-o-o!"* he yelled, his voice echoing over the treacherous mountain.

Kristina was safe now, but the Magic Warble was gone, and this time there was no way either of them could retrieve it. Kristina felt it was her fault they'd lost it, and she knelt down beside Werrien. "I'm so sorry, Werrien."

"Sorry for what?" Werrien asked.

"If I wouldn't have fallen over the cliff, you wouldn't have had to come and look for me," she said, choking on her tears. "And then you wouldn't have had to lean over the edge of the cliff, which in turn caused the Magic Warble to fall out of your shirt. It's my entire fault that this happened. I should have never been given the gift from Miss Hensley. She should have realized that I wasn't one to whom the Magic Warble could be entrusted."

Werrien looked up with tears in his eyes. He wanted to say something from his heart, but before he could speak, he saw something at the cliff's edge. It was Roage, and gripped tightly in his talons was the golden case.

"Roage!" Werrien said, enthusiastically.

"I think it's high time you two got moving along," Roage said, as he rolled the golden case over to Werrien.

Kristina was happy to have the Magic Warble back, but at the same time, she felt that Werrien was about to tell her something important. Now, she'd probably never know what that was. She quickly pushed the thought out of her mind when Werrien turned to her and said, "We'd best be moving on. This episode has lost us quite a bit of time." He tucked the golden case back in his shirt and turned to the raven. "Thank you, Roage. I will never forget this."

Once again, the two children began their grueling upward climb, but they hadn't gotten very far when they heard Roage's familiar caw behind them again. They turned around to see that he was still standing at the edge of the cliff.

"What is it, Roage?" Kristina called out.

"Oh, I was just wondering if you might have forgotten something," Roage answered.

Kristina and Werrien looked at each other, puzzled. Then Kristina suddenly realized what it was. "Raymond!" she said franticly. She made her way back down from the mountain again. "How could I be so absent-minded as to forget Raymond?" she went on. She searched all about the area where she had last seen him, but he was nowhere to be found. "He must have gotten buried!" She began digging in the snow. Roage cawed, but Kristina ignored him and kept on digging. He cawed louder again and finally got her attention. She stopped digging and looked over at him. "Roage, can't you see, if I don't find Raymond fast, he could freeze to death."

"If you would stop digging, maybe I could help you find him," Roage said.

Kristina stopped digging.

"I suggest you take a look over the cliff's edge," Roage said.

Kristina's stomach sank as she thought about looking over the edge of the cliff and possibly finding Raymond dead. She cautiously went to the edge of the cliff, and even though it was extremely hard for her to look over it, she knew she had to do it—and be brave about it. She crept up to the snowy edge and then, with her eyes tightly shut, she poked her face over it. When she opened her eyes, the biting wind blew in her face. She looked down, expecting to see Raymond's dead body, but to her surprise, she found him sitting on a very small piece of rock that jutted out of the cliff's snowy wall. The rock was barely big enough for even Raymond's little body.

As the harsh wind and snow blew at him, he yelled up to Kristina, "It's about time you came for me! I'm freezing to death down here!"

"Oh, Raymond, I'm so glad you're okay. Just hold on, and we'll get you back up here in a jiffy," Kristina said.

She quickly pushed herself away from the edge of the cliff and stood up. She turned around and saw Werrien, who was waiting for her a short way up the mountain. "Werrien, I found Raymond!" she called out.

Werrien headed back down to the cliff's edge, and Kristina showed him where Raymond was. "Kristina, I'm glad that you found him, but how in the world are we going to get him back up here?" Werrien asked.

"Well, I was kind of hoping that you could help me out with that," Kristina said.

"Believe me, I'd like to, but unfortunately he's too far down," Werrien said.

"Couldn't you hang your cloak over again so that he could climb up it?" Kristina asked.

"No, the cloak isn't long enough."

"Well, there must be some way," Kristina said.

"Would you like me to get him?" Roage interrupted.

Werrien and Kristina stopped talking and turned their attention to Roage.

"You mean, pick Raymond up with your claws?" Kristina said.

"Well, I could try to pick him up with my beak, but the taste of rat really appalls me," Roage answered.

"I think you should let Roage get him, Kristina, unless you can come up with a better idea, besides, we really need to get going," Werrien said.

Kristina looked once more over the cliff's edge again and tried to think of another way to get Raymond, but she just couldn't come up with anything. "Raymond," she called down to him. "Raymond, can you hear me?" There was still no response. She quickly stood up, turned to Roage, and said, "Be gentle with him; he's my best friend."

"I won't let you down, or should I say, I won't let *Raymond* down," Roage said.

The raven flew over the cliff's edge, and a few minutes later, he came back up. Raymond was gripped in his talons, and Roage laid his limp body down in the snow.

- 34 -

The Dream

When Kristina saw Raymond's body lying on the cold, snowy ground, she gasped and ran over to him. She gently lifted him up and cradled him in her arms. She checked his body to see if Roage might have left any claw marks on him, but there were none to be found. "You must have died from exposure to the cold," she cried. "I'm so sorry, Raymond. I shouldn't have taken so long to make the decision to let Roage rescue you." She closed her eyes and began to sob.

Roage, who was standing beside her, noticed Raymond's nose twitch. "Your friend is not dead," he said.

"Oh, yeah? What do you know?" Kristina snapped back at him.

Suddenly, Raymond let out a loud sneeze, blowing the snow that had fallen in his face into the air. He shook his little head and looked up at Kristina. "Why do you always have to wake me? I was having such a wonderful dream. I was flying like a bird, high in the sky, soaring effortlessly over treacherous mountain peaks," he said, with a relaxed smile on his face. Then he stretched out his limbs and opened his mouth very wide in a yawn, revealing his two large front teeth.

"He's quiet the exaggerator—flying like a bird, soaring in the air," Roage said.

"Well, I'm just glad he's alive," Kristina said. She gently placed him back in his protective container.

As she was closing the lid, she heard Raymond's echoing voice say, "Do I have to go back inside this cold contraption? I think I would sleep much better somewhere else."

Kristina smiled as she slammed the container's lid shut. Then she opened it slightly and said, "I think you'll sleep just fine, Raymond. If you can handle the cold from down the cliff, you can certainly handle sleeping in this container." Then she closed the lid again.

Raymond didn't seem to be affected by the bone-chilling cold; he slept soundly in his protective container. But the harsh winds were almost unbearable for Werrien and Kristina as they began climbing again. Kristina had never experienced such cold conditions, and she was beginning to have serious doubts that she could hike much farther. She wouldn't tell Werrien, of course. She felt that she had caused enough trouble as it was. *I'll keep going until I pass out or drop dead, whichever comes first*, she thought.

Not long afterward, her legs gave out, and she fell forward. Werrien tried with all his might to pull her up, but he had very little strength left, and so she lay there, and the snow began to cover her.

"Kristina, you've got to get up or you'll freeze to death," Werrien said.

"I can't make it. You'll have to leave me and go on your own," she said weakly.

"I can't leave you. You're the only one who can deliver the Magic Warble to its resting place." He wouldn't have left her, even if it weren't so, but being a typical teenage boy, he couldn't bring himself to say it. When she didn't respond, he sat down beside her. "I guess we'll both just sit here and die together," he said.

All was silent, except for the sound of the howling wind, and as Werrien sat there, looking at nothing but the white snow falling, he began to grow extremely tired. He started to imagine that the snow covering them was a soft down blanket. He even imagined it to be very warm and cozy. Then his mind began to drift off, and he suddenly found himself on a warm sandy beach looking over a clear blue sea. It was so beautiful and inviting that he ran toward the water, but then, when he was just about to dive in, he heard the strong, familiar voice of his father say, "*Turn around, son. You must go back. You must do what is right, even though it seems impossible to you.*" Werrien stopped dead in his tracks—he knew he must listen to his father's voice, but the water was so inviting, and the air was so warm that he didn't want to obey. He just stood still, looking at the beautiful, clear blue sea, as if hypnotized by it. It provoked him so much that he decided not to obey his father's voice. He would dive in, but just before he did so, a tall tower appeared in the water. The sun was so bright that he had to squint. Suddenly, the clear blue sky and water began to change. They turned a cold, gray color, and the water grew rough and turbulent. The warm sand under his feet became cold and hard, and the air grew ice-cold. He looked toward the top of the tower, through a window he saw a beautiful woman. Her complexion was very pale, and she looked very sad. He new right away that the woman was his mother, and his heart ached in his chest. He was deeply saddened to see her sitting in the window, looking so sad and pale from lack of sunlight, but then the tower faded away, along with his mother and the cold, cold sky. The rough, turbulent water changed back to a bright, crystal-clear blue sea. His feet began to sink into the warm, soft sand, and it wasn't too long before his feelings of sadness faded away. He began to feel happy again, and he wanted to go swimming and have fun in the crystal-clear blue sea. A dolphin jumped up out of the sea and playfully tried to coax him to come in and play. It did flips and swam backwards, flapping its front fins together. The dolphin brought a smile to Werrien's face, and he wished, more than anything, that he could dive in the water and play with it. But he knew it was not the right thing to do, so he turned around and began to walk away from the water. As he did so, the sky began to change back to gray, and a cold wind blew at him, lifting the sand up and blowing it in his face. It made it hard for him to see or walk, and so he began to run. The wind grew stronger, as if trying to push him back to the sea, and it took every bit of his strength to run away from the sea. Then, suddenly, he felt something sharp pinching the skin on his ankles. He looked down to see many large, slimy, rotting crabs, all grabbing at his ankles with their sharp claws. He looked up again and saw that they were coming at him from every direction, thousands of them circling around, closing in on him with their slimy claws, open ready to pinch him. It was a terrifying sight, and the smell was horrendous. He lost his balance and fell backwards, yelling, "*No-o-o-o-o!*" As he hit the ground, he suddenly felt so cold that he thought he might be frozen solid. But he sat up to find himself back on Mount Bernovem, covered in snow.

Werrien realized that being at the seaside had only been a wild dream, but as for hearing the voice of his father, and seeing his mother in the tower, that had been very real to him. It impacted him so much that he decided he wouldn't give up climbing the mountain, no matter what. And even though he was extremely cold, it was actually a bit of a relief to be back on Mount Bernovem, compared to being attacked by slimy, stinking, rotting crabs. Unfortunately, his relief wasn't long lived, for lying beside him, looking very pale and almost completely covered in snow, was Kristina. Guilt overcame him. *What have I done? Have I been so stupid as to fall asleep and let her freeze to death?* The thought of this made him so angry with himself that he began to feel the familiar rush of adrenaline pump through him. It gave him a little bit of strength, enabling him to stand up and begin to remove the snow that had covered her. Raymond's container lay on the slope next to Kristina, and as Werrien was removing the snow from her nearly lifeless body, its lid popped open. A few seconds later, a very sleepy Raymond stuck his head out into the frosty air. But the icy wind blew at him and chilled him to the bone. The weather conditions were just too cold and miserable for him to venture out, and so he pulled his head back inside. Before he closed the container's lid, a handful of snow came at him and hit his face. He shook his head, and then peeked outside again. He looked around suspiciously to see where the snow had come from.

He took notice of Werrien, just off to the right of him, removing the snow from Kristina. "Hey, watch where you're throwing that nasty cold stuff," Raymond said. When Werrien didn't respond, Raymond finally took notice of Kristina. He figured that there must be something very wrong, so he quickly made his way over to Werrien. "What in the world is going on here?" he asked.

"Can't you see with your own eyes? Kristina is buried in the snow!" Werrien replied angrily.

"Yes, of course I can, but why did you let this happen?" Raymond asked.

"Instead of sitting there asking questions, why don't you lend me a hand?" Werrien said.

Raymond quickly jumped on top of Kristina and began helping Werrien to remove the snow from her. When they had gotten most of it off, Werrien felt her wrist, to see if she still had a pulse. She did, but it was weak.

At least she is still alive, he thought.

"What are we going to do?" Raymond asked.

Werrien really didn't know what he could do for her. He could barely stand the miserable cold weather himself. He thought for a brief moment and then said, "Hurry! Get back in your container."

Sensing that this was no time for arguing or questioning, Raymond obeyed and quickly went back inside, and Werrien closed the lid after him.

Not knowing where he would get the strength, Werrien picked up Kristina's limp body and started up the mountain, taking one strenuous step at a time. The biting wind blew in his face, and he desperately tried to think of a way to help her, but being so tired and weary himself, his mind was a complete blank. To make matters worse, that familiar spirit of fear began taunting him again, knocking at his mind, and generously offering him thoughts. *"What are you supposed to do now? You hardly have any strength left yourself. You think you can carry the girl up to the top of the mountain? And so what if you get her to the top? You know fully well that the spell can only be broken if she places the Magic Warble in its resting place. Can't you see? She's not going to be able to do that. Stupid boy, all this hardship you are putting yourself through is really just for nothing."*

The words "for nothing" repeated in Werrien's mind. Then his foot gave way on an icy spot beneath the snow, and with Kristina still clutched in his arms, he fell forward and began to slide down the mountain. As they went whizzing down, all he could do was close his eyes and hope not to slide off one of the mountain's many cliffs. Finally, his left foot hit against something hard, and it brought him to an abrupt stop. When he opened his eyes, he saw nothing but the white slope rising above him. He turned his head very slowly to see a jagged rock protruding out of the snow. This was what had stopped his fall, but it was what lay beyond the rock that made his heart jump into his throat. Another steep cliff, with a drop twice as deep as the one Kristina and Raymond had fallen over, lay just beyond the rock. Even worse, he was now lying on top of Kristina. He needed to somehow change his position. He managed to turn onto his side without lifting his foot off the rock, but after that, there was nothing else he could do. Kristina was still unconscious, and so he couldn't use his arms to pull himself up the slope. If he let go of her, for even a split second, she would most assuredly slide down, and go over the edge of the cliff. And if he took his foot off the rock, they'd both slide down over the edge. All he could do was lie very still on the ice-cold slope, and hope for a miracle.

- 35 -

The Battle on the Slope

Werrien closed his eyes and was about to drift off when he felt something touch his shoulder. He turned his head very slowly and saw that Ugan and Retzel were kneeling over him. Ugan quickly lifted Kristina up off the icy slope. Then Retzel reached down to Werrien and helped him to stand up.

"Are you okay?" Retzel asked, his bulgy eyes looking very concerned.

"I'm fine. It's Kristina I'm worried about," Werrien replied.

Ugan felt Kristina's pulse in her neck. "She's still alive," he said, relieved.

"How long has she been unconscious?" Retzel asked Werrien.

"I'm not sure because I dozed off," Werrien answered.

"It's a good thing Roage told us to follow you two," Retzel said.

A strong wind blew at them. "We'd best get out of this area, before all of us get blown over this cliff," Ugan said.

Ugan carried Kristina up the slope. Retzel picked up Raymond's container from the snowy ground and followed him. Werrien was just about to follow also, but then he noticed something on the

212

ground where Kristina and he had been lying. It was a little pouch. He picked it up. *This is Leacha's. Kristina must have had it*, he thought. He untied its tassels and looked inside it. "Fairy blossom!" he said.

"Hurry up, Werrien. We need to find a spot that's sheltered from the wind," Ugan called down to him.

Werrien quickly closed the little pouch and put it inside his cloak. He made his way up to where Ugan and Retzel were standing.

"Does one of you have a canteen?" he asked.

"I do, inside my cloak," Ugan replied. Since Ugan's arms were holding Kristina, Werrien reached inside his cloak and took out the canteen. "I'm sorry to say that there is only a little bit of plain water inside it. The zelbocks have destroyed every trace of fairy blossom, even the small amount that had been growing on the lower mountain," Ugan said.

Werrien opened the canteen, took the little pouch out of his cape, and poured the small amount of dried fairy blossom into the canteen. He put the lid back on and sealed it tight. Then he shook the canteen to mix the fairy blossom with the water.

"Is that fairy blossom?" Ugan asked.

"Yes," Werrien said.

"Do you know how fortunate you are to have that? Not a single dwarf, gnome, or fairy has a trace of it left," Ugan said.

"I didn't think we had any either, but then I found this little pouch on the slope where Kristina had been lying," Werrien said.

"We must give it to her right away," Retzel said, his eyes growing wide with anticipation.

"That's my plan," Werrien said, unscrewing the cap off the canteen again.

Ugan held Kristina in his arms, and Retzel helped to open her mouth while Werrien poured a small amount of the fairy-blossom water mixture over Kristina's lips. Her mouth moved a little, and she seemed to be drinking it fine, but she didn't wake up.

"You'll have to give her some more," Ugan said, looking slightly confused.

Werrien poured a little more into her mouth, and again the three of them eagerly waited to see if this time it would be enough to wake her. Her lips moved a little again, but she still didn't wake.

"Could the fairy blossom be losing its magic powers?" Werrien asked Ugan.

"In all of my life, I have never heard this to be possible," Ugan said.

"You must give her some more," Retzel said nervously.

"This is the last of it," Werrien said, as he slowly poured the few remaining drops into her mouth.

Kristina's lips moved again, and then, like the sun breaking through the clouds on a dreary cold day, a pinkish-rose color filled her cheeks, and she opened her eyes. At first, she saw six faces staring down at her—of course, there were really only three, but she was seeing double. Slowly, the six faces turned into three, and she smiled as she began to recognize them. "Werrien, Ugan, Retzel! Is everything okay?" she asked, as if nothing at all had even happened to her.

"It is now," Werrien answered, smiling down at her.

Feeling puzzled as to what was going on, Kristina asked Ugan, "Why you are holding me?"

Ugan chuckled. "It would take much too long to explain right now, child. I'll leave that up to Werrien to tell you about it a little later. Right now, we need to get going."

It was then that he heard a voice that he was all too familiar with: "Werrien will have plenty of time to explain all kinds of stories to her, *in the afterlife that is!*"

The four of them looked up the mountain to see the wicked Queen Sentiz and three of her disgusting zelbocks standing above them. She was wrapped in her bear stole, and the look on her pale face was a mixture of utter disgust and hatred. As Ugan slowly put Kristina down on the ground, the queen looked at him and said, "And you two good-for-nothing traitors will be joining them." She turned to the three zelbocks and yelled, "*Seize them!*"

As the three zelbocks started down the mountain, the lid to Raymond's container popped open. Raymond stuck his head out of the top of it, and being unaware of what was going on, opened his mouth very wide in a yawn. He looked up to see Retzel, who had his container tied around his waist. "Oh, fancy seeing you again," he said nonchalantly.

214

Suddenly an arrow flew toward them and hit Raymond's container, right below the lid. Raymond's sleepy expression quickly turned into a look of terror.

"You best get back inside there, if you want to keep your head," Retzel said to him urgently.

Raymond's head quickly disappeared back into the container. Then he reached up with his little paw and pulled the lid down. Another arrow came at his container, and this time, it hit it directly in its center, denting it and tossing Raymond around inside. At the same time, one of the other zelbocks shot an arrow at Werrien and hit him directly in his chest. Fortunately, the chainmail vest he was wearing stopped it from penetrating his skin. He pulled the arrow out and threw it down the slope. Then he turned to his left and saw an arrow heading straight for Kristina's head. It was moving so fast that there was absolutely nothing he could do to help her. The arrow was less than an inch from her, when suddenly, from out of nowhere, Roage swept down from out of the sky and snatched it up in his talons. It caught Kristina by surprise, but she had no time to dwell on it. Out of the corner of her eye, she could see Ugan, with his knife drawn out, defending himself from the third zelbock, which was lunging toward him. Luckily, Ugan was able to duck out of its way. He turned quickly and thrust his knife into the zelbock, stabbing it in the middle its back. It fell to the ground and tumbled down the snowy slope until it finally disappeared into an abyss of white.

Queen Sentiz stood up the slope, nervously watching as Werrien went to help Kristina, who was now drawing out her knife. Another zelbock was quickly approaching her, holding a spiked flail. It began to spin it violently in circles above its head. Then it let it go, and the flail flew toward Kristina's head. Werrien pushed her out of the way, just in the nick of time. The flail missed her head by less than an inch and fell to the ground. Then it rolled down the mountain until it disappeared out of sight. With their knives drawn out, Werrien and Kristina both stood up to face the gruesome zelbock.

It, too, had a knife and was backing them up to the edge of the same cliff where they had almost gone over not long before. When it had them very near the edge, it thrust the knife at Werrien, but he was quicker than the zelbock and able to duck out of its way. The zelbock tried again to stab him, and this time Werrien slipped and fell very near the edge of the cliff. Fortunately, Kristina was able to get away from the cliff's edge, but Werrien was not so fortunate. With a wicked grin on its face, the zelbock stood over him, revealing its rotten teeth. It began to laugh, and a greenish-gray drool dripped out of its mouth. Werrien could smell its foul breath, which came out of its mouth like smoke into the ice-cold air. It lifted its knife high up, and then began to bring it down to stab Werrien in his chest, but halfway there, Kristina stopped it by thrusting her knife into the back of its neck. The zelbock dropped its knife and fell forward. It would have fallen on top of Werrien, but he was able to push it over him, and it tumbled over the cliff's edge. Kristina reached her arm out to Werrien and helped him up. Then they both turned to see the last zelbock, the largest one, holding both Ugan and Retzel up in the air by the scruff of their necks.

"We need to help them," Werrien said.

They started off toward the zelbock, but then Werrien said, "Stop! I have an idea."

Kristina waited expectantly, as Werrien yelled to the zelbock, "Hey, you great big oaf!"

The zelbock quickly turned his attention to Werrien.

"Don't you know you're wasting your time on them? Isn't it us you want?" Werrien shouted.

Seeming a little puzzled, the zelbock looked at Ugan and then Retzel. It dropped them onto the snow and began to make its way toward Werrien. Werrien headed back toward the cliff. The snow was falling so hard that the zelbock couldn't see the cliff's edge.

Werrien began to tease and entice the zelbock. "What's taking you so long, you overgrown, mutated dwarf?" he yelled. He quickly glanced beyond the zelbock to see Queen Sentiz, still standing a distance up the slope, intensely watching everything.

"Watch out, Werrien!" Kristina yelled.

He looked back toward the zelbock and saw that it was charging as fast as it could down the slope toward him. Then when it got close enough, it let out a loud horrifying growl, jumped up in the air, and hurled itself toward Werrien. It was just what Werrien hoped it would do. He ducked down as it flew at him and went clear over him, headfirst, over the cliff.

Now that all three of the zelbocks were dead, Werrien's next plan was to go after Queen Sentiz, but when he looked to where she had been standing, she was no longer there.

"Queen Sentiz has left!" Werrien yelled to Ugan and Retzel.

"Yes, she has and is most assuredly on her way to the Magic Warble's resting place. We must get there before she does. I know she will do anything she can to stop you from delivering it," Ugan said.

Ugan's judgment about Queen Sentiz was most certainly right, for she had already made it back to her tent, which was not far from the place where the Magic Warble needed to be placed. When she entered her tent, extremely angry and covered from head to toe in snow, she found Rumalock sitting in her very own plush chair, with a warm woolen blanket wrapped around his shoulders. He was looking through the Book of Prophecy and sipping a cup of hot fairy-blossom tea. He looked up to see her enormous stature standing across the tent from him. The snow that had stuck to her bear stole made her look like some kind of snow monster. Not recognizing her, Rumalock was startled and jumped up out of his chair.

"How could you just sit there, warm and cozy, while I stand here freezing to death," the queen growled through chattering teeth.

"Oh, it's you, my dear lady," Rumalock said, seeming somewhat relieved after finally recognizing her voice.

"Get this snow off me at once, before I tear all your clothes off and throw your pathetic naked body out of this tent!" she yelled.

"Oh yes, of course, my queen." Rumalock scurried up on a chair so he could reach her shoulders, and he began removing her bear stole. Then he took the woolen blanket that he had wrapped around his shoulders and placed it around her shoulders. Feeling stiff and cold, Queen Sentiz slowly made her way over to her plush chair. Once she was seated, Rumalock handed her a mug of steaming-hot fairy-blossom tea.

"Now, now, that's much better," he said, in his most soothing voice, trying to calm her nerves. "At least now that you have finished off those two brats, all we have to do is get back to your warm and cozy palace," he continued, while massaging her cold bony shoulders.

Queen Sentiz took a large gulp of her tea and then turned toward Rumalock and spit it directly in his face.

"Ow-w-w!" Rumalock winced, as the hot tea splattered in his face.

"I thought you were at least smart enough to read. Didn't that stupid book tell you that the boy and girl killed three of my strongest zelbocks?" the queen barked.

Rumalock rubbed his eyes. "No, my dearest queen, I must have overlooked that part, or else it hadn't showed on the page yet."

"It's just as I figured. I always said you brainless dwarfs are good for nothing."

There was silence, except for the sound of the wind howling outside the tent and the tapping of the queen's claws on the side of her tea mug. She finally broke the silence, saying "We'll have to resort to our last defense."

"Oh yes, yes, our last defense," Rumalock said enthusiastically.

Queen Sentiz took another large gulp of her tea. Then she turned to him and said, "Well, don't just stand there. Go out and get them." Rumalock continued rubbing her bony shoulders, but she pulled herself away from his soothing hands and stood up. She turned to face him. "Well, what are you waiting for? Get going, lazy dwarf."

Rumalock nervously twirled his beard around his finger, as he usually did when trying to remember something. Then, fearing the outcome, but knowing he must, he asked, "What was it exactly that you wanted me to do with the other three children, dearest queen?"

Queen Sentiz's temper began to rise as she stared down at him with a trembling face. She turned pink, then red, and finally purple. Her eyes began to bulge out of her head, and her thin lips shriveled up to almost nothing. Rumalock lifted his arms over his head and then shrunk to the floor, as if to defend himself from what might possibly be his own death. As he waited for what seemed to be his unavoidable fate, all he could hear was the sound of his own heart beating and the queen's loud breathing through her flared nostrils. He was expecting something hard to come down on him and crush him. But nothing did.

Instead, an odd thing happened—Queen Sentiz suddenly regained her composure, and her face went back to its normal pale, gaunt appearance. She took a deep breath and calmly said, "I realize that I must be more patient with your inferior species, no matter how trying it is."

Rumalock suspected that she really just didn't want to deal with going out in the cold to get the children, which she'd have to do if he were killed. Regardless, he slowly moved from his curled-up position on the floor with his arms over his head and turned his head to look up at the queen. "Do you really mean it, dearest queen? Will you take time out of your precious day to explain it to me once again?"

"Yes, yes, now get up," she said. Rumalock slowly rose to his feet and stood before his tall dictator, who cast a long dark shadow over him. "Now listen to me very carefully. I want you to go out of this tent, to the place where the three children are being held, and let them know that we will be going for a little hike," she said calmly.

"Yes, my lady," Rumalock said.

There was silence again, and Rumalock didn't move.

"Well, what are you waiting for? For hell to freeze over?"

"No, of course not, we wouldn't want that," Rumalock said, as he started for the tent flaps.

While he was untying the flaps, the queen said, "I think you might be needing these."

Rumalock turned around, and she threw three ropes on the floor at his feet.

"Do you think these are really necessary?" he asked.

The queen's eyes began to bulge again, and her lips began to shrivel.

"Yes, I suppose they are," Rumalock said, answering his own question.

As he trudged up the mountain toward the tent where Davina, Graham, and Hester were being held, the harsh wind blew at him and made it very difficult for him to walk. He fell down and had a very hard time getting back up. Finally, he made it to the tent.

Inside, the three children sat huddled close together in a crate. They'd each been given a small dwarfs cape, but they had nothing else to keep them warm. Even though it was freezing outside, they still had the strength to argue with each other.

"Quit breathing your stinky breath on me. It smells like road kill," Hester said to Graham.

"Would you rather have me move to the other side?" Graham asked.

"I would, but then we'd probably freeze to death," Hester said.

"Then don't complain," Graham said.

"I don't know about you two, but if someone doesn't get us out of here soon, we're going to turn into ice statues," Davina said through chattering teeth.

Graham caught sight of the tent's door flaps moving. "Someone's coming," he said in a loud whisper.

The three of them couldn't see who it was because it was dark in the tent. Rumalock entered, carrying the ropes. He dropped them on the floor, which startled Hester, so that she huddled even closer to Graham. Rumalock lit a lantern, and the children peered through the crate's bars, trying to see who he was. Hester was the first to notice that it was Rumalock.

"It's about time you showed up. Do you realize that you and your fellow little people are going to be charged with child abuse?" she said.

Rumalock didn't answer but went to shut the tent door flaps because the icy wind was blowing in through them. Then he picked up the ropes and the lantern and walked up to the crate to get a better view of the three children. "You look very cold," he said to them.

"Please, could you get us out of here?" Davina pleaded.

"I'll tell you what. If you cooperate with me, I will take you to a much more comfortable and warmer tent for some hot cocoa and a bite to eat," Rumalock said.

The three children looked at each other, and then Hester said, "I suppose we'll cooperate."

"Good, then I will let you out, one at a time," Rumalock said. He unlocked the crate. "Boy, you come out first." Graham went out of the crate. "Now turn around and put your hands behind your back," Rumalock said.

"What for?" Graham asked.

"Listen, I can leave you here in the cold if you don't do as I say," Rumalock said.

"Just do as he says," Davina blurted out, shivering.

Graham put his hands behind his back and Rumalock tied them. Then he let the girls out, one at a time, and tied their hands behind their backs as well.

"Why are you treating us like criminals?" Hester asked.

"It's the queen's orders," Rumalock said. He quickly picked up a whip that had been leaning against the table and snapped it in the air. "Now don't try to run away. It's nothing but a stormy blizzard outside, and there is no one out there to help you."

221

The three children were so cold, and their teeth were chattering so loudly that they didn't even try to respond.

Rumalock looked at them through his squinty eyes and said, "Very good."

He walked back to the tent's entrance and untied the door flaps. A gust of bone-chilling wind blew in, directly at them. "After you," he said, indicating that they should pass by him. The three slowly exited the tent, and Rumalock followed.

Once outside, they heard a voice behind them say, "Are my lovely guests enjoying their stay?"

They turned around to see Queen Sentiz.

- 36 -

The Golden Goblet

The howling winds and falling snow showed no mercy on Werrien, Kristina, Ugan, and Retzel. They could now see the very top of Mount Bernovem. Werrien took the map out again to try and find the exact place where they needed to deliver the Magic Warble. The map showed that its resting place was in a small cave on the north side of the mountain, near its peak.

"I was up here once before, a long time ago, with my father so I might be able to recognize the place from the map. May I have a closer look at it?" Retzel asked Werrien.

Werrien handed the map to him. Retzel held it very close to his eyes to get a better view, but a very strong gust of wind blew at them and swept the map right out of his hands. The four franticly grabbed for it, but it was no use—it was quickly carried away by the wind, down the mountain.

"I'm so sorry," Retzel said, feeling very guilty for letting it go.

No one said a word, but it was clear from the look on each of their faces that no one expected to find the Magic Warble's resting place now.

"I have caused you all nothing but trouble," Retzel said sadly.

"Wait a minute—what's that over there?" Werrien said, pointing up the mountain.

"It looks like a wolf," Ugan said.

The animal stared down at them, then turned around and disappeared into the side of the mountain.

"It must have gone into a cave," Kristina said.

"Let's follow it," Werrien said.

It took every bit of their strength to reach the spot where they'd seen the wolf disappear, but it was worth it when they found the cave. The entrance was about three feet wide, just big enough for a dwarf or someone about Kristina's size to fit through. Werrien stuck his head inside it, and from a short distance away, the wolf stared at him with its light-green glowing eyes. It began to growl, and then it suddenly came charging toward him. Werrien quickly pulled his head out and backed away from the entrance. The wolf stuck its head out the opening and continued to growl, revealing its large white fangs. "What do you want?" it asked in a gruff voice.

"We are looking for the resting place of the Magic Warble," Werrien said.

"You will only be able to enter if the chosen one is among you, any imposters I will fight to the death," the wolf said.

"She is here with us," Werrien said.

The wolf's eyes shifted from Werrien to Kristina. "You will need to show me the Magic Warble before I can let you in," the wolf said.

With very cold, shaking hands, Werrien brought the golden case out from underneath his shirt. Then he held it out toward the wolf so the animal could examine it.

The wolf sniffed it. "Yes, this is the golden case that was placed in the hollow of a tree many years ago." The wolf turned around and directed them, "Follow me."

The five, including Raymond, who was now awake and fully alert in his container, followed the wolf into the cave. There was no light inside, and their surroundings became so pitch black that they couldn't see even a glimpse of the wolf ahead of them.

"Stop," the wolf said suddenly.

They all did as they were told. There was complete silence, except for the wind whistling outside the cave.

"Dwarf," the wolf directed, "to your right is a torch. Take it."

Ugan was the only dwarf, so he felt in the dark to his right, and just as the wolf had said, there was a torch leaning against the cave wall. "How am I to light it?" he asked.

"The walls in this cave are covered with a flammable substance. Scrape the top of the torch against the wall to light it, but be very careful—once it is lit, you must not let it near the walls or the ceiling again, or the entire cave will go up in flames. Make sure you stay in the middle of the tunnel, so that you do not go to close the left or the right."

This made Ugan very nervous, but he did as the wolf told him to do, and the torch lit up instantly. The five continued following the wolf, and as they walked, he explained to them that the reason why the cave walls were flammable was to protect the Magic Warble. After it was placed in its resting place, if someone were to try to steal it, the wolf could easily ignite the cave and kill the thief.

"What would happen to you?" Kristina asked the wolf.

The wolf's glowing eyes met hers. "I would die also," he said very seriously.

Kristina felt the butterflies begin to flutter in her stomach as she realized once again how serious this mission was.

Nobody said another word but cautiously followed behind the wolf. Not long afterward, the wolf turned to face them again. "We are now where the Magic Warble needs to be placed," he said.

All five of them looked around, but they couldn't tell anything special about this place. Nothing seemed any different from other areas of the cave they had passed. But then Kristina took notice of a certain spot to the left. It was an indentation in the wall.

"Ugan, please shine the light over there," she said, pointing to the spot. Ugan quickly shined the torch light, and she saw that there was a shelf there with an arched top built into it. "Come here and take a look at this," she said to the others.

The shelf had a thick, dust-covered cobweb sprawled throughout the inside of it. Ugan moved the torch slightly and the light shifted to reveal a large black spider sitting in the upper right corner of the shelf.

"Are we to lay the Magic Warble down inside the shelf?" Kristina asked the wolf.

"There is a golden goblet sitting in the bottom of it. The Magic Warble will need to be placed in it, but first, you must get the poisonous spider out of the way," the wolf replied. Werrien remembered the spider that had tried to attack him in the underground hideout. He recognized this type of spider, and it's venom was the most lethal.

"Ugan, bring the torch to the shelf and burn the spider," Retzel said.

"No," Werrien said, grabbing hold of the torch to stop him. "We can't risk setting the cave on fire." He took his knife and tried to stab the spider with it, but he missed, and the spider swung out on its web toward Werrien's face. He ducked out of its way, and the spider landed on Kristina's shoulder. Kristina slowly turned her head to see the huge black spider sitting on her shoulder with venom beading out of its fangs.

"Don't…move…as much as…a muscle," Ugan said slowly. He brought the torch close to the spider, and Kristina could feel the intense heat from its flame. She closed her eyes and swallowed nervously. Soon, the spider, not being able to stand the heat, hopped off her shoulder and swung back toward the shelf. This time Werrien was quicker than the spider, and he stabbed his knife right through its middle while it was still swinging.

"Shish kebab, anyone?" he said, holding the spider over the flame. The spider burned to a crisp, and its ashes fell to the ground.

Kristina and Werrien quickly went to look inside the shelf again. There seemed to be the shape of a wine goblet there, but it was covered in a thick cobweb. Werrien took his knife and quickly wound up the spider webs with it, as if he were winding spaghetti around a fork. Then he gave a quick yank, and all at once, the entire web came out. They could see the golden goblet sitting at the bottom of the shelf. Ugan and Retzel came closer to look at it. Then Raymond crawled out of his container and onto Retzel's shoulder to get a better view.

"You must not delay placing the Magic Warble in the goblet. I sense time is about to run out," the wolf instructed.

"Yes, yes, of course," Werrien said, and he quickly brought the golden case out from underneath his shirt. It was very warm, and it pulsated and almost seemed to vibrate. Werrien carefully opened its lid, and they all saw that the Magic Warble had reached its final color: red.

"Kristina, you must take the Magic Warble and place it in the goblet," the wolf said.

Kristina reached into the golden case to lift the Magic Warble out, but just before she touched it, a voice cried out that she knew all too well.

"Wait! Please don't do it!"

They all quickly turned to see the tall figure of Queen Sentiz. She was standing behind Davina, holding a knife to the girl's throat.

Kristina was about to ask Davina how she had gotten to Bernovem, but then she remembered Rumalock telling her,

"Whoever has touched the Magic Warble, or even the case it was stored in, will be brought here."

"If you place the Magic Warble in its resting place," Queen Sentiz said in a calm yet eerie voice, "your friends will surely die."

What did she mean, "friends"? thought Kristina.

Ugan moved the torch a little to the left and the light revealed other figures standing a short distance behind Queen Sentiz. It was Rumalock, and he was holding Hester at knife point; beside him stood a zelbock who was holding Graham at knife point as well.

"Why are you doing this?" Kristina asked Queen Sentiz.

"I don't have to explain anything to you, you pathetic brat. Just roll the Magic Warble over to me, and I will spare your friends' lives," the queen said.

Davina, Hester, and Graham were no friends of hers, but even so, Kristina knew that she couldn't just let them die. She looked at Werrien to see if he might have any ideas, but as far as she could tell, he had none.

"You'd better do as she says," Werrien said.

Werrien's reaction seemed odd to Kristina. It just wasn't like him to give up so easily, especially after all they had been through to get to this point. How could they just hand the Magic Warble over to the wicked queen and possibly lose everything they had struggled so hard for? It just didn't make any sense. Even so, she really didn't know what else to do, so she took the Magic Warble out of the golden case. Then, just before kneeling down to roll it over to Queen Sentiz, she looked one last time at Werrien.

"Trust me," he whispered softly.

Everyone's eyes were fixed on the Magic Warble as Kristina knelt down and rolled it over to Queen Sentiz. When it got close enough to her, the queen pushed Davina to the ground and reached down with her long red claws to snatch it up. And just as she grabbed hold of it, the wolf jumped out from the dark crevasse in which he'd been hiding and leaped up onto Queen Sentiz, pushing her to the ground. She fell backwards and dropped the Magic Warble. When it hit the ground it rolled back toward Kristina, who bent down and scooped it up. Then she turned to face Werrien.

"You must do it now, before it is too late!" he said urgently. Kristina saw that the Magic Warble's deep red tones were fading into a lighter orange-red.

"Its power is beginning to decline!" Werrien said.

Kristina placed her hand into the shelf and was about to lay the Magic Warble in the gold goblet, but again she was stopped by another voice: "You'd best not be doing that." Ramon stood a few feet behind Kristina and Werrien, holding his cupped hands out in front of him. "If you drop that thing in that cup, I'll not hesitate to squash your annoying little friend like I would a bug," he said.

Kristina looked again to Werrien for any ideas, but this time he definitely had none. They both new that they couldn't let Ramon kill Clover, and beside that, what a horrible sight it would be if he did squash her like a bug. There was no choice, other than to hand the Magic Warble over to Ramon. So once again, they took their hands away from the shelf and reluctantly, Werrien held the Magic Warble out toward Ramon.

Ramon stared at it with a conniving smile on his quirky face. "Place it on the floor," Ramon said.

Werrien did as he was told. Then Ramon called for one of the zelbocks to tie Werrien's and Kristina's hands behind their backs.

"Now take them to sit by those other three brats," he ordered the zelbock. The zelbock led Werrien and Kristina toward Davina, Graham, and Hester. "There is one more thing I must have," Ramon went on, "if you want me to let your pretty little friend live."

"We've already given you everything we have," Werrien said angrily.

"Not quite," Ramon said, while brushing his dirty finger over Clover's hair.

Clover, angrier then a hornet, beat her tiny fists down on Ramon's closed hand.

"What else could you possibly want?" Werrien asked, feeling disgusted with his greedy requests.

Ramon's smirk grew into an evil, lustful smile, and he glared at Kristina as if he could devour her with his eyes. "If you want your little fairy princess to live, then I must have Kristina as my bride," he said, his eyes growing wide.

When Kristina heard these words, she felt like she might throw up. "I'm much too young to get married! And besides, I'd rather die then have to marry you," she blurted out.

"Well, then, have it your way," Ramon said, his lustful grin turning into an angry frown. "I will squash you slowly after I deal with the Magic Warble," he said to Clover.

He plopped Clover back into his canteen and then sent the zelbock to tie Werrien's and Kristina's feet. Then he knelt down to pick up the Magic Warble, but as his hand got close to it, it turned from lukewarm to hot, and there was no way he could touch it. This made him even angrier, and he stood up, drawing his dagger out of its sheath. "Wait! I've changed my mind. Release the boy instead. I have decided to let him have the honor of destroying it—and the honor of squishing the fairy as well," he said.

"Not a chance," Werrien said, adamantly.

"Well, then, I guess I'll have no other choice other than to kill you right now," Ramon replied.

Kristina noticed that Ramon's canteen was wobbling to and fro on the ground behind him. The lid suddenly popped off, and Clover flew out. She flew very fast past Ramon, and he swiped the air, thinking she was nothing more than a cave bat.

He turned to Ugan and said, "And you, you little traitor, I'll deal with you soon, but for now, bring that torch closer so I can see where I'm going to stick my knife in the peasant boy."

Ugan slowly made his way toward Ramon.

"Hurry, lazy dwarf! I don't have all day," Ramon snapped impatiently. He then told the zelbock to bring Werrien to him, so the zelbock snapped its long whip on the ground in front of Werrien. But Werrien didn't move; instead, he looked up at the zelbock and because he was much angrier than scared, he spit in its face. This infuriated the zelbock, and it wiped the spit off its face with the back of its hand, and then grinned, revealing its rotten teeth. Then it snapped its whip again, this time hitting Werrien.

"Leave him alone, you evil, rotting creature!" Kristina yelled.

The zelbock quickly turned its attention to Kristina and brought its whip down toward her, but Kristina was able to duck out of its way. Werrien managed to loosen his hands from the ropes and at the same time, Clover flew up behind Ramon and gently took hold of a few strands of his hair. Then, with a hand gesture, she told Ugan to bring the torch closer. Once the flame was close enough, Clover placed Ramon's hair in it.

Unaware that his hair had caught fire, Ramon sniffed the air and said, "What is that horrible smell?"

Rumalock looked up at him and yelled, "Oh no! Your Highness, your hair is on fire."

In a panic, Ramon began to run in circles, but this only made the flames burn even stronger. He ran toward the entrance of the cave, with Rumalock following close behind.

Werrien quickly untied his and Kristina's feet. "Come on," he said, grabbing her by the hand and pulling her up. The two of them ran to the Magic Warble, and Werrien quickly scooped it up into the palm of his hand. They were just about to run with it to the shelf in the cave's wall when Kristina felt something ice cold grip her ankle. Queen Sentiz was lying on the cold ground, trying to pull Kristina to the ground.

"Give it to me, or you'll never escape this cave!" she croaked.

Retzel, who had been standing in a dark spot of the cave, holding Raymond, took notice of this and quickly ran to help Kristina.

"Nobody lays a hand on my master," Raymond said angrily, and when they were close enough, he leaped into the air and landed on the queen's head. He dug his nails into her scalp and then jumped onto her hand and bit it. Queen Sentiz screeched in pain, and finally loosened her grip from Kristina's ankle. Once Kristina was free from the clutches of the queen, Werrien and she made their way toward the shelf. But *again* they were hindered, this time by a sudden strong wind heading towards the entrance of the cave. It tried to pull them away from the shelf. Werrien gripped Kristina's hand even tighter to stop her from being taken away by the wind. After it blew past, they quickly made their way back to the shelf, and Werrien gave Kristina the Magic Warble.

She put her hand back on the shelf and then—finally—placed the Magic Warble in its final resting place.

But all was not well, for as it dropped into the golden goblet, Werrien looked at the tunnel that led to the entrance of the cave, and he got a sick feeling in his stomach.

"What's wrong?" Kristina asked him.

He didn't answer; instead, he pushed Kristina to the ground and with his own body, he shielded hers. Kristina didn't see what happened after that, but she felt an intense heat.

The Curse Is Lifted

An enormous explosion took place when Ramon brought his burning hair too close to the flammable walls.

After the intense heat subsided, Werrien and Kristina looked up to see a bright, colorful light radiating from within the shelf in the wall. They quickly peered inside the shelf to see the Magic Warble spinning around in the golden goblet. As it spun, it changed into all the colors it had previously displayed. They watched in awe as it spun faster and faster, until they couldn't see its shape anymore, only its many colors intermingling and swirling throughout it.

"What do you think is happening to it?" Kristina asked Werrien.

"I have no idea," he answered.

They felt the ground beneath them begin to tremble, and then shortly after, Kristina saw a rock the size of a football falling from the ceiling, directly above Werrien.

"Look out!" she shouted.

Werrien jumped out of the way, just in time. "We have to get out of this cave, and fast!" he said.

Kristina glanced over at the other three children, still huddled together on the ground. "Hester, Davina, Graham! Get up! We need to get out of this cave before the ceiling caves in on us."

Werrien, Ugan, Retzel, and Kristina started toward the tunnel that led to the entrance of the cave, and as they hurried past the other three children, Kristina stopped and offered her hand to help Hester up. But even in a life-threatening situation such as this, Hester was too prideful to accept it.

"Well, then have it your way," Kristina said, knowing how Hester felt by the sour look on her face. "If you can't accept my help, then just get up yourself and follow us—that is, if you want to get out of here alive." Then Kristina and the others continued on down the tunnel.

"Who does she think she is, trying to act like she's some kind of hero to us? We'll do just fine on our own," Hester said, as the three of them stood up and reluctantly followed Kristina.

Kristina and the others hadn't gotten very far when they heard a loud crashing sound behind them. They turned around to see that a great many rocks had fallen in between them and the other three children.

"We have to go back and help them," Kristina said to Werrien, but almost instantly, there was a loud rumbling sound and more rocks came crashing down, this time very close behind them.

"If we don't get out of here now, we, too, will be trapped or even crushed by the rocks," Ugan said.

Raymond poked his head out of Retzel's shirt. "Kristina's right. We have to go back and help the other children. If something happens to them, none of us will ever be able to live with ourselves."

Was that Raymond speaking, the one who was scared of everything? Kristina thought.

"Raymond's right; we can't just let them die in there," Werrien agreed. "Ugan, Retzel, and Kristina—you three go on ahead of me, and I'll go back and get the other three."

"If you're going, then I'm going, too," Kristina said.

There was more rumbling, and then more rocks fell to the ground. Ugan quickly handed Werrien the torch. Then Retzel, Raymond, and Ugan went on ahead to escape the crumbling cave.

They were making their way out when Raymond crawled out of Retzel's shirt and leaped to the ground.

"Hey, where are you going?" Retzel called out after him.

"I've got a rescue mission to attend to!" Raymond's voice echoed as he scampered away into the darkness of the cave.

"Wait, you can't go!" Retzel shouted.

But Ugan grabbed him by the arm and said, "Let him go. It will be good for him to experience a little danger."

Retzel agreed, and the two headed for the entrance of the cave.

Werrien and Kristina made their way back into the dark cave with the dimly lit torch. They climbed up the pile of fallen rocks, and Kristina began calling out for the other three children.

"Hester, Graham, Davina! Can any of you hear me?" Her voice echoed loudly, but unfortunately, there was no answer. Then, suddenly, the ground beneath them began to tremble again.

"Kristina, if we don't get out of here now, we'll die, too," Werrien said.

"What do you mean, die, too?" Kristina said, shocked by his statement. She felt her stomach lurch. "They couldn't have died; they're much too young!" She felt very strange and tears began welling up in her eyes. *How can I feel such sorrow and guilt for possibly my worst enemies on earth?* she thought.

The ground trembled again, and Kristina fell backwards. She would have landed with her head on a very sharp rock, but Werrien grabbed her by the arm and stopped her fall.

"Kristina, we really need to get out of here!"

Kristina used her sleeve to wipe the tears from her dirty face, and then sadly agreed. Werrien climbed down from the rock pile, and Kristina was about to follow when she suddenly heard a faint voice calling her name. She turned around quickly, and her eyes panned the darkness, hoping to find any signs of the other three children. Instead, she caught sight of two very small glowing eyes back in the cave.

"Raymond? Is that you?" she called out.

"Yes, come quickly," he replied.

The ground began to quake again, but this time it didn't even

235

faze Kristina. She crawled down the heap of rocks and made her way over to Raymond.

"What are you doing out here all alone? Don't you know how dangerous it is in this cave? If a rock falls on you, you'll be crushed in an instant," she lectured her pet rat.

"I thought you'd at least be happy that I found them," Raymond said, his confidence bubble slightly deflated.

"What? You found them? But where are they?"

"They're not directly out in the open. Come on; follow me and I'll show you where they are," Raymond said as he scampered over fallen rocks and went deeper into the heart of the cave.

Kristina followed behind Raymond, but because of the darkness, she soon lost track of him. "Raymond, where are you? I can't see you anymore," she called. She was beginning to get really scared and wondered if what she was doing was all worth it. Then she saw Raymond's glowing eyes.

"Over here!" he called out.

She made her way over to him, and he led her into a deep crevasse in the cave wall. Huddled together inside it were Hester, Graham, and Davina. Hester was crying.

"Are you guys okay?" Kristina asked.

"Does it look like it?" Davina snapped, as if Kristina were stupid.

"Are you now willing to accept my help?" Kristina asked.

"I suppose, if we must," Hester said, in between sniffles.

Kristina reached out her hand to Hester and helped her out the crevasse. Graham and Davina followed. Now they could see the light of the torch coming toward them.

"Werrien, I found them!" Kristina said excitedly.

"That's great! Now come on—we need to hurry and get out of here."

They started to follow Werrien, but then Hester stopped and said, "Wait! Where's Graham?"

Everyone looked around, but they couldn't see him.

"He was just with us a minute ago," Davina said.

Werrien moved the torch around to see if he could spot him anywhere, but the cave walls began to shake, and he lost his balance.

While steadying himself, the light shined directly on Graham. "Look! There he is," Werrien said.

They watched as Graham headed in the opposite direction.

"Graham, you're going the wrong way!" Hester yelled franticly.

But Graham either didn't hear her or wouldn't listen.

The cave shook violently again, and more large boulders began to fall from the ceiling. Kristina picked up Raymond. Just as he was crawling inside her cloak to hide, Werrien saw a large boulder heading straight for Kristina's head. He pulled her out of the way, and it hit the ground and shattered, sending small sharp chunks of rock in all directions. One razor sharp chunk hit Davina's thigh. She let out a loud screech, sounding like someone had stepped on a cat's tail. Then she pulled out the shard to reveal a good-sized gash in her leg.

"Follow us," Werrien shouted to her and Hester.

Davina held one hand on her cut leg as she and Hester followed Werrien and Kristina toward the entrance of the cave. Rocks fell continuously, and the violent shaking didn't cease, but they all made it safely out—except Graham.

"We can't just leave Graham in there," Kristina said.

"If he gets hurt, it serves him right," Davina said, her voice straining from the pain in her leg.

"The brat shouldn't have gone the opposite way," Hester said coldly.

"Can you think of any reason why he did?" Werrien asked Hester and Davina.

"No, not really," Davina said through chattering teeth.

"Wait a minute," Hester said excitedly. "Remember he kept saying that he felt sorry for that ugly, scary-looking woman who brought us here?"

"Are you saying you think he was heading to Sentiz?" Werrien said.

While they were talking, the wolf suddenly came toward them. "Follow me," he said hastily.

"We can't leave! My dumb cousin's in the cave," Hester said.

"We must leave this area now, before the cave blows," the wolf said.

Then he turned and began to descend the mountain. The children followed him down to a large rock, at least three times the size of them in height, that protruded out of the slope. Already standing behind it, shielded from the wind-driven snow, were Ugan and Retzel. They had no sooner joined them when the ground beneath them began to quiver and quake, and then a tremendous explosion took place. Snow, ice, and rock spat high up, obscuring the already cloud-covered sky. The atmosphere went dark, and the blistering wind grew even stronger. Then there was a fearful wrenching sound, and the snowy slope around them began to crack and separate. Deep crevices began to form that resembled slithering snakes going in all directions. One crack came toward them and went directly between Hester and everyone else. Hester let out a blood-curdling scream when the snow she stood on began to separate from where the others stood.

"Grab hold of my hand and try not to panic!" Werrien yelled, reaching out to her.

Hester didn't answer; she only looked down to see the snow separate even more. Her face turned as white as a ghost and she seemed to freeze up like the icy ground beneath her.

"Hester, please, grab hold of Werrien's hand," Kristina insisted.

"I can't. I'm too scared!" she yelled. She began to cry hysterically.

Without giving it another thought, Kristina jumped over to her and took hold of her arm. She looked her straight in the eyes and said, "Its okay, we're going to jump together."

As Hester stared back at Kristina's eyes, her stone-cold glare seemed to melt. She shook her head to focus better, and said, "Okay, okay, I'll do it, if you promise not to let go of me."

"I promise," Kristina said. Kristina linked her arm with Hester's, and then she said, "On the count of three."

"Are you sure?" Hester asked nervously.

"Yes! Now here we go—one, two, three!" Just as they jumped, the chunk of snow they had been on broke away completely and tumbled down the mountain until it finally disappeared into the abyss of white below them.

Other large hunks of snow, rock, and ice hurled past them and over them. It felt like the land of Bernovem was coming to an end.

They all stood crammed together, like sardines, on the small chunk of snow behind the large rock, and the only thing they could do was wait, and wait, until finally, the avalanche stopped. At that instant, all the ruckus, rumbling, and tumbling of snow and debris, along with the violent roaring of the wind, subsided and there was dead silence. They all looked up to the sky to see that the snow had ceased falling and the vicious wind had died. The clouds began to separate, and the sun suddenly pierced through them. It was so bright that they had to squint. The clouds quickly evaporated, and the sky turned bright blue.

"It must have happened!" Werrien said excitedly.

"What must have happened?" Davina asked, while shielding her eyes from the sun.

"The curse over Bernovem has been lifted," Ugan said, looking amazed.

The sun began to warm them, and they got so toasty that they took off their cloaks. Raymond crawled on top of Retzel's shoulder to bask in the sun. While enjoying their newfound warmth, they felt movement under their feet, and they looked down to see the chunk of snow beneath them melt before their very eyes. They all sank down, about three feet, and found themselves no longer on snow but on very wet, flattened grass. Everywhere around them, patches of snow began to dissolve and small streams formed and ran down the mountain. There was no more need to stand behind the large protruding rock, for most of the snow on the mountain had melted. Kristina was the first one to venture away from the rock, and when she was no longer behind it, she could see the top of the mountain perfectly.

"Wow!" she said, astonished. It was the most unusual yet beautiful sight she had ever seen in her life.

Werrien quickly joined her, and he, too, couldn't believe his eyes. Then Ugan, Retzel, Raymond, Davina, and Hester also joined them, and they all stood in awe.

"What is it?" Kristina asked, without taking her eyes off it.

239

"The Magic Warble, its grown into the Rainbow Tree," Werrien said.

"Hey, isn't that where that cave was?" Davina asked.

"It certainly was," Ugan said.

"Where did it go?" Hester asked.

"Well, what happened was that after Kristina placed the Magic Warble in its resting place, the curse broke, and the Magic Warble grew back into what it originally used to be, years ago: the Rainbow Tree," Ugan said.

"It grew right through the cave," Retzel added.

The Rainbow Tree was different from any other tree that Kristina, Davina, or Hester had ever seen, and though its shape was very similar to that of an oak tree, it was much larger than even the largest one on earth. It was made out of a vibrant, shimmering rainbow crystal, and it had many, many limbs and many, many branches on the limbs. Its branches reached so high up into the sky that they could not tell where they ended, and its color was that of a rainbow. The tree shined like the sun in the sky, but it was different than the sun because it didn't hurt their eyes when they gazed upon it.

"Can we go up to it?" Kristina asked Werrien excitedly.

"Maybe Graham's up there, waiting for us," Hester said enthusiastically.

"Let's go," Werrien said.

They made their way back up the mountain, this time with ease, for the biggest obstacles in their way were only small brooks created by the melted snow. On their way up, they noticed that the closer they got to the Rainbow Tree, the greener and fresher the grass became.

"Look at the grass. It's sprouting up everywhere," Kristina said, amazed by the sight of it.

"And look at the little red flowers growing all around us," Davina said excitedly.

"It's the fairy blossoms," Kristina said.

The fairy blossoms were growing all around them before their eyes. Other plants and flowers began to grow, too, and by the time they all reached the base of the Rainbow Tree, the mountainside was covered in stunningly beautiful wildflowers of whole ranges of colors. The tree itself gave off a lovely warmth, and it brought about a feeling of utter joy and happiness.

As the group stood beneath it, they suddenly found themselves become very happy, and smiles came across all their faces—all except for Hester's.

"Maybe Graham somehow escaped out the back of the cave. Once the cave started crumbling, I remember seeing a small hole with light shining through it from outside," Kristina said to Hester, trying to be optimistic.

"There is one positive side to not finding him up here. At least we haven't found him dead," Davina said bluntly.

The longer they all stood under the tree, the more joyful they became, even Hester. Then, as if from hearing a hilarious joke, Retzel began to laugh. And then Werrien, seeing how funny Retzel's face looked when he laughed, also began to laugh, and soon after that, they all found themselves laughing, including Hester. Raymond joined in and became so excited that he leaped off Retzel's shoulder and onto the ground. Then he bounded happily over the lush green grass. Davina became so joyful that she forgot about the pain from the cut on her leg. She even tried to do a cartwheel, but being not very coordinated, she ended up falling before she finished it. When she got up, she was amazed to see that her leg was completely healed. "Look, everyone, my leg is better," she said excitedly.

"That's because you fell in a cluster of fairy blossoms," Ugan said.

While everyone was frolicking and having fun, they were suddenly interrupted by a familiar caw. They saw Roage, flying high above them in the bright blue sky. He glided down slowly and landed on a branch of the Rainbow Tree.

"It's good to see you, Roage. Come down and join us," Werrien called up to the raven.

Roage cawed loudly again and then left the tree branch. They watched as he glided down effortlessly with his wings stretched fully out. It seemed he was going to make a landing on the other side of the tree, so Werrien and Kristina quickly went to the other side to greet him.

- 38 -

The Necklace

When Werrien and Kristina reached the other side of the Rainbow Tree, they found Roage standing on the ground under it.

"The spell has been broken, Roage," Werrien said excitedly to the raven.

"Yes, it has," Roage agreed. He stretched out his wings as far as they would possibly stretch and began to flap them vigorously. They moved so fast that they became a blur.

"What is he doing?" Kristina asked Werrien.

"I'm not sure," Werrien answered.

As Roage continued to flap his wings, his form suddenly began to change. His neck stretched longer, and his body grew much larger and taller. His wings began to change into the form of human arms, and at the tips of the wings, human hands began to emerge. His thin, scaly legs grew longer and larger, and his talons changed into human feet. Last of all, his face changed into that of a man's face. Werrien looked at the man Roage was turning into, and when his face was fully formed, Werrien suddenly recognized him.

"Father?" Werrien gasped.

"Werrien, my son," his father, King Warren, responded. He held out his arms and Werrien ran and embraced him.

"I thought you were dead," Werrien said.

"Oh, no, I've been under a spell that was cast upon me," King Warren said.

"So Roage was actually you?" Werrien said, amazed by the reality of it.

"I know it's hard to believe, but yes. I was turned into a raven many years ago, when you were a very small boy," King Warren said.

"I guess that explains why you were such a great help to us," Werrien said.

"I wanted to help you even more, but I was so limited, being a raven. I'm just glad that I planted the golden case in the trunk of the tree before the spell was cast upon me," King Warren said.

"I wondered how Roage knew about the golden case," Werrien said.

Suddenly, they heard a loud howl, and they turned to see the wolf. As it trotted toward them, it, too, began to change into a man.

"Uncle Corin!" Werrien said.

Corin walked up to them, and father, son, and uncle embraced.

While they talked, Kristina stood nearby, waiting. King Warren glanced over at her. "Come here, Kristina," he said to her.

Kristina felt nervous about meeting King Warren because of the times she had been short-tempered with Roage.

"It so nice to finally meet you *in person*," King Warren said, warmly, offering his hand to shake.

As Kristina shook King Warren's hand, she noticed that Werrien looked very much like him and that they both had the same hair color, very blue eyes, and very similar facial features.

"It's very nice to meet you, too," Kristina said shyly, avoiding eye contact.

"I'm sorry, but is something the matter?" King Warren asked, noticing her apprehensiveness.

"I feel that I need to apologize for not being so nice to you, when you were a raven," Kristina said.

"Well, let me tell you what I think. If I had to go through what

244

you went through, I would have acted no differently than you did," King Warren said with a serious yet kind look on his face.

Kristina could tell that King Warren was a good-hearted man, and so she began to feel more at ease. While they conversed, Ugan, Retzel, Davina, Hester, and Raymond came to their side of the tree.

"What are you two up to? You've been gone a long time," Raymond said, just before bounding over the grass toward them.

"Hey, guys, I want you to meet Werrien's father, King Warren, and his uncle Corin," Kristina said to all of them.

After everyone was introduced, Kristina explained to King Warren and Corin that while they were escaping the cave, Graham went in the opposite direction and never made it out with them.

"I'm worried he might be dead," Hester said nervously.

"When I was still Roage, I soared high above this mountain, and I saw all of you escaping. Unfortunately, I also saw Sentiz escaping down the backside of the mountain as the cave began to break apart. There were others with her, but I couldn't quite make out who they were due to the dust and debris that filled the air and flowed over them," King Warren said.

"Do you think Graham may have been one of the others?" Hester asked.

"It's quite possible, but if he was, I don't know which would be worse—his dying in the cave or escaping with her," King Warren said.

They decided to head down the mountain, and this time, all that surrounded them was lush green grass, wildflowers, little brooks, busy bees, and butterflies that flew in and out of the flowers—a very nice contrast to the cold, treacherous, icy slopes. It was such a lovely hike that even Hester seemed to forget about Graham for the time being. When they neared the bottom, they could see a large crowd waiting to greet them. There were many gnomes, dwarfs, fairies, and animals, all cheering. Some were holding small children on their shoulders, and others held poles with brightly colored streamers, which they waved back and forth. Others enthusiastically waved their arms in the air. They were chanting "Long live the chosen one, Kristina, and long live the true prince of Bernovem, Werrien."

When they actually got close enough to see their faces, Kristina noticed Leacha standing near the front of the crowd, and not too far from her were Taysha and Lisheng. Taysha whinnied happily, and she and Lisheng trotted up the hill to meet them. They both lowered themselves down for Kristina and Werrien to climb up onto them. Werrien looked at his father to see if he and his uncle would like to have the honor of riding the horses the rest of the way down the mountain, but before he could even say anything, King Warren said, "You and Kristina best get on those horses fast. You don't want to keep that anxious crowd waiting. We'll do just fine walking down with the rest."

So Werrien mounted Lisheng, and Kristina, Taysha. Then they rode down to meet the crowd. Werrien rode directly to Leacha, and when he got to where she was, he jumped down to greet her. Leacha ran toward him with tears in her eyes and her arms open wide.

"My dear child, I'm so glad you returned safely and in one piece," she said while squeezing him tight.

"And I'm so glad to see that you are well also," Werrien said, returning the embrace.

When Leacha finished embracing Werrien, she turned to Kristina and embraced her as well. "Our little chosen one! My what a brave girl you have been," she said, smiling so hard that her eyes disappeared into the folds of her fat cheeks. "Did the fairy blossom come in handy?" she whispered into her ear.

"Oh, yes, as a matter of fact, if I hadn't had it, we probably wouldn't have made it back," Kristina said.

"I'm so glad I was able to give it to you," Leacha said happily.

King Warren, Corin, Davina, Hester, Ugan, and Retzel, with Raymond sitting on his shoulder, joined Werrien and Kristina, and when the crowd found out that King Warren was back, they went wild with happy cheers, hollers, and hoots. Then a certain dwarf blew on a large ivory horn. The sound it made was so loud, it silenced the noisy crowd.

"Make way for our queen!" the dwarf said.

Both Werrien's and Kristina's stomachs went queasy, for they both thought of Queen Sentiz. But from the spot where they stood, the crowd separated to form an open path, and the queen suddenly appeared. There was no need for them to worry, because it was not the horrible Sentiz but the true Queen of Bernovem, Lafinia.

"Mother!" Werrien shouted.

He and his father quickly made their way toward her, and all three embraced each other.

The people in the crowd lowered themselves down on one knee, including, Kristina, Hester, and Davina.

When the three finished embracing, the crowd stood back up and cheered wildly.

Then the certain dwarf blew again on the ivory horn and said, "Now let us all head to the celebration!"

A beautiful horse-drawn carriage, adorned in ornate gold, appeared at the back of the crowd.

"Your coach is ready, my king, queen, and prince," the dwarf said.

King Warren, Queen Lafinia, and Prince Werrien headed toward it. They were just about to get in it, but Werrien suddenly stopped and said, "Wait a minute. I'll be right back."

He could see Kristina standing with Hester and Davina, and he went to her. "Come on; I want you to meet my mother," he said, taking her by the hand. The two of them ran back toward the horse-drawn carriage. When they arrived at it, a gnome, dressed in a purple velvet outfit with gold piping on the neck and sleeves, opened the carriage door.

Kristina went in first and when she saw Queen Lafinia sitting inside beside King Warren, she felt butterflies in her stomach. She hadn't realized how beautiful the queen was when she'd seen her from a distance. She was slender, with long flaxen hair, just like her own; delicate, yet strong facial features; and radiant teal-blue eyes that matched her teal-blue velvet gown with mother-of-pearl accents.

Kristina sat down across from the queen and king. Werrien entered the carriage and sat down beside Kristina.

"Mother, I'd like you to meet my friend Kristina. She's the one who was chosen to deliver the Magic Warble to it resting place," Werrien said.

Queen Lafinia smiled warmly. "I am so happy to finally meet you. Our family has been waiting for many, many years for the return of the Magic Warble, and now that it has finally come and brought peace to our land, I can be nothing but forever grateful to you." She took Kristina's hand, kissed it, and then she placed something in it. Kristina opened her hand to find an elegant golden necklace with a shimmering rainbow crystal attached to it.

"It's the most beautiful necklace I have ever seen," Kristina said, dazzled by its splendor.

"It's for a girl who is just as beautiful," King Warren said.

The crystal glistened and sparkled just like the Rainbow Tree, and its many colors swirled about the inside of the carriage.

"May I?" Werrien asked, holding his hand out toward her.

Kristina put the necklace in his hand. He opened its clasps and placed it around her neck. Then she lifted it in her hand again to admire it.

"This necklace is going to take you home," the queen said softly.

Kristina was so enthralled with the crystal's beauty that she didn't seem to hear what Queen Lafinia had said.

"Kristina," Werrien said, gently nudging her shoulder.

"Yes?"

"My mother was just saying that this necklace is what is going to bring you home," Werrien said, looking seriously into her eyes.

"It is?" Kristina seemed a little caught off guard by this statement. She turned her head to stare out the carriage window, and as she gazed upon the lovely green meadow they were passing, it began to sink in that her time of being in Bernovem was coming to an end. She would have to leave her newfound friend Werrien, and would never see him again. The thought caused a tear to well up in her eye and slowly trickle down the side of her nose.

"Is something the matter Kristina?" King Warren asked her.

Kristina quickly wiped the tear from her nose. "No, I was just admiring the pretty scenery."

"It is very lovely, isn't it," Queen Lafinia agreed, her eyes tearing as well.

"How is the necklace going to bring me home?" Kristina asked.

"When the crystal turns a deep red, it will take you home," Queen Lafinia said.

"And what about the others? How are they to get home?" Kristina asked.

"They also will be given a crystal that will take them home," Queen Lafinia said.

The carriage came to a sudden halt and the door swung open. Loud cheers flooded into the carriage, and the same gnome stuck his head inside. "The crowd anxiously awaits you," he said to the four of them. As Werrien, Kristina, and the king and queen exited the carriage, they could see that the sun was receding behind Mount Bernovem, and it was a very lovely sight.

"Would you please follow me?" the gnome asked Kristina.

Kristina looked to Queen Lafinia to see if this was the right thing to do. The queen nodded, and so Kristina followed the gnome. He brought her to a tent in the meadow, not far off from the crowd. When they arrived at it, he opened the door flap, bowed, and waved his hand for her to enter. Inside the tent were Bronya and Neela, busily sewing the last stitches on a beautiful fuchsia and moss-green gown. They were so busy that they didn't even notice that Kristina had entered the tent.

"Hello," Kristina said.

Both girls looked up, and when they saw that is was Kristina, they instantly laid the dress down on a chair and quickly went to her. "We have just finished the dress you are to wear to the party. Come with us and try it on," Neela said cheerfully.

Both girls helped Kristina into the dress. While Neela was fastening the back of the bodice, Bronya brought a chair for Kristina and suggested that she sit down so that they could fix her hair. The two rosy-cheeked, plump gnome girls brushed and combed Kristina's hair, sprayed it with herbal hair remedies, and braided parts of it, all the while discussing how lovely her pale blond hair was and that any gnome girl would do practically anything to have it. Once they had her hair exactly as they wanted it, Bronya pulled out a number of hair pins from a woven basket. Then Neela picked up a vase that was filled with fairy blossom and carefully plucked a handful of the freshest, brightest-colored ones for Kristina. They continued working on Kristina's hair, pinning in the fairy blossoms. When they finished, Bronya hurried to get a long mirror for Kristina to view herself. Kristina could hardly believe it was her own reflection that she was looking at. This definitely didn't look like the little girl with the mismatched socks, too-short pants, and crookedly buttoned sweater. The bright fairy blossoms matched the fuchsia and moss-green dress perfectly, and the crystal around her neck sparkled vibrantly, reflecting all the colors she wore.

"She sure looks radiant," Bronya said to Neela.

"I'd say like the portrait of Queen Lafinia, when she was her age," Neela said.

The tent door flaps began to shake, and Bronya went to see who it was. It was the same gnome who had brought Kristina to the tent. "Is she ready?" he asked Bronya.

"As ready as she'll ever be," Bronya answered.

As Kristina exited the tent, Werrien was standing right outside, and when the two of them laid eyes on each other, both were amazed.

Interrupted Once More

"You think I look stupid, don't you?" Kristina asked Werrien, feeling quite awkward in her dress and new hairstyle. At home, she had worn a dress maybe three times in her entire life.

"As a matter of fact, I was thinking how nice you look," Werrien said. "And what about you? I saw how you looked at me." Werrien also was dressed up, in a white shirt, royal blue tunic, black breeches, and black shoes. "Could it be that you think I look stupid, dressed like this?" he asked.

"Well, you do look a few centuries behind the times, but I must say it does suit you," Kristina said.

"Oh, I see, you're saying the clothes suit me, but you still haven't said whether I look stupid in them," Werrien teased.

Their conversation was interrupted when a red carpet came rolling up to them. Kristina moved out of its way, but there was really no need—the carpet stopped right at their feet. Hundreds of dwarfs, gnomes, fairies, and animals lined up on each side of the carpet.

"I feel like a Hollywood celebrity," Kristina said to Werrien.

"Like a what?" Werrien asked.

"Oh, nothing. It's just an Earth thing," Kristina said.

Suddenly there was a loud *boom*, and when they looked up to the sky, it was filled with fireworks bursting in all directions. They were different from the fireworks that Kristina would see at home, because instead of disintegrating in the air, the tiny sparkling lights actually fell to the ground and landed there. When they fell toward Kristina, she quickly dodged out of the way, thinking that they might burn her skin. Werrien found it very amusing, watching her try to avoid them, and he began to laugh.

"Oh, yeah, it would be real funny if I got burned," Kristina said, annoyed.

"You think that they'll burn you? Whatever gave you that crazy idea?" Werrien said. He jumped directly under a few of the falling sparkles, and when they landed on him, they burst into tiny sprays of what seemed to be sparkling colored water. "They really only tickle a little," he said, smiling boyishly. "Come on! Try it!" He continued jumping under more of them.

Kristina quickly joined him, and when the multicolored sparkles landed on her, she burst out laughing. "They *do* tickle," she said gleefully. Then she smelled something wonderful, like fresh spring flowers. "What is that scent?" she asked.

"It's the sparkles. When they burst open, they let out a fragrance," Werrien said.

Something on the other end of the red carpet caught Kristina's attention, and she turned to see Hester in a robin's egg blue gown, with a matching bow in her hair; and Davina in a pumpkin-orange gown. Both girls were running toward her and Werrien. Kristina thought they looked like football players coming in for a tackle. They both stopped running when they reached Kristina and Werrien, and they stood there, panting.

"Wow! I see you guys got dressed up also," Davina said, still trying to catch her breath.

"We both got crystal bracelets," Hester bragged, as she held out her wrist for Kristina to see.

The sparkle from Kristina's crystal necklace gleamed and caught Davina's eye. "Holy moly! Look at the rock on her neck. It's got to be three times the size of ours," she said to Hester. Hester's eyes grew wide with envy.

"Are you two all right?" Kristina asked. "You seem really tuckered out."

"Are we all right?" Davina said excitedly "I'd say a lot better then just all right. You've got to come and see all the food."

Kristina hadn't eaten anything more than the food that Leacha had given them for their journey, and Werrien had only had the soup from the gnome girls, so they were both very hungry. She looked to Werrien.

"What are we waiting for?" he asked. "Let's go."

The four of them ran down the red carpet, past the crowd on both sides that was cheering and partying. At the end of the carpet, they came upon a very long table that was lined with many ornate golden chairs. The table was set with the most beautiful silverware, tall candles, flower arrangements, and of course the food Davina had been so excited about. All kinds of dishes, such as shrimp, crab, oysters, and clams, were set on fancy plates. Beside them were colorful vegetable and fruit platters and numerous kinds of edible nuts and cheeses, soups, sauces, breads, rolls, fancy finger foods, and crackers. And the desserts! There were many desserts—cakes, cookies, puddings, molds of wobbly jelly, parfaits, pastries, and candies. In the very center of the table was a punch bowl with an ice fountain in its center. The fountain spouted bright-red fairy-blossom punch, which came up from the center of the punch bowl, ran down the sides of the ice, and then returned to the punch bowl. As the children were admiring the beautifully set table with its entire splendor, a dwarf came toward them carrying a golden tray topped with tall, slender glasses full of bubbly red fairy-blossom punch. Werrien took two glasses off the tray and handed one to Kristina and the other to Hester. Then he took two more off, one for Davina and one for himself.

"May I lead the honored guest to her seat?" a dwarf asked.

"Why, yes, of course," Hester said, holding her hand out limply and pointing her nose to the sky.

But the dwarf didn't go to Hester; he walked right past her, rolled his eyes at her hoity-toity attitude, and went up to Kristina. "Would you come with me, my fair young lady?" He bowed slightly and held his arm out to her.

Looking a little surprised, Kristina smiled brightly and took the dwarf's arm. He led her to the very end of the table and pulled out the chair for her to sit down. Once she was seated, the dwarf pushed her chair up to the table. Then he turned to Werrien and said, "Come with me, Your Highness, and I'll escort to your seat at the other end of the table."

"Actually, I'll do just fine to sit here beside our honored guest," Werrien said.

"As you wish," the dwarf said. He bowed to Werrien and turned to face Davina and Hester. Davina and Hester were standing a little way back from the table with slightly soured looks on their faces. They knew Kristina was the one who had saved Bernovem, but they were jealous of her special treatment.

"Please follow me, girls?" the dwarf said, as he turned and led them to the table. Davina and Hester followed the dwarf to the chairs across the table from Werrien. They waited for the dwarf to pull out their chairs, but he didn't; instead, he just waved his hand for them to sit down. Once Davina and Hester were seated, King Warren, Queen Lafinia, and Uncle Corin were escorted to their seats at the opposite end of the table. Then Leacha and the gnome couple, who had given Kristina the basket of food during her journey, were brought to sit by Davina and Hester.

Kristina suddenly recognized the cat that had led her to the Salas Prison. It came prancing down the carpet, followed by an old gnome man who walked very slowly. He was hunched over and needed a cane to help him walk. The cat stopped at the end of the red carpet, said something to the gnome, and then pranced toward Kristina, with the gnome following it. It stopped beside her chair and stood there, purring loudly, while it waited for the old gnome to catch up with it. When the old gnome finally made it to Kristina, the cat said, "I want you to meet my master."

The old gnome cleared his throat and said, "I am here to celebrate this lovely day, only because of a miracle, and that miracle is because of you." His bright hazel eyes twinkled with joy. "You see, child, I was on my deathbed when my cat, Rone, came to me with a small amount of fairy blossom. I was merely seconds away from dying, but then he put it in my mouth, and I was given another chance at life. I just wanted to tell you how very grateful I am to you." The old gnome got down on one knee, took one of Kristina's hands, and placed a kiss on it. The dwarf then escorted the gnome and his cat to their seats at the other end of the table. Other guests also were escorted to their seats—Ugan, Retzel (with Raymond sitting on his shoulder), Retzel's wife, Mitzi, and their child, Stompfy (who looked like he was feeling a lot better).

Raymond was admiring the new crystal necklace he wore around his neck, and when he finally took his eyes off of it, he noticed Kristina sitting at the end of the table. "There you are!" he said. He jumped off Retzel's shoulder and onto the table, knocking over Retzel's fairy-blossom punch, but Retzel caught the glass before it spilled all over the gold-and-white lace tablecloth. Raymond zigzagged between the delectable dishes, only stopping once to eat a sweet pickle skewered to an olive, and some sort of sea urchin.

"Raymond, where are your manners?" Kristina whispered loudly. "You just can't go tromping between the food dishes to come and talk. You're embarrassing me."

Hester turned to Davina. "Oh, my gosh!" she said nervously. "There's a swarm of glowing bees coming this way!"

Werrien chuckled at the wide-eyed look on Hester's face. "That's not a swarm of bees. It's the fairies coming to join us," he said.

"Don't they look beautiful." Kristina said as they watched the fairies move like twinkling balls.

King Oreadas, with Clover and Looper at his side, led the fairy colony to the table. They made their way to the fountain in the middle of it and encircled it. Then one by one, they landed at the base of the punch bowl, where there were tiny velvet pillows of all colors set around it—one pillow for each fairy. Beside the pillows were tiny plates, and on top of the plates were cutlery and glasses for drinking, so small that they were very hard to see.

Kristina turned her attention back to Raymond, who had snuck a chocolate-dipped strawberry and was busily stuffing it down his throat.

"Now what were you saying?" Kristina asked.

"I was just about to ask you…"

Kristina didn't hear his next words, because a dwarf was blowing on the ivory horn. Its sound was so loud that it startled Raymond, and he quickly crawled under the edge of an oyster platter. The platter tilted and the oozing, smelly delicacies nearly slid off onto the tablecloth, but Werrien caught the edge of the platter before they did so.

"Ladies and gentleman, may I have your attention?" the dwarf said. The guests fell silent. "I would like to propose a toast to our true King and Queen of Bernovem!" He lifted high his glass of fairy-blossom punch. The guests now filled every seat at the table, and all of their glasses went up in the air. The fairies' glasses went up as well, filled with drops of punch that had splattered off the fountain. The dwarf cleared his throat and continued, "May our beloved king and queen be blessed with wisdom, strength, power, and happiness and may they reign long over our precious land, Bernovem." He brought his glass down and took a sip of it, and the rest of the guests did the same.

Kristina tugged on Raymond's tail to get him out from under the platter. "What is it you want to ask me?" she asked.

"I just wanted to say—"

"One more toast before we eat," the dwarf said, raising his glass in the air again. "This is to the chosen one, who delivered the Magic Warble to its resting place." He turned to face Kristina, and all the guests turned in their seats to face her, too. Kristina swallowed nervously. She quickly pulled Raymond onto her lap, so he wouldn't be seen on the table. "I want to tell you how grateful we are to you, for coming into our land and saving it from that horrible Sentiz." The dwarf's eyes sparkled as he looked at Kristina. "You, my dear Kristina, will always be remembered in Bernovem." Then he took a sip from his glass, and the rest of the guests did the same. "Now, let us feast!" he said.

Kristina looked down at Raymond sitting on her lap. "Hurry up and tell me what you want to say!" she said.

Raymond sat up on his hind legs to look up at Kristina. With his ears slightly back, he swallowed nervously and said, "I was thinking I might—"

Before he could finish, a dwarf and a grubby boy on a horse galloped up to the table and stopped abruptly beside Kristina. All eyes fell on the grubby boy sitting behind the dwarf—it was none other than Graham Kepler.

- 40 -

A Rock with a View

The dwarf dismounted the horse and then helped a very weak and hungry Graham down as well. Graham was too embarrassed to look at the guests who were staring at him; he kept his gaze on the ground. When Hester saw him, she jumped up from her chair.

"Graham! Where have you been?" she demanded angrily.

Graham didn't answer.

From at the other end of the table, King Warren stood up and said, "Please allow the boy to clean up and change. Then he will be fit to join us."

The rest of the guests mumbled in agreement but not Hester. She gave Graham an angry glare before sitting back down in her chair.

The dwarf led Graham to one of the tents to clean up and change, and the guests all began eating the delectable food that was in front of them. Kristina and Werrien watched as Davina piled her plate with every single type of food she could get her hands on. Hester skipped the main courses and loaded her plate with sweets and pastries, the whole time complaining that Graham had caused her to worry unnecessarily. As for Raymond, he made himself a pile of nuts, cheese, and fruit and was so busy eating that he forgot all about telling Kristina what he wanted to say to her. Kristina enjoyed the feast and tried foods she had never tasted before, like olives and sharp cheeses, and she found them to be quite tasty.

As the guests enjoyed good food and conversation, Graham finally showed up at the table with his face washed and his hair slicked back. He wore new clothes—black breeches, long white socks, black shoes with shiny silver buckles, and a red vest that overlapped a white shirt with ruffles around the collar and sleeves. In the center of the ruffles, at chest level, sat a tiny crystal pin that held the ruffles in place. When Davina saw Graham, she began to laugh, revealing the food that had gotten stuck in her braces.

"Cute, Graham! Real cute," she said, inadvertently spitting some food toward Werrien's face. Werrien ducked, and it hit Graham on his vest.

"Why don't you say it instead of spraying it," Graham said disdainfully.

"There's a chair for you on the other side of the table," Werrien pointed out to Graham.

Graham sat down between Hester and Davina. "If I'd had it my way, I'd have never come back," Graham said haughtily, while piling large amounts of potatoes, bread, cheese, and crackers on his plate.

"Where did you go?" Hester asked. "I can't believe that we were actually worried about you."

"Speak for yourself," Davina said, while stuffing her mouth full of jumbo shrimp.

"I don't owe any of you an explanation," Graham sneered. He didn't want anyone to know that he had escaped down the back of the mountain with Sentiz.

~ ~ ~

While he was still tied up in the cave with Davina and Hester, Sentiz was on the ground, close by him. She threw small pebbles at him to get his attention, and when she finally did, his eyes met hers and he suddenly remembered her from the boat ride to Treachery

Island. She whispered to him that if he would help save her, she would let him live in the palace with her and she would allow him to be next in line to the throne. As Graham listened to her voice and gazed into her dark eyes, she began to hypnotize him. Under her spell, he began to feel that he would do anything for her, even if it meant risking his own life. He decided not to tell Hester and Davina about Sentiz; instead, he would wait for an opportune time to sneak away when the girls had their backs turned. But when the cave walls started crumbling and there was no light to see even a few feet ahead of him, he never found his opportune time that is until when the other children were escaping. Werrien held the torch, which gave Graham just enough light to see down the cave, and that is when he went to her. He found Sentiz and helped her out the back of the cave. Once outside, they met up with Ramon and Rumalock, and they escaped from the mountain. They traveled until they came to the Indra River, where there was a raft near its bank. Rumalock, Ramon, and Graham helped the injured Sentiz onto the raft, and then got on themselves. Soon after, they began to cross the wild river. While on the raft, Graham couldn't help but notice that Sentiz's appearance began to change. Her face no longer had that smooth pale complexion that he'd thought was so beautiful; now, it looked older and wrinkled. And she began to develop warts, one on her right eyelid, and another under her left nostril. Her eyebrows grew bushier, and her buck teeth became pointier—and then one fell out of her mouth, right before his eyes. Her mouth shriveled and sunk in, and her whole body became smaller and frailer. Her shiny black hair became thinner and turned a dull gray. Graham didn't find her attractive any longer, but he was still glad he had helped her, for now that she was old and feeble, it meant that he was closer to becoming the King of Bernovem.

All was going well on the raft ride until Ramon turned to Graham and said, "I don't think we'll be needing you any longer." Then he pushed Graham off the raft, into the icy cold turbulent water. After that, all Graham could remember was being wakened by a dwarf, who'd found him on the river's bank shivering and near death. The dwarf opened his canteen and gave Graham a drink of hot fairy-blossom tea. Then he placed a warm woolen blanket around him. When Graham had regained a little of his strength, the dwarf helped him onto his horse planning to bring him back to the other children. Graham wondered about Sentiz and what she had said about him being able to live at the palace and be next in line to the throne. He didn't believe that she had anything to do with his being pushed off the raft. No, it was that stupid oaf of a son of hers. He was surely jealous.

Now, Davina and Hester continued to interrogate Graham as to where he had been, but he wouldn't tell any of it. Their continual bickering was getting on Kristina's and Werrien's nerves, and they found it hard to enjoy their dinner. They watched Davina shovel food in her mouth and Graham pour so much gravy on his potatoes that it ran over the sides of his plate.

Kristina suddenly felt the crystal around her neck warm up, which she had forgotten about until now. She took it in her hand and saw its rainbow of colors swirling around inside of it. Then she looked over at Davina's and Hester's bracelets. The colors were also swirling inside their small crystals, but the two of them were too busy eating and squabbling to notice. She looked over to Raymond's necklace and then to Graham's pin, and the same was happening. As she watched her own crystal, staring into its dazzling colors, all the clinking and clanking of glasses and cutlery and the celebrating and arguing around the table seemed to grow distant. She began to feel very relaxed and peaceful, and the colors in the crystal seemed to entrance her. She felt something on her shoulder and realized that it was Werrien's hand.

"Would you like to go for a ride?" he asked. "There's something really neat that I'd like to show you."

"Yes, I'd like that very much," Kristina said feeling relieved to be able to get away from the other children. She rode Taysha, and Werrien rode Lisheng into the meadow. They rode until the clamor of the celebration grew faint and the sound of the sea grew louder. The scent of flowers mingled together with the scent of sea water filled the air. The moon illuminated the tall green grass ahead of them. A large rock came into view, and Werrien led the way to it. Once there, he dismounted Lisheng and then climbed on top of the rock. Kristina dismounted Taysha, and Werrien helped her up onto the rock as well. Ahead of them, beyond the bluffs and cliffs, was the Citnalta Sea shimmering in the moonlight.

"Have a seat," Werrien said.

Kristina sat down beside him and just as she did so, the crystal began to warm up again. She took it in her hand to look at it. The rainbow of colors were swirling around, just like before.

"What's happening with it now?" Werrien asked.

"The colors are swirling," Kristina said. As she spoke, the colors began to change. "Wait a moment; I spoke too soon. It's turning pink."

"May I see?" Werrien asked.

Kristina showed him the crystal. "It will be turning red soon, won't it?"

Werrien didn't answer but instead gazed out at the sea.

"What an awesome view," Kristina said.

"This is the place I come when I want to think," Werrien said.

"I can see why," Kristina said.

"See those mountains off in the distance?" Werrien pointed toward the northwest.

"Yes, barely," Kristina answered.

"Well, beyond them is the land where my people come from," Werrien said.

"What's it called?"

"Tezerel," Werrien said.

A cool breeze blew by, bringing with it the scent of the fragrant flowers.

"Werrien, what would happen if I took off the necklace?" Kristina asked.

"Well, it's quite simple; you wouldn't be able to go home," Werrien said.

"What if I took it off and then put it back on later? Could I stay longer that way?" Kristina asked.

"I'm not sure, so it's probably best not to take the chance. Besides, why would you want to stay longer?"

Kristina looked back out to the sea. She wanted to tell Werrien that he was the best friend she had ever had and that if it weren't for her own family at home, she would much rather stay in Bernovem. But she just couldn't bring herself to say it.

Werrien heard a faint humming sound, and he looked over his shoulder to see two small, glowing balls of light coming toward them. "Looks like we've got visitors," he said.

It was Clover and Looper. They flew up to the rock and landed on it in front of them. "He wants to speak to Kristina and says it can't wait," Clover said.

"What is it, Looper?" Kristina asked.

"Oh, not me, it's him down there," Looper said, pointing to the ground at the bottom of the rock.

Kristina looked over the edge of the rock to see Raymond sitting at the base of it. "Raymond, is everything okay?"

"I never got to finish what I wanted to say to you earlier at the table," Raymond said.

"Oh, that's right, let me come down and get you," Kristina said. She jumped down from the rock, and then picked up Raymond and handed him up to Werrien. Then Werrien helped her up again, and they both sat back down.

"So now that you have my undivided attention," Kristina said, "what is it you want to tell me, Raymond?"

Raymond swallowed apprehensively. Then his eyes shifted back and forth between Werrien and Kristina.

"Well, what is it?" Kristina asked again.

"I've been offered a chance to stay on in Bernovem with Retzel's family," he said.

263

Kristina chuckled. "No way, Raymond," she said, surprised he would even ask.

"I thought it was a stupid idea myself," Raymond said gloomily.

Seeing Raymond downhearted made Kristina sad as well, and she thought about him having to go back home to his cage. Then she thought about him not being able to talk like he was able to in Bernovem. He could have such a better life here, and he'd definitely have more freedom—and he could live with a very loving family.

"I guess it's selfish of me to want you to come home," Kristina said softly. Retzel and his family were now walking through the grass toward the rock. "Raymond, I can't think of any reason for you to come home with me, other then my own selfish ones," Kristina said.

"Loving me isn't selfish," Raymond said quietly.

"No, it's not Raymond, and because I love you, I have changed my mind. You can stay here—if that's what you really want."

Raymond's face lit up. "Are you sure?" he asked.

"Yes, Raymond. Now don't ask me again, or I just might change my mind." She picked up her beloved pet and hugged him gently. "Well, I guess you'd better not keep your new family waiting," she said. Raymond looked to the meadow and saw Retzel and his family waiting for him. "I'll take you down now," Kristina said. She scooped Raymond up in her arms and brought him down from the rock. "I guess this is good-bye," she said, tears welling up in her eyes.

"I'll always love you," Raymond said, his teeth chattering as he began to get choked up. With that, he turned away and headed to his new family.

"Wait! Come back," Kristina called after him.

Raymond turned around and made his way back through the tall grass. "I thought you might change your mind," he said.

Kristina knelt down and picked him up again. "I don't think you'll be needing this," she said, removing his necklace. Then she put him back in the grass and watched as he ran happily toward his new family.

Very soon after, Looper and Clover flew down from the rock. "Well, kid, I wish we didn't have to leave so soon, but we do need to get back or our father will start to worry," Looper said.

"I'm sure going to miss you," Kristina said to him.

"And I'll sure miss you," Looper said, trying not to cry.

Kristina turned to Clover. "Hey, listen, Clover. I just wanted to say that I'm sorry for all the times I irritated you."

Clover looked a little embarrassed. "I think it's actually me that owes you an apology," she said softly.

Kristina held her hands out, and Clover and Looper each landed on one. "I'll never forget you two," she said.

"And we'll never forget you, either," Looper said.

"How could we? You're famous in Bernovem," Clover added.

Kristina smiled humbly. Then Clover and Looper lifted up off her hands. Just before flying away, they encircled her head, leaving what seemed to be a crown of sparkling dust to fall all around her. She watched as Retzel, with Raymond on his shoulder, and his wife and child disappeared into the tall green grass, followed by the fairies.

Werrien helped Kristina back up on the rock. "That was very kind of you," he said.

"What was?" Kristina asked.

"Letting your best friend go," Werrien said.

"I think it's the hardest thing I've ever done," Kristina said.

"I think I'm feeling the same way," Werrien said, with tears in his eyes.

Kristina felt goose bumps on her arms. Nobody had ever claimed her as being a friend, let alone a best friend.

The crystal suddenly warmed up again, and this time there were no swirling colors or even a light pink color. No, this time the crystal had reached its final color, a deep, dark, rich red.

"Werrien, you're my best friend," Kristina whispered as she embraced him, but just as her arms encircled him, he disappeared into thin air.

~~~

Jingle, jangle went the familiar and annoying sound of the alarm clock. Kristina reached her hand out of bed and gave it a good whack. Then she stuffed her head under her pillow and dozed off again. A few minutes later, her squeaky old door opened, and her mother, Ingrid, poked her nose into Kristina's bedroom.

"Kristina, you need to get up. Your grandma Ursie will be here in less than two hours, and I'm really going to need your help tidying up the place," she said.

Kristina pulled the pillow off her head and sat up abruptly. Holding her covers up to her neck, she stared at her mother with a wild gaze in her eyes.

"Must have been some dream. Are you okay, dear?" her mother asked.

Kristina swallowed nervously and shifted her eyes quickly to Raymond's cage and then back to her mother. Raymond's cage door was wide open, but luckily her mother didn't notice.

"You look a little pale. Maybe you're coming down with something."

"Actually I don't feel very good. My stomach's upset and my throat hurts."

"Well, in that case, I'll just have to get your father to do the vacuuming."

"Thanks, Mom," Kristina said, lying back down and pulling the covers over her head.

Her mother shut the door to her room, and Kristina waited for the sound of her footsteps to disappear. Then she felt her neck. There was nothing hanging around it, and she was not wearing the elegant fuchsia and moss-green gown she had on in Bernovem. No, it was just the old sweater she had buttoned wrong and the same short pants she had worn on the last day of school. She threw off her covers to find just what she had suspected: one light pink and one white sock. She looked at the floor beside her bed and saw her old sneakers.

Might all I experienced have been only a wild dream? she wondered. She looked over at Raymond's cage with its wire door wide open, and her stomach churned. Her heart pounded faster as she got out of bed and went over to it. "Raymond, are you in there?" she asked apprehensively.

Raymond always came out when she called his name, but this

time he didn't. She looked inside his wooden house, but it was empty. Did Raymond stay on in Bernovem, or did he only escape from his cage? She was feeling really confused.

Next she looked for the hatbox that Miss Hensley had given her. At first she couldn't see it anywhere, but then she spotted it on the floor next to her dresser. She quickly opened it. Inside, there was the little leather sack. She untied its tassels and looked inside, but it was empty. Then she noticed something she hadn't noticed before. In the corner of the hatbox was a small, tarnished silver ball, the same size as the ball she had found before. But unlike the other one, this one had a seam, and there was a clasp on the seam to open it. She lifted the clasp, and as the tarnished ball slowly opened, a tune began to play. Inside the ball were two tiny figures—a blond-haired boy and a blond-haired girl—standing on top of a rock, turning in time to the tune. The boy was dressed in the same clothes that Werrien had worn to the party, and the girl was dressed in a fuchsia and moss-green gown. The crystal necklace around the girl's neck shimmered brightly.

About the Author

Victoria Simcox lives with her husband and three children, in Western Washington. Besides being a writer she is an elementry school art teacher.